Morrow's Con

Opening Gambit

D1707313

Earl James

Pluribus Enterprises
4005 20th Ave West #133
Seattle, WA 98199

Edition #1

ISBN: 9798366211345

Published by Pluribus Enterprises 2022

Life is like chess. You never know where the game is going until you get there.

PART ONE

PART ONE

1

It wasn't planned.
It was thrust upon him.
He didn't disagree or fight it at all.
It effectively deployed his natural talents.
He found that he liked the idea and was confident.
The job sounded simple to do, entertaining, and safe.
It was none of those things.

Morrow vacuumed the back seat of the town car and then reached down and started cleaning the floor. It didn't need it. He had done the same three days ago, and no one had driven the car since then. But today, it would be. His boss, Arnie Westcott, the number two highest-ranking member of the Santangelo crime family in Phoenix, would be riding in one of the cars tonight, and he didn't want to be the one who failed to clean it properly. Those who failed tended to have a short career in Westcott's enterprises.

Westcott had four drivers working for him. Three of them doubled as mechanic assistants in the garage. It gave them something to do between driving duties. The one driver who didn't do extra work was David Clooney, a veteran of over twenty years with Westcott. The others, Wade Connell and Rafe Wright, had more seniority but were still relatively new and inexperienced.

Tonight, the word was out that Westcott would need a driver and that driver would be named about an hour prior to departure. Morrow had been with Westcott for nearly six months before he got his first call, but since then, he'd been tabbed three or four times. It was an honor, and all the drivers secretly vied for the chance to be the boss's driver for the day. Driving some of the thugs around on their various misadventures seemed far less glamorous.

Morrow finished cleaning and turned off the vacuum. The radio was blaring in the garage. An announcer was doing the pregame show for the Diamondbacks, who were in Pittsburgh playing a night game against the Pirates. Morrow smiled inwardly as he listened and marveled at how his spirits were always lifted in April as baseball season began again.

After moving to Phoenix a few years back, he adopted the D-Backs as his team and spent many an evening listening to the broadcasts. Phoenix's team was starting strong, and hopes were high. Of course, in baseball, every team's hopes were high in April. Morrow's left lip twitched as he reconsidered that thought. *The Royals are 8 and 17, last in the AL Central, so it's unlikely they're hopeful,* he thought, almost saying it out loud to himself.

"Sure would like to see them sweep the series," Rafe said, smiling widely at Morrow.

"Dream on, they're bums," Wade called out from forty feet away. He had a mischievous look in his eyes as usual. He enjoyed riling Rafe.

"Might get your wish, Rafe," Morrow said.

"And he might not," Wade said.

Morrow placed the vacuum in storage and looked around for something to do. It was five o'clock, technically quitting time, although this wasn't the kind of job with a timeclock.

Clooney walked in and bellowed out, "Wade, you're wanted. Bring a car around to the front entrance."

Wade leaped up and looked at Morrow. "You done with this one?"

Morrow nodded.

Wade jumped in and pulled the town car out of the garage. The door closed behind him.

Morrow glanced at Rafe, and their eyes connected. Rafe was bummed. He'd hoped he'd be picked to drive Westcott's car. Morrow tilted his head and shrugged his right shoulder subtly as if to say, "No big deal. You'll probably get the next one."

Rafe nodded and flashed a resigned smile.

2

Morrow washed his hands at the sink, gazed at the clock, and decided to call it a night. He had a modest room within the compound, a building away, with the bare essentials. It was enough for him. He didn't need much. He finished drying his hands and was about to bid Rafe a good night when Clooney walked in from the far side of the garage and boomed out again, "Morrow, get a car and circle around front."

"I thought Wade got the call tonight," Morrow said.

"Wade's driving team B. You got the man himself. Don't fuck up." Clooney turned and left.

Again Morrow glanced at Rafe, knowing he felt like the one left out of the action. Trying hard to put a happy face on it for Rafe's sake, Morrow said, "Poor you. You'll just have to go home to that beautiful wife of yours and your amazing kids and have a delicious meal."

Rafe's face broke into a huge grin, and he said, "Yeah, poor me. See ya later, sucker."

Morrow smiled back at him and nodded. Smiling never came naturally to Morrow. When the occasion required it, he'd give it his best shot. It was never done well, but then he reminded himself, *I got no right to be smiling anyway.*

2

Morrow pulled up in front of the mansion. He drummed his fingers on the wheel as he watched the front door. As it opened, he exited the vehicle, went around to the passenger side, and opened the back door. Westcott came down the stairs and entered the town car without as much as a glance in Morrow's direction. That was fine with him. All he wanted to do was keep a low profile and stay under the radar.

Morrow got back into the driver's seat and started to pull out of the compound. They passed through the front gate after the cursory check by the guards, and Morrow edged the car up to the intersection.

"Chandler," Westcott said.

Morrow turned right.

Westcott immediately protested. "Chandler's the other way."

"Yes, sir, it is," Morrow replied.

After a few seconds, Westcott said, "So…"

"So, it seems smarter to go to the left, but I've timed it. If we go right, we catch Interstate 10 down here at Casa Blanca within three minutes. Going right, it takes almost eight more to get to the interstate."

Westcott stayed silent for the next minute, then asked, "Who asked you to make that decision?"

"Sir, there's still only twenty-four hours in a day, and you're a busy man. I figure if I can help you do something faster, you'd want that."

Westcott said nothing else until Morrow exited the interstate and turned east on 202. "Another shortcut?"

"Yes, sir. We can get off at Alma School Road and be in the heart of Chandler in just a few minutes."

"You don't even know where we're going in Chandler," Westcott said.

"No, sir, I don't. But I know you're not the shy type, and you'll tell me where to go when you're ready."

That brought a brief smile to Westcott's face. When they exited the highway, he said, "Take a right at the first light. You'll see a bar called Marly's with a flashing orange light on the roof. Turn right into the alley at the end of her block and pull up behind our other car."

Morrow did as ordered and came to a stop behind Wade's town car. Within seconds, four of Westcott's bruisers piled out of the car and started walking forward toward a similar-looking car facing them in the alley.

Four large men exited the front car on the other side of the alley and stopped in a firm line ten feet in front of their bumper, just as Westcott's men did the same.

Westcott and Morrow exited their car to get a better view.

"Ever seen one of these, Morrow?"

"Not sure I know what I'm looking at, sir."

"What's your guess?"

"Looks like a brawl to me," Morrow said quietly.

"It is. Over there, behind the first car, is Damon Barger. He runs the north side of Phoenix. We run the south. We both work for the same—um, the same company." Westcott paused and let that sink in. "Now, what do you think?"

"It's interesting," Morrow said, pausing a moment longer to think. "My best guess is you two fellows have had a disagreement over something, and both agreed that this is the way it'll be settled. Maybe, what, last man standing wins for his team?"

Westcott nodded and continued to watch his men as they prepared for battle.

Morrow recognized only one of the men. His name was Dale, and he stood a full head higher than the others. Morrow talked with him once a few months ago and marveled at how strong he was for a string bean of a man. He was fast and wiry with a wingspan of almost seven feet. There were a slew of NBA players who couldn't top that.

Those long arms were a huge advantage in a boxing match, but, according to Rafe, Dale had kickboxing experience as well.

The other three thugs were guys he'd seen around on the compound but didn't know by name. They wore T-shirts: one gray, one dark blue, and one black. They appeared ready to start rumbling.

The Westcott four looked at each other as if they were checking to see if the other teammates were ready.

They sauntered forward, and Barger's men did the same. A few of Barger's thugs switched positions in their line, apparently lining themselves up with an opponent they liked. Suddenly, the Barger clan moved quickly. Gray and black shirt were fighting one man each, but the other two turned on blue shirt, double-teaming him, while Dale stood alone, frozen for a second while he assessed which one of his teammates needed the most help.

He was closest to black shirt, so he jumped into the fray and knocked the Barger man to the ground. He popped back up again quickly just as the double-teamed Westcott fighter was knocked out cold and fell to the ground.

Four to three now.

The double-teamers went after Dale. Blows were delivered, and arms were swinging by all seven of the remaining battlers. Before Morrow could take his next breath, two more of Westcott's men went down and didn't get back up again.

"Shit!" Westcott uttered under his breath.

Dale was the last Westcott man standing, and he was fighting furiously. His speed and size made him formidable for even four opponents. He unleashed a powerful kick into the jaw of a Barger fighter, and the man went down like a brick, unmoving. He smashed another one in the face, knocking him to the ground. He looked dazed.

"Look at that man fight," Westcott said.

Dale took a smash to the gut and doubled over. The other upright fighter grabbed his arms, pinning them back. The Barger man on the ground seemed to be shaking it off as he rose again. The end came just seconds later. While the one man locked Dale's arms back, the other two pummeled him with one blow after another. Dale's legs gave way, and a few more hits finished him off. He fell face-first onto the alley pavement.

"Dammit!" Westcott muttered. "Well, Dale put up a good fight. Not sure I can say much about the others. Looks like this round goes to—what are they doing?" He pointed to the three remaining Barger fighters. They were in a line walking purposely toward Westcott and Morrow.

"I think that's our cue to leave," Morrow said.

Westcott didn't argue. As the three men increased their pace, Westcott hustled back to the town car. Morrow did the same.

"Get us out of here, Morrow. I don't know what they think they're doing, but it doesn't look good."

Morrow started the engine, threw the car into reverse, and glanced back at the three approaching men one more time. They had stopped next to a dumpster. One of the men was reaching behind it. He started pulling something out.

"Oh, fuck!" Westcott yelled. "He's got a fucking bazooka!"

Morrow pressed on the gas pedal, driving backward down the long alley toward the street at thirty miles an hour. He blasted on his horn to warn pedestrians. At that moment, a woman holding a child's hand froze in place almost in the middle of the sidewalk. Morrow slammed on the brakes, then looked back at the three Barger men.

One of the men had the bazooka on his shoulder, and another was loading it from the back.

Morrow smacked the horn again, and the woman snapped out of her fear. She picked up the child and ran back out of Morrow's view. He hit the gas again and yelled, "Hang on!"

He blew past the entrance to the alley, into the middle of West Pecos Road, honking all the way. Turning the wheel quickly, he gunned the engine and backed out into the lane to the left.

He could almost feel the blast from the projectile as it ripped past them and hit a parked Ford cargo van on the other side of the street. The van exploded, sending fiery parts everywhere in the area. Flaming pieces of the van landed on other vehicles while pedestrians screamed in terror and took cover. Morrow glanced at the woman and child and saw they were shielded by an SUV and out of danger.

He shifted and sped straight ahead, figuring the brief view of them passing was too little time for Barger's boys to get off another shot.

Westcott was on the phone in three seconds, barking orders to Wade and then to his second in command back at the compound.

Morrow turned onto 202 at Alma School Road. The two of them rode in silence until Morrow connected with Interstate 10.

"You don't say much, do ya, Morrow?"

"Never been much of a talker, sir."

"Well, you're a hell of a driver. And you were right. That's how Barger and I settle things. He made a move last week into what's always been considered my territory. Kind of a gray area, though. Our boss likes that we settle disputes without anybody getting killed or any cops noticing what we're doing. So this is how we've done it for four years now. I guess those days are over."

Morrow nodded. "Looks like Barger doesn't want to play by those rules anymore."

"I guess not."

"So, now what? War?"

Westcott sighed. "I'm all for resolving problems with a minimum of violence. Talking it out is even better, but I imagine that was never really an option with someone like Barger."

Morrow said nothing else. He knew Westcott's analysis was right.

Westcott rode the rest of the way in deep thought. He remained quiet but eyed Morrow from behind. He noted that he wasn't the muscular type. Maybe six feet tall, probably 180. Short black hair, piercing eyes. Not an imposing man, yet he had a serene air about him.

Morrow pulled the car up to the front stairway of the Westcott mansion. Before he could get out to open the boss's door, Westcott asked, "Why are you working here, Morrow?"

Morrow mulled over a variety of responses and settled on the truth instead. "I got a record—from when I was young and dumb. I don't want any trouble. I'm happy to be able to do a good job and not draw any attention."

When Westcott didn't reply, Morrow opened his door, exited, and came around to the passenger side, smoothly opening Westcott's door for him.

Westcott got out and turned to Morrow. "So, I see how you handle yourself, and I heard what you did for Rafe. That could have been an attention grabber. Seems you are a—a conflicted man."

Morrow swallowed hard. Nothing was worse than having people think about him. Making eye contact with his boss, he quietly replied, "Aren't we all."

3

The next morning, Morrow was cleaning another car when Rafe arrived. Rafe stood a few inches taller than Morrow and carried twenty pounds more as well. He was the son of parents who had emigrated from Nigeria a few years before he was born. He grew up as American as anyone else and spoke very little of the old language. His parents assimilated quickly, and his father even owned his own cab company for a dozen years before he passed away.

"You beat me here every day, Morrow," Rafe said.

"I only gotta walk about a hundred yards to get here, remember."

Rafe chuckled and asked, "You should move where we live. Closer to the action there. Living on the compound ain't real livin', man."

"I think we've had this conversation already, Rafe. You know me. I'm fine right here. Can't beat the rate, and I'm only fifty yards away from the kitchen."

"Ah, the real reason. You like that Gail girl that works the night shift."

"Yup. I like her 'cuz she's generous with the leftovers."

Rafe laughed out loud. "That reminds me. My wife is cooking up a pie this week. She says she'll make one for you too. Wants me to ask what kind you like."

"Rafe, that's nice, but she doesn't need to do that. You guys already thanked me ten times over for helping out. It was no big deal. I'm fine. No need to keep thanking, OK?"

"Shit, man. I wanna thank you too. She's been in such a good mood since you got the landlord to leave our rate alone and let us stay there. And you know what happens when Leesa's in a good mood?"

"What?"

"Man, I gotta tell ya? She's been giving me some extra lovin' lately, and that's why I'm smiling every day."

It was Morrow's turn to chuckle. He didn't laugh often, but this solved the mystery he'd been pondering. "Don't you got some work to do, old man?"

"This old man could whip your white ass any day of the week," he called out as he walked past Morrow to the next car in line.

The rest of the week went smoothly for Morrow. But while he attended to the cars, Westcott and his army of men struck back at Barger with a variety of small hit-and-run attacks that spared lives but not much else. His message had been sent, and relations between the two family execs settled back to normal.

At Friday's quitting time, a serious-faced Rafe approached him and said, "You up for a beer tonight?"

"A cold one sounds good to me," Morrow shot back.

Morrow arrived at the Indianhead Pub, a few miles from the compound, at six o'clock. Rafe was already on his second beer when his friend walked through the door. He slipped into the booth on the other side of the table and flagged the waitress down. Pointing to the beer that Rafe was having, he raised his index finger and mouthed the word "one."

She returned in record time with the beer and a come-hither look aimed at Morrow. After she took his order and left, Rafe looked at his friend. "Did you see that?"

Playing dumb, Morrow asked, "See what?"

"She looked at you like you were the answer to a lonely gal's prayer."

"Rafe, I've known you for a while now. I don't care about how she looks. I care about you and the look I've been seeing for the last two days. What's on your mind, 'cuz you look troubled."

Rafe moved closer to the table and took a look around. Leaning in towards Morrow, he said, "That's kinda why we're here. I got me sumthin'. I think I got me a chance to make some real money."

"I'm listening," Morrow whispered back.

"This guy I know has a gig. Some rich Jewish dude collects paintings, and he had one stolen from him years ago. Now he thinks he knows where it is, and he kinda needs somebody to, you know, steal it back for him."

"Why tell me?" Morrow asked.

"This guy, the guy with the gig…"

"What about him?"

"Well, the thing is, I don't really trust him. He needs people to help, but I keep getting the impression he just wants somebody else to get hurt or do the dangerous stuff. And even if we do, I don't know. I'm not so sure I'd get my cut."

"Same question, Rafe. Why tell me?"

"Well—" Rafe stopped talking and downed the rest of his second beer, then motioned to the bartender that he was ready for another.

Morrow waited patiently.

"Well, I was thinkin'. I trust *you*. You seem like a guy who knows how to get things done. Maybe you could go offer your services to the Jewish guy, and then I could work with you and get a fair cut. It sounds like he's paying a lot."

"Sounds like the guy with the gig already has it. How much did he promise you?"

Rafe got his third beer, took a long sip, and waited for the waitress to be long gone. Then he stretched his six-foot-two frame even more, moving his head less than a foot from Morrow's. "He said I could make twenty grand."

Morrow pursed his lips and nodded back as though acknowledging that twenty grand was, indeed, a small fortune to a man like Rafe.

"But he has the gig already," Morrow restated.

"I don't know. I mean, it was last week when he told me about it, and now I'm not hearing from him anymore. Maybe he got cold feet. Or maybe he checked it out, and it looked harder than he thought. Nothing's happening, so I thought maybe we could kinda jump in there."

"Why do you think this is up my alley, Rafe?"

"Jeez, Morrow. The way you talked the landlord into not kicking us out, you know, with the whole 'posing as a city employee thing' and telling him about the city's awards and incentives for keeping us po' black folk with a roof over our head and all." Rafe couldn't hide his sly grin as he greatly exaggerated their condition. "I mean, he bought it, didn't he. We got a new lease, and we're solid for two more years until the kids get out of school. And you did it without any rough stuff. You're just smart that way and a good talker, and you're creative. I mean, Leesa and I still laugh every time we think about how you conned him."

"I told him the truth. There *is* a city program that rewards landlords for equitable standards. I may have exaggerated how, um, robust it is. Hell, it's been on the books for four years, and the city hasn't made one award yet. But most of it was true."

Rafe scratched his head. "It's real? Why would they pass a law like that and then not ever use it?"

"Votes. That kinda stuff helps 'em look good and righteous and get re-elected. I just dusted it off and made it sound like it was active and all."

Rafe slapped his hand on the table and howled. "See! See! That's what I'm talking about. Hell, I bet you could talk that guy into handing over the painting to you for, uh, I don't know, brownie points or something."

Morrow shook his head. "That's different. Any painting worth stealing is worth some serious money. No one will hand it over willingly. But—"

A smile crossed Rafe's face. "Yeah? But what?"

"But it might be worth looking into. This Jewish guy got a name?"

4

It was Sunday. The fifth of May. Trees were budding, flowers were blooming, there was a sweetness in the air, and Morrow was about to begin a new adventure. This fine Sunday morning, he strolled up the front walkway leading to the home of Jacob Almeda. It was nothing short of a mansion. Three levels of brick, stained glass windows, and an entryway with sixteen-foot wooden doors complete with oversized, metal doorknockers. Tentatively, Morrow took hold of one of them and tried to knock on the door softly. Nothing about what he did sounded soft. Morrow felt the vibration directly through his feet.

As he listened to his knock and its echo inside the building, he could make out footsteps coming closer to the door. It opened to a man who appeared to be the butler. Morrow wasn't sure. He'd only seen butlers in old movies or PBS specials.

"May I help you?"

Standing there in a pair of navy-blue slacks and suit coat, a white shirt, and a subdued blue tie, Morrow said, "I was hoping to speak with Mr. Almeda about a painting."

The butler eyed him carefully and then allowed him to step into the foyer. "I will see if Dr. Almeda is available."

Doctor, huh? Morrow pondered.

Morrow shifted his weight from one foot to the other as he watched the time slip by. When fifteen minutes had passed, the butler returned and led him through a long grand hallway and into what appeared to be a private den. Bookshelves lined the left side of the room while fifteenth-century paintings filled the opposite wall.

A diminutive man, certainly in his sixties, entered the room. He was neatly groomed and attired in a gray suit and maroon tie. His hair was solid white, and he sported a neatly trimmed beard.

14

He walked up to Morrow and extended his hand. "I'm Jacob Almeda. To whom am I speaking?"

Morrow shook his hand. "I'm Dan Thompkins, and I'd like to speak with you about a painting. In fact, specifically about the painting you had stolen from you several years ago."

Suddenly, the older man stood up straighter, and a light flashed in his eyes. "Are you an artist or a collector?"

"Neither," Morrow answered simply.

"Perhaps you're a reporter or an insurance rep? If so, I have no time for this." With that, he turned and began to walk out of the room.

Morrow called out after him. "Sir, I'm none of those things. What I am is the man who can get *Gabriel's Steed* returned to you."

Almeda stopped in his tracks. He walked back into the den, past Morrow, and sat down at a small table. He rang a bell, and the butler appeared within seconds.

"Do you think you'd enjoy a glass of Cherry Port, Mr. Thompkins?"

"That sounds perfect."

With a glass of port in their hands, Almeda walked Morrow through a full tour of the home. Incredible pieces of art hung on every wall, some of which Morrow recognized as Grand Master work.

"What do you think, Mr. Thompkins?"

"I'm actually a bit blown away. This is a fantastic collection. I thought some of these were in museums and—"

"Oh, I thought you understood," Almeda interrupted him. "I don't display the real thing. These are all copies made by very good artists, and they truly are art themselves. But everyone knows these are forgeries or commissioned copies."

"They look old and so incredibly impressive," Morrow said, meaning every word.

"Thank you. They *are* impressive; however, most would retail for only twenty G's or so. A few perhaps as high as thirty."

"That actually sounds like a lot of money to me," Morrow replied. "I had no idea that there was a market like that for fakes."

Almeda nodded. "It's good we discussed it."

"Well, sir, I'm not educated in the arts, but I would still say you have an outstanding collection." As they continued their walk, they had a long discussion about the origins of *Gabriel's Steed*. Almeda described the artist, Francesco Bandeaux, as an obscure painter whose work was largely disappointing. He explained that the artist's other paintings were selling for less than what some fakes of *Gabriel's Steed* went for.

Then he told Morrow what he believed to be true about where *Gabriel's Steed* was being held.

Seated back down in the den, Almeda poured another two glasses of port and quizzed Dan about his background and degree of experience in procuring art pieces, which Morrow breezed through, drawing from his experiences, creatively constructing a whole imaginary life on the fly. Lying came naturally to Morrow, and although not generally perceived as a positive attribute, he reasoned his occupation made it mandatory for his survival.

Almeda followed up with a description of his own circumstances. "So, that is the situation, Mr. Thompkins. I don't have a lot of time. The painting is almost certainly in the hands of the fence, Conrad LeBlanc, and it is, no doubt, well-guarded. In just four weeks a collector from the east coast, a man reputed to be mob-connected, arrives to buy it. My only hope of getting my painting back is to, um, procure it before then."

"Four weeks is not a lot of time," Morrow said.

"No, it isn't. It's one week less than five weeks, and that's all the time I offered the last gentleman. He declined."

Morrow took his last sip of the port. "I guess I'll just have to hurry. My price will be six hundred thousand with fifty up-front for expenses."

"I can afford four hundred, maybe four fifty, but that's all."

He's offering me the job already. He's got no choices. If I say no, he'll have even less time for the next guy.

"I understand. I want to thank you for your fine hospitality and wish you the very best. I can let myself out." Morrow rose from his seat and took eight paces towards the door before he heard Almeda speak.

"Perhaps I can do five twenty-five."

Morrow turned around slowly. "Sir, I am the one who can do this. No one else can, but I can. I usually don't dicker."

"You say that, but you have no credentials or references."

Morrow provided a small chuckle for Almeda's sake. "Doctor, you know as well as I do that no client of mine will even acknowledge knowing me. And after I do this for you, you will purposely forget my name. The kind of business we do is based on professional trust. After I'm paid, I won't remember your name either."

Almeda nodded and followed up with one more question. "Mr. Thompkins, or whoever you are, I assume you've done your homework, and you know of my reputation?"

"I did, and I do," Morrow lied. *The homework will have to wait until later.*

"I'm desperate to gain back my painting. It means the world to me. Failure isn't an option. I, um, I don't handle failure well. If you accept this role, I'll pay your six hundred thousand, but I expect the original *Gabriel's Steed* to be handed over to me by no later than Sunday, June 2nd."

Morrow walked back over to where Almeda was seated and extended his hand. "Then we have a deal."

5

Birds seemed chirpier than usual as Morrow left Almeda's mansion with a check for fifty thousand dollars in his pocket, striding to his car. He loved this feeling. It wasn't making a boatload of money that pleased him. It wasn't the anticipation of success that was ringing his bell. He knew what it was, and he allowed himself an extraordinarily brief smile of appreciation.

He used to wonder about himself. About why he reacted so strongly to moments like these. He didn't wonder anymore. It was clear what he enjoyed about the process. It was the planning. It was the opportunity to use his imagination to dream up a game plan to win the day. He knew the next twenty-four hours would be exhilarating. Others might engage in daydreams about what to do with all that money, but Morrow was way past that. He couldn't wait to sit down at a bar with a pen and notepad and start his list of bullet points—who he'd need, what he'd need, what the sequence of steps would be, how he would do a clean wrap, and how he would get away with it.

Morrow parked in front of a bar he'd never been in before, just off Powell Street. The lighted sign above flashed *Park Place Pub*. He took a step in. No one would call it a park, and it barely qualified as a place. It looked more like some entrepreneur found an unleased space and shoehorned a bar into it. It was cramped and dark, but at two in the afternoon, the place was nearly packed. It was the kind of place Morrow liked. A place he could be without being noticed. A lone table next to the front window was open with one stool next to it. He needed light to write, so he took a seat immediately. He pulled out his notepad, opened to a blank page, and titled it GSG. Thus began the planning for the *Gabriel's Steed* Gig.

18

A woman in her fifties stopped at his table and with a stern face said, "Sorry, we don't allow any work to be done here."

Morrow looked up at her and waited for her to smile. She didn't.

"I, uh, I like to doodle and—"

"Gotcha!" the woman said, laughing. "You can work all you want, but only if you order something."

Despite his usual predilection to restricting joviality, Morrow laughed too. "You did get me. You looked mighty serious. Are you taking my order?"

"I'm takin' it and makin' it."

"In that case, I'll get a Jack neat and a pint of your best IPA."

The woman flashed him a knowing smile as though he had ordered her favorite combination as well. She headed back to the bar.

Minutes later, she returned with his bourbon and chaser and said, "You gonna be a regular around here?"

"I might. Never know."

"Then I should introduce myself. I'm Sadie Ervine, owner, operator, and janitor."

"Sadie, I'm Morrow, and I'm glad to meet an entrepreneur like you."

Sadie gave him a nod and returned to the bar.

Morrow turned to his notepad and wrote, *Sadie's Bar – May 5, 2019.*

His pen poised in his hand, he hesitated for a moment. This was it. His first full-fledged con—his opening gambit. Instinctively, his thoughts ebbed back to Edwin. Those had been the years. Fresh out of prison after serving three ugly years for being the driver in a heist he knew nothing about, he moved to Phoenix, and Edwin took him under his wing. He learned everything there was to learn about running a con, and now it was his turn to completely run his own.

Morrow flashed back to the day before Edwin died. That was the day Edwin finally gave him rule number ten, the last one. He'd said, "It's all about one buck. Just one. Take the pressure off yourself. Budget the con to pay you one dollar. If you did it right, you'll make a lot more." He explained that as long as you take care of your team and walk away with at least one buck in your pocket, it's a win. Anything more is gravy.

Morrow allowed himself an inside smile as he remembered that day. *One buck. One buck, Morrow. I can do that.*

During the next two hours, his creative juices flowing, Morrow planned out the play's rough outline. He decided he'd need six people, and Rafe would be one of those. For the other five, he quickly jotted down his first choices.

Morrow flagged down Sadie and ordered a BLT, fries, and a seltzer water.

Sadie arrived with it fifteen minutes later and said, "Here you are. So, I'm nosey. What you working on?"

Morrow eyed her for a moment and replied, "I'm outlining a daring caper to steal the Hope Diamond."

"Good," Sadie said. "I'll leave you to it."

Morrow jotted down some final notes, finished his meal, and paid his check. "See ya, Sadie. Could you reserve that back booth for me and some friends tomorrow afternoon, say two o'clock?"

"Kinda dark over there."

"I know. It's perfect."

At 1:50 the next day, Morrow arrived and took a seat in the U-shaped booth, facing the front door. If he sat right on the end, he could see people as they walked in and could summon them to the back.

First to arrive was Chuck Young, one of the muscle men. Chuck was in his mid-twenties, with a chiseled body and a Marine haircut. Morrow knew exactly how he would use Chuck, but even if he didn't, it always paid to have an enforcer on the team.

Next in the front door was Paul Nash. He was the forger, and his job was to paint a B+ copy of *Gabriel's Steed*. He could do an A+, but he'd need more time and more money, neither of which Morrow had.

Bubba Baine entered, holding the door open for Jenny Caldwell as they both arrived at the same time. Bubba was a giant of a man who would work with Chuck, playing the muscle men in Morrow's plan. Jenny was the computer whiz needed for the grand finale. She was five-foot-two but wore heels and a short skirt. Nothing like the typical programmer, but she was the brightest mind that Morrow knew. As he watched her approach, he flashed back to that moment a year ago when he'd made a modest move on her, testing her interest. She'd put her hand on his chest and said, "Whoa, boy. Rein in the hormones. I do business only. Got it?"

Almost against his will, an ever-so-brief smile escaped his lips and then disappeared. "Bubba, Jenny, welcome."

They sat down in the booth and gave a tepid "hi" to the others. No one knew each other, but everyone mumbled or nodded their hellos.

As Morrow started to say something, the front door opened. Rafe's heavy frame blocked the afternoon sun as he entered and spotted Morrow. Immediately behind him came Walter Hyde. The gray-bearded Walter was sixty-two and an actor on stage in the Phoenix area. Never a leading man, he filled his time with bit parts and became a sought-after character actor. His favorite role was playing the evil business antagonist, and he naturally looked the part. In real life, he was one of the gentlest men on the planet.

The two of them joined the others at Morrow's circular table and neatly filled up every bit of space available. Sadie appeared with a round of mineral waters and a vegetable plate as Morrow had instructed.

Not wasting any time, Morrow looked around the table and was pleased. Every one of them was his first choice for the role they agreed to play. "So, let's get to it," he said.

"Take a look at this." He passed around six copies of the glossy PR flyer from the Sedona-Hamilton Art Museum. It announced the amazing opportunity for locals to visit and see the Francesco Bandeaux painting of *Gabriel's Steed*. The photo of it failed to do justice to the work's magnificence, but art fans would understand that. Seeing it in person was, according to most aficionados, an awe-inspiring sight.

"*Gabriel's Steed* was displayed at the museum for six weeks and then transported under guard back to the original owner who loaned it to the museum. It never completed the trip. The truck was stopped and taken over by parties unknown. Bandeaux's masterpiece was never seen again. Now, though, there are rumors that a fence named Conrad LeBlanc has it in his possession and is holding it for sale to a rich collector. The original owner has hired us to get it back for him."

"We're going to break in and steal it?" Chuck asked.

Morrow scratched his neck and said, "No, that seems kinda violent. I think it'd be better if he just willingly gave it to us."

"Right!" Paul said. "And maybe the sun will rise in the west for a change."

"Maybe it will," Morrow replied. "I'm going to paint this gig in broad strokes for everyone and discuss it in more detail with each of you one on one."

He looked around the table again and, in a slightly lower voice, said, "In four weeks, a Baltimore mobster will fly into town and land at one of the area's minor airports, then he'll drive to the LeBlanc mansion and close the deal to buy the painting. Except I'm going to identify the airport in advance, and he's going to run into delays in trying to leave the airport. And while he is being delayed, Walter—a consummate actor, I might add—will take his place, pulling up in front of LeBlanc's office/home in a black limo. That'll be about the time that Mr. Mob would have shown up if he'd been on time. He'll get out with Chuck and Bubba playing the bodyguards and with Jenny playing his assistant."

Morrow paused to take a sip of his mineral water. "Now we don't know yet how much Mr. Mob agreed to pay, so we will be doing some research on that, but, Jenny, why don't you explain how we're going to pay for the painting and get it turned over to us in less than ten minutes."

Jenny reached into her pocket and pulled out an odd-looking piece of equipment. "This is something I've nicknamed the Dream Stealer. When I get it within five feet of another computer, it wirelessly sends an image of what's on the computer's screen to my computer. With a few keystrokes, my computer screen replaces his, looking identical."

Morrow jumped in. "That's when Walter will say to LeBlanc, 'I'm ready to make the transfer. Are you ready to receive?' We're anticipating that will cause LeBlanc to turn his head and look at Walter, right, Jen?"

"Yes, and that's when I'll key this button on the Dream Stealer, and his screen will flash, go black, and then recover. But what he'll see then is really our reproduction of his bank account. We'll show a bogus million dollars, or whatever they agreed to, rolling into LeBlanc's account. When it does, he'll hand over the painting, and we're gone. All I have to do is stay close to his computer until we're all out of there. Once I'm more than five feet away, his real bank account will show back up, and the money he thought he got will be gone too."

Morrow added, "Then we return the painting to the rightful owner, collect our fee, pay everyone here, and we can celebrate with a drink knowing we righted a wrong and got paid for it too."

He looked around at his team members and asked, "Questions?"

Everyone started to speak at once.

Morrow held his hand up and pointed to Rafe. "This is the man who brought this opportunity to our doorstep, so he should go first. Rafe, what you got?"

"What if it doesn't work?"

"What if what doesn't work?" Morrow asked.

"What if Jenny's little gizmo has a glitch or something else happens that makes the Dream Stealer fail?"

Morrow looked to Jenny.

Realizing this was her question to answer, she said, "Well, first of all, I built this thing, and I don't think it will hiccup or experience a glitch. I've tested it many times, and it never fails."

Undeterred, Rafe pushed harder. "What if he has some kind of airwave blocker around his building? You know, like the cops can shut off cell phones in a specific area during a terrorist crisis."

Jenny glanced at Morrow and said, "It's actually a decent question. Morrow's going to go inside and become a client of

LeBlanc's. It's not likely he could do that, but we'll make sure by having Morrow test a call out while he's there."

"So the device will work on any Windows or Mac computer, right? You tested both?" Rafe asked.

"I did. It's a very good plan that Morrow has. We've already discussed my part, and nothing he wants to do is unrealistic. It's actually quite easy."

Morrow started to point to Paul, but Rafe wasn't done yet. "What if he has a computer that runs on Linux?"

Jenny's jaw fell partly open. "Um, shit, Morrow, he's right. I haven't tested for that."

Morrow nodded. "This is good. This is how we become a winning team. Rafe, good thinking. We need to keep analyzing the plan and make sure we cover everything. Jenny, you do some testing and make sure it's foolproof. Rafe is right. If it fails while we're there, it's a disaster. We'll only have a few minutes before the real Mr. Mob shows up to buy his painting. He won't be pleased with us, to say the least."

The table grew very quiet. A few somber glances were exchanged.

Morrow broke the silence. "Relax, everyone. This is how it works. We keep thinking and questioning whether our plan holds water or not. Now I want to say something. Each one of you has a unique skill that our team needs, and each of you was my first choice. I know that other than Chuck and Bubba, no one knows anyone else here, but you are the cream of the crop, and I'm willing to go to any amount of effort to work with all of you. Now, Paul, you had a question."

One by one, they shared their thoughts and asked probing questions about the process. Many of the questions followed the same what-if pattern that Rafe had started with. Morrow fielded them all and made notes, identifying problem areas and backup plans they would need.

An hour and fifteen minutes later, Morrow signaled Sadie for a round of drinks. The team relaxed and took a few minutes to get to know each other. Morrow seized the opportunity to lean over and talk to Jenny. "I need one other thing from you."

"No, I won't be your date to the prom, Morrow."

Morrow chuckled and said, "Wow, one little mistake, and you never let me forget it, do you?"

Jenny smiled back at him. "You're fun to tease. You're so serious all the time. I like to see if I can ambush you and get a smile or a laugh. I think you need that sometimes."

Morrow nodded. "You're so cruel. Taking advantage of such an easy target. But, actually, I really do need one more thing from you."

"Name it."

"I, um, never really got around to doing any research on our client. Things have moved pretty fast, but I should have done that already. Would you use your internet surfing skills and reach out to your contacts to learn what you can about him?"

"Jacob Almeda is the name, right?"

Morrow nodded.

"Not a problem," Jenny said. "I'll get on it right away...well, after I do some more testing on the whole Linux thing and stuff."

Morrow turned to the others and said, "That's it for today. Sadie needs this booth for some serious customers, not ne'er-do-wells like us. I'll be in touch with each of you this week to go over the details of what you'll be doing. Four weeks from now should be payday, so let's get to work."

The team broke up, all leaving within minutes of each other.

Morrow went over to the bar to settle the tab with Sadie. It added up to only fifty-some dollars. Morrow placed a fifty and a hundred-dollar bill on the counter and waved to Sadie. "Sorry, that wasn't the kind of meeting that leads to a big bar tab. I'll make it up to ya."

"Just give me the Hope Diamond, and we'll call it square."

Morrow rolled his eyes.

6

24 days left.

"Red, you got an insurance investigator named Sawyer here in the lobby waiting for you," the desk sergeant said.

"I'll be down in a minute," Detective Clyde Fuller replied. Fuller started with the Phoenix P.D. nineteen years ago and had been a detective for the last eleven years. He was the most veteran officer in the department, and he mulled that over for the hundredth time as he walked down the stairs to the lobby. Quietly, to himself, he muttered, "If I'm so fuckin' veteran, why do I get all the boring cases?"

Knowing there was no answer to give himself, he put on his professional face and tried his best not to take it out on the insurance investigator.

Looking around the room, it didn't take long to spot his quarry. A man with a briefcase in a blue suit, white shirt, and a tie sat patiently on the far chair.

Fuller walked up to him and put his hand out. "I'm Detective Fuller. You must be Sawyer."

The man rose to his full five-foot-eight height and shook the detective's hand. "I am. Morgan Sawyer. Do you have an office where we can talk?"

Five minutes later, they were seated in conference room B and Sawyer had half the contents of his briefcase splayed out on the table. He handed Fuller a copy of the Sedona PR flyer about *Gabriel's Steed*.

Staring at Fuller as though he were trying to judge his age, Sawyer asked, "Do you remember this case? The transport truck and the guards disappeared along with the Bandeaux painting."

"Yeah, I remember it. It wasn't my case, but I watch the news like any other person. What was so special about that painting anyway? I never understood that."

"Bandeaux was a seventeenth-century painter of no importance. He created hundreds of paintings, mostly religious, and there are still sixteen of them left in various museums in Europe and the U.S. Most art critics think of those sixteen—well, mostly they *don't* think of them. They are considered of no value except that the painter, Francesco Bandeaux, is famous for one painting and one only—*Gabriel's Steed*. It's considered a masterpiece."

"Why?" Fuller asked, feigning interest, and making a mental note of Sawyer's formal speaking style.

"Many reasons," Sawyer gushed. "The vibrant colors, the look in the steed's eyes, the exquisite reflection of the horse in Gabriel's shield, and the overall aura. You cannot look at the painting without feeling engulfed by it. One critic said it made him sense, for the first time, his own insignificance."

"Spoken like a real narcissist," Fuller mumbled.

"Anyway, it is a remarkable piece of work, copied many times, but never truly captured. But what makes it all so important is that it was painted by Bandeaux, a man of so little talent. Many say he must have seen a vision from heaven, or he was infused with the Spirit when he painted it. In any case, when it was stolen, its value was pegged at nearly two million dollars. Now, with all the mythology that goes along with it, the Steed is valued at close to six million."

Fuller didn't respond. He was hoping Sawyer would get to the point.

Looking a bit flushed, an ebullient Sawyer shook his head and said, "It *is* an amazing story and all because a very low-level artist created it. In our day and time, we would call him a one-hit-wonder."

"You mean like Buster Douglas?"

"I'm sorry, who?" Fuller asked.

"Buster Douglas. He upset Mike Tyson for the Heavyweight title."

Sawyer scrunched up his face. "Oh, sports. No, no, this was *art*. You know, something that lasts centuries."

"Art, huh? You mean more like Norman Greenbaum and 'Spirit in the Sky.'"

Sawyer scratched his head and replied, "I do not know what you are talking about, but let me get to the point of why I am here."

Fuller smiled.

"I am here to talk to you because it is rumored that *Gabriel's Steed* is here in Phoenix. We believe it is held by a fence of stature and that it is likely he will sell it soon. We paid out two million dollars when it was stolen to a Mr. Jacob Almeda, and so now we stand as the new rightful owner, and we could gain that amount back and more if we gain possession of it."

"We? As in the insurance company?" Fuller asked.

"Yes, and we think we know where it is. We would like you to help us get it."

Now, Detective Clyde Fuller, his orange-red hair flopping on the top of his head, moved closer to the investigator. *Finally, something interesting to do.*

7

Morrow took a deep breath as he sat in his Toyota, parked half a block away from the front door of the LeBlanc mansion. He could feel the perspiration starting to form on his forehead. Today was the real start of the con, and he was feeling the pressure and loving every minute of it.

He walked himself through his initial conversation and felt comfortable with it. He'd already sent Jenny into the foyer once, pretending to be an assertive salesperson who dismissed the no solicitation signs. He knew there was a tall receptionist, prim and proper, at the front desk who immediately ordered her to turn around and leave. Jenny put up a good fight and even blurted out the first line of her sales pitch before she was cut off and unceremoniously led back to the door. Morrow expected a similar response.

For the third and last time, he swiveled the rearview mirror around to view himself. His tie was yellow and didn't quite complement his blue-checkered suitcoat and slacks. He started to straighten it and then decided it was better as it was. He wanted to look like a man with no flare for style, like someone who wanted to dress well but was unable to discern if he had or not. It was the first dropped hint that he was harmless, simply not sharp enough to ever pull a fast one on the great Conrad LeBlanc.

Morrow got out of his car, went around back, and cautiously picked up his painting from the trunk. He secured the brown paper wrapping around it and began walking up to the mansion. With his game face on and doing his best to temper any light in his eyes that might display a higher intellect, he took the front stairs one at a time.

Unlike Jenny, who barged in the front door, Morrow knocked three times and stood there calmly. He could hear high-heeled footsteps coming to the door.

Jen was right; the receptionist was tall and a bit severe looking. She had short blond hair and wore glasses, and Morrow's first thought was that she wasn't the smiling type.

"Can I help you?"

"Yes, I'm Chuck Dawes. I'd like to see Mr. LeBlanc. I have a painting that—"

"Do you have an appointment?" the woman asked, cutting him off.

"Well, no. I just assumed he wouldn't mind getting more business, so I brought—"

"Come back when you have an appointment." With that, she shut the door in his face.

Morrow pursed his lips and knocked on the door again.

This time, the woman opened it partway and said, "No, I do not set up appointments in person." Then she handed him a card and slammed the door shut.

Recognizing defeat when it slapped him in the face, Morrow returned to his car. He carefully placed the painting face up in the trunk and got behind the wheel.

Shit. That was really anticlimactic. At this pace, I may need a week to get in the door. I only have twenty-three more days, and I just wasted one. Slick.

Pulling out his cell phone, Morrow dialed the number on the card. It was a recording. He waited until the tone beeped so he could leave a message.

"Hi, this is Chuck Dawes. I'd like to make an appointment, preferably for this afternoon or no later than tomorrow morning. I have a painting that I'd like to sell, and I need a dealer with, um, Mr. LeBlanc's, uh, particular skill sets to assist me in finding buyers." Morrow gave his number and signed off. He sat in his car, almost unmoving, thinking to himself that setbacks were normal for any con and he simply experienced his first on day one.

Day two wasn't better. He continued to wait for a return phone call. He left two more messages trying to convey his sense of urgency. It didn't work.

The call came at eleven thirty at night. The voice and the cadence were familiar, and Morrow instantly realized it was the receptionist.

"Mr. Dawes?"

"This is Chuck Dawes." Morrow drawled his phony last name a bit.

"This is Ms. Velloitte in Mr. LeBlanc's office. I was expecting to get your voicemail, but as long as I have you, please tell me exactly what it is you want to see my boss about."

"Ms. Bellylot," Morrow started, trying to get a rise out of her. "I have a—"

"Velloitte! It starts with a V. It's our family name going back generations." She nearly screamed it into the receiver as she interrupted him again.

"Oh, I'm sorry. Well, I was about to say, I have a painting that was painted in the 1600s, and its value is over forty thousand dollars to private collectors. But I need help reaching those people. So I'd like to show it to Mr. LeBlanc and pay him his usual fee to, you know, perform his magic."

"Mr. Dawes, Conrad LeBlanc does not deal with small commissions like that would net. I'm sorry, but I doubt he would be interested in it."

Sensing she was about to hang up on him, Morrow leaped in and said, "Wait! There's more. This is just the beginning. I'd gladly pay double his commission on this one, so he will help me with my future, um, fortuitous acquisitions."

Silence on the line ensued, and Morrow thought he could hear the wheels in Ms. Velloitte's brain turning.

"I should make it clear we do not deal in any stolen goods. That would be illegal."

"This painting's not stolen. Why would you say that? I can show you the bill of sale from Kendelton's Gallery in Tucson. They needed the cash, and I needed a painting with a high upside."

Again, silence reigned. "Who is the artist?"

"Oh, his name is, um, let me find my notes. I think Mr. Kendleton said it was Bando, um, Salvador Bando."

A long silence ensued. Finally, Ms. Velloitte said, "Perhaps you meant Bandeaux? That's E-A-U-X at the end. Francesco Bandeaux?"

"Yeah, well, I don't remember that first name, but I thought he said Salvador Bando. That sounds more right to me."

Ms. Velloitte's sigh could easily be heard through the phone. "Are you a baseball fan, Mr. Dawes?"

"Yeah, sort of."

"Sal Bando played third base for the Athletics in the nineteen sixties and seventies. I can assure you that he never painted in the seventeenth century. It was probably Francesco Bandeaux, and if it was, you've probably been bamboozled. Bring it in tomorrow and show me. If it is truly his work, then I will allow you to meet with Mr. LeBlanc. Can you be here at ten a.m.?"

"I can be there at eight a.m.," Morrow tried, hoping to gain more time back on his schedule.

"See you at ten." She hung up before he could get another word in.

Morrow turned off his cell phone and poured himself a shot glass of Jack Daniels. Quietly to no one but himself, he muttered, "I'm in."

8

22 days left.

Morrow showed up at 9:55 the next morning and knocked politely on the door. The ever-stern-looking Ms. Velloitte opened the door and allowed him into the foyer.

Chuck Dawes wore white slacks and a white suit coat, a style popular in Phoenix's overwhelming heat. He complemented it with a dark blue shirt and the same poorly knotted yellow tie he wore the other day. The effect was, once again, of a clueless man trying just a bit too hard.

"Ma'am, good morning to you," Chuck said.

The receptionist looked at him with a hint of disgust and said, "Follow me."

She led him to her office and motioned for him to sit down on the guest couch. Placing the artwork carefully on her desk, she unwrapped the painting slowly and looked it over. "Well, I'll be. Mr. Dawes, what you have here is a very unspectacular painting of no real value. However, due to other news in the art world, it may be worth more someday."

"So, it sounds like I got a good deal. I told Kendleton that I wanted to get something cheap and sell it for more," he said, trying and succeeding to sound ignorant.

Without as much as a glance at her guest, Ms. Velloitte said, "I'd say you succeeded. This is very odd, indeed." She pulled out a magnifying glass and looked very intently at the lower right corner of the painting.

"Whatchya looking for?" Chuck asked.

"Shh!" was all she said.

Morrow waited patiently for what felt like half an eternity but was only three minutes.

She turned to him and asked, "There it is. Amazing. It's authentic, all right. You have that bill of sale?"

Chuck fumbled in his vest pocket and pulled out a poorly folded single page, handing it to her. She looked it over and said, "This seems valid. Why did he agree to sell it to you, though, for only eighteen thousand dollars?"

"He seemed unhappy. He said his deal fell through, and he needed the cash. He said he made a profit on it, but it could net forty grand on the open market. He seemed surprised that he hadn't been able to sell it. I figured, you know, it was a good risk. Is it?"

Ms. Velloitte nodded. "Surprisingly, yes. It is a real Francesco Bandeaux work. Not one of his best, by a long shot, but still valuable in its own way."

"So, I can meet Mr. LeBlanc now?" Morrow asked, trying again to make Chuck appear somewhat clueless.

"No, I handle all of his sales myself if they are under a hundred K. How much do you wish to sell it for?"

Thinking fast, Morrow said, "I was hoping to get a hundred and twenty for it."

Ms. Velloitte pursed her lips and stared at the man in the poorly fitting suit. "That's not what you just said. You said forty K."

"That's what Mr. Kendleton said. I say it can be a lot more. I don't want to be leaving money on the table, you know. I'd really prefer to deal directly with Mr. LeBlanc."

"Perhaps you simply don't like women."

"Oh, no, I love women. I just don't like getting the bum's rush."

The receptionist turned back to the painting and began to rewrap it. "Well, I'm sure you'll find someone better who can help you." She handed the painting back to him and said, "I'll show you out."

Chuck shook his head. "I'm not leaving until I see Mr. LeBlanc. You show him the painting and tell him I'll pay triple his normal fee for his, um, sales help. Tell him I won't leave until he agrees, or he, himself, tells me to leave."

Appearing unflustered, Ms. Velloitte said, "We'll see." She walked out of the room, and Morrow began planning his best verbal pitch to LeBlanc.

A minute later, she returned with six feet, six inches of muscle beside her. "Lucas, would you help Mr. Dawes to the door?"

Jumping instantly to his feet, Chuck put his hands up, palms facing the man, and said, "Now, wait a minute! I came in here—"

A giant fist flew in Chuck's direction with no warning, smashing into his jaw and knocking him to the floor. As he fell, he swung the painting against the receptionist's desk, emitting a crack like a ball-peen hammer hitting a brick. Chuck's thud on the floor came next.

"You idiot!" Ms. Velloitte yelled, staring at Lucas. "I said help him to the door. I didn't say kill him. Get out of here."

Morrow watched, quite entertained, as the man-mountain scampered away like a pooch with his tail between his legs.

Expecting Ms. Velloitte to come to his aid and assist him off the floor, Morrow was only mildly surprised to see her attention and affection focused on the painting rather than him. "Oh, my God, what have we done?"

She unwrapped the painting slowly and exhaled as a closer look at the damage proved only the frame had suffered any indignity. "Oh, we can fix this. I'm very sorry, Mr. Dawes, I only wanted—"

"What's happening here?" Conrad LeBlanc said, walking into the room. "I heard all this racket and wanted to see for myself."

Still half-sitting on the floor, Morrow struggled to get up. Mr. LeBlanc approached him, hand extended. Morrow gladly accepted the help to get him upright. "Mr. LeBlanc, it was nothing, really. I'm just a very clumsy man. Chuck Dawes is my name. I slipped and hit my head and the painting on the desk."

Knowing a lie when it was well-spun, Conrad accepted his story graciously and said, "Well, nonetheless, we'll replace this frame for you and—my, that is a fine painting. Did you wish to sell it?"

Smiling, Chuck said, "Yes, sir, I do. I'd like to get a hundred twenty for it or whatever the highest price you can land for me."

LeBlanc glanced at his assistant. "Well?"

"It's a legitimate Bandeaux. It's one of the—"

"Did you say it's a Bandeaux?" LeBlanc demanded.

"Yes, sir, but, sir, it is just one of his, um, unknown ones. It's not, you know, the one that, you know, everyone talks about."

Looking at his new poorly dressed client, LeBlanc said, "Of course it isn't. He wouldn't—well, I mean, the Steed has been missing for years. What is this one called?"

"The bill of sale says it's *A Study in Amber*. I've seen it before. In a Nashville gallery. Last I heard, it was for sale in Dallas. Mr. Dawes here bought it at a Tucson gallery."

"Isn't that a bit odd? How much?"

Ms. Velloitte shook her head. "Not really. This one and another of Bandeaux's have been floating around various galleries in the U.S., being sold and resold. Mr. Dawes got it for eighteen thousand. The gallery told him he might be able to fetch forty grand for it." She gave a quick roll of her eyes that only LeBlanc could see.

"I think it's worth a lot more," Chuck said, smiling like an idiot.

"Absolutely! Let's aim for the stars. There's always a generous buyer out there somewhere. Mr. Dawes, are you up to taking a stroll through my own collection and discussing how this works?"

"You bet! Lead the way," Chuck said as he stole a victory glance at Ms. Velloitte and used his handkerchief to wipe away the blood from his lips.

LeBlanc gave his newest client the grand tour. Morrow viewed high-quality copies of every painting LeBlanc had ever sold. As they walked, LeBlanc told him a short story about each one. They lined the walls of what only could be described as a room resembling a giant ballroom. Morrow imagined the ghosts of dancers from a hundred years ago, waltzing to the musical creations of the day.

After thirty-five minutes of touring, LeBlanc turned to him and said, "Are you an art lover, Mr. Dawes?"

"Sir, I am not a sophisticated gentleman like you, but I know beauty when I see it, and I have greatly enjoyed this tour. Which one is your favorite?"

"Oh, I've always been partial to that Dipre over there in the far corner. However, right now, I have a painting so incredible and so rare that I start every day staring at it. I absolutely love it and fear that any attempt at creating a good copy will fall so flat I will never enjoy it the same."

"Wow! That must be some painting. Where is it?"

Appearing lost in his thoughts, LeBlanc shook his head and said, "What?"

"Uh, I was just wondering where it was. I'd love to see it," Chuck replied, trying not to display anything more than mild interest.

"Well, I keep that in the safe. It's an original, of course, and just like yours, it will be stored in safe keeping until it's sold. Come on, I'll show you where we'll place your painting too."

Chuck returned to the office and picked up his painting, carrying it very gently. Rejoining LeBlanc, they walked together to a gray door where LeBlanc paused and called the guard to post him at the top of the stairs. He whispered something to him and then picked up a black cloth item and looked at Chuck. "You'll have to put this over your head. Security, you know. No one gets to see where the safe room actually is. Just hang on to my shoulder and follow me."

Slowly, they descended the stairway, and, once in the basement, LeBlanc led him around a series of twists and bends. Morrow sensed that it was a contrived, circuitous route designed to confuse him and give the impression that the safe room was farther away than it actually was.

Finally, they stopped, and Morrow could hear LeBlanc applying a key to a lock. A door opened, and his host said, "Follow me. Once inside, I'll take your hood off so you can see."

The door closed behind them and locked. Morrow could tell that a light came on. LeBlanc took hold of the bottom of the hood and lifted it off Chuck's head.

"There we go. And here we are."

Chuck blinked a few times and asked, "This is it? The safe room?"

"No," LeBlanc replied. "It's a corridor leading to the safe room."

The walls on each side were filled with shelving, holding nothing other than household supplies. No paintings. Looking forward, Chuck said, "It's a dead end. Where's the entrance to the safe?"

"Turn around and look at the lightbulb hanging there," LeBlanc ordered.

Chuck did as he was told and immediately sensed LeBlanc reaching out to the near side. Suddenly, a slight whirring sound came from behind him, and he turned back around. The dead-end wall was sliding away to the far side, exposing a metal safe door and a control panel on one side.

"I have four million dollars' worth of goods in here. You can't expect me to make it easy on anyone, can you? After all, I have to protect your painting now as well."

"Pretty slick," Chuck said, staying in character. *Glad the plan doesn't call for breaking into this puppy,* he thought.

LeBlanc placed his thumb on a reader screen, and then, shielding the view from Chuck, he entered five numbers on the keypad. The metal door swung open. LeBlanc's phone beeped, but he ignored it.

In what seemed like some kind of ritual, LeBlanc pushed the heavy metal door as far open as possible and then said, "Come on in. I hope you don't get claustrophobic. It's a bit small but totally impenetrable."

It *was* small. The corridor leading to it was far bigger. There were scores of paintings on both sides of the short walkway, on shelves and leaning against the walls. All sizes and types. Most were encased in glass or wrapped in paper and sealed tight. All had a notation on them—a name and a number.

LeBlanc stopped four feet in and turned to Chuck. "This is where we'll put yours, Mr. Dawes. On the paper, I'll mark Dawes 120. Your name and your desired sale amount. I apologize again for the incident that caused your frame to break. Naturally, we will fix that with a duplicate of this current frame."

"I appreciate that. So, not to rush you, but how long do you think it will take to find a buyer?"

LeBlanc smiled at his new client and said, "That will depend on you. I will forward every bid I get to you. I imagine at some point you will accept. Could be two weeks or two years."

Acting unhappy about the vagueness of the answer, Chuck nodded anyway and said, "Well, it is what it is. I guess we'll find out."

"Not that you asked, by the way, but this is all temperature-controlled and will keep your painting safe as can be. I am the only one with the code and the thumbprint to open it. The floor, walls, and ceiling look like wood, but we have three steel three-inch plates surrounding the room. There is no safer place for your painting, so do not concern yourself with worry."

"I like it! I'm feeling better already, Conrad," Chuck said, trying hard to stay in character.

As they exited the vault, Chuck suddenly said, "Hey, I almost forgot. Is your favorite painting in there? Can I see it?"

LeBlanc hesitated as he stood at the door. Then, forcing a smile onto his face, he said, "I normally don't do that, but I like you, Chuck. You seem like a nice man, and you passed graciously on your chance to blame Ms. Velloitte for what Lucas did to you, so I think you've earned it."

He walked two steps into the small vault and turned to the right. He moved three paintings to the side and, there, in all its glory, was the twenty-four by forty-inch favorite encased in glass.

"This is the painting called *Sunrise in Siena* by Emil Jarvone. I adore it. I admit I don't want to sell it, but I know I have to. For now, though, it's wonderful to be able to start every day gazing upon it. I love it. Just love it."

"It's impressive. I mean, even a klutz like me can appreciate it," Morrow said, only half-kidding.

They stared at it for a moment more, then LeBlanc closed the safe, and they walked back to the other end of the corridor.

"Before I put your hood back on, I apologize for the theatrics, but I need to make sure I protect all my clients' art, including yours."

Then, partly out of hubris and partly out of caution, LeBlanc said, "You should also know that I have twenty-four–hour armed guards here in the building and a sophisticated alarm system that sounds off if anyone attempts unauthorized access to either the mansion or the safe. When it goes off, I get a text to alert me, even if I'm not home. The police, once notified, will be here within four minutes. The precinct is less than six blocks from here. Even if anyone was successful in getting inside and getting past the guard, they would have to find the corridor and break into the safe before the police arrived. It's impossible." LeBlanc smiled at Chuck as if congratulating himself on his precautions.

"Sounds good to me. I mean, I'm only into this thing for eighteen grand, but I feel better already."

LeBlanc placed the hood over Chuck's head again and led him upstairs. Once off the stairs, he removed the hood. Ms. Velloitte stood there as if she had been waiting for them all this time. Morrow found it unnerving.

A moment later, after signing the sales contract, holding only the receipt that Ms. Velloitte gave him, Chuck Dawes left the LeBlanc mansion and headed to his car. Checking his silenced phone for messages, he spotted a text from Jenny. WE NEED TO MEET TONIGHT. SAME PLACE. 8 PM.

Not exactly thrilled that Jenny seemed to be taking over control of the con but amused at her encouraging sense of urgency, Morrow texted back, C U THERE.

He was ready. The visit could not have gone any smoother. He had a lot to share with her.

9

Morrow arrived at the Park Place Pub on time as usual. Punctuality meant something serious to Morrow, and he felt a tinge of failure whenever he was late, which wasn't often.

Walking toward the back of the pub, he spotted Jenny waving to him. She was overdressed for a hole-in-the-wall bar like this one, but then, he mused, she seemed overdressed anywhere she went.

As he came within a few steps of the booth, Morrow realized she wasn't alone. *Surprises are never a good thing*—the thought flashed through his mind in a millisecond.

Reaching the booth, he saw that Jenny had assembled the whole team. He glanced at each of their glum faces and said, "If this is a surprise birthday party, you're about three months late."

No one smiled.

Jenny spoke first. "Have a seat, Morrow. You may want to have a drink too. We've got a problem."

Morrow motioned to Sadie, mouthing the words "Jack and a chaser." Turning back to the team, he said, "Well, don't keep me in suspense. What is it?"

"Morrow, you fucked up. You didn't do your research. Or maybe you did and you didn't want to tell us what you know. That's even worse."

"You're talking in riddles, Jen."

"Then I'll get right to it. You asked me to check around about our client. Did you think I wouldn't find the dirt?"

"I was *counting* on you finding the dirt," Morrow replied. "I mean, how bad could it be? He's an old Jewish art dealer. What, he sold a fake to somebody, or he stole something? Hell, everybody has some dirt in their past."

Walter butted in. "He's connected, Morrow."

"What? How connected?"

Jenny pushed a printout of a newspaper article in front of him. "This shot was taken more than twenty years ago. That's your client there, sans the beard."

"So? He bought a painting. Where's the crime?" Morrow asked.

"Look who else is on the dais. On the far right."

"Oh, shit! Well, wait, there could be a dozen reasons—"

Jen cut him off. "That's what I thought, so I made some calls. They confirmed it. He's connected to the Russian mob."

Morrow rubbed his chin. "Well, sorry, I didn't know. But, really, I'm still not sure—"

"It gets worse," Jenny said. "He has a reputation. Turns out that he doesn't tolerate failure very well."

"Does anybody?" Morrow asked. "Anybody here at this table enjoy failure? Raise your hand, I'm doing a survey here."

"Look, Morrow," Bubba began. "We signed on for what looked like a fun little gig. No rough stuff and a nice payday, helping out an old man. But what Jen said is right, and it changes everything."

Jenny added, "Morrow, the word on the street is that anyone who fails Almeda disappears. I mean, for good."

"Maybe he started the rumors himself. You know, to, um, incentivize people," Morrow mused.

Jenny shook her head. "I wouldn't bring this up if it weren't substantiated by multiple sources. *Gabriel's Steed* was stolen as it was being transported from a Sedona museum back to Almeda. He hired the owners of an armored car service to do the job for him. Those two men are still missing. This guy doesn't like to lose. So here we are."

Morrow took a swig of Jack and washed it down with his beer. He looked around the table and pondered his response. Knowing it was inevitable, he decided to bring it up himself. "So, I should assume you guys no longer want to play?"

Chuck Young spoke first. "Morrow, you're a straight shooter, and I like working with you, but I don't really need this in my life. I'm sorry, but I'm gonna have to bow out."

Walter was next. "Me too, Morrow. I'm a minor-league con guy. This is the big leagues, and I shouldn't be playing up here."

Morrow nodded and looked at the others. Bubba bailed next, and he was followed quickly by Paul and Jenny. Only Rafe was left. Morrow tried to make it easy for him. "Rafe, you got family. I get it."

Rafe just nodded and said "sorry" with his eyes.

"OK, then," Morrow said, attempting to sound chipper about it. "I'll, uh, I'll move to plan B. No hard feelings." He left the booth and called back over his shoulder, "I'll get the drinks tab."

The others filed out slowly, saying nothing more.

Morrow sat at the bar and ordered another round for himself.

Sadie served him and watched as his team left the building. "No more team?"

Morrow just shrugged and downed his last shot of Jack in one pull. Staring back at his reflection in the mirror, he raised the beer in a silent toast to himself. *Nice job, Morrow. You have twenty-one days left to complete the heist, you're already off to a slow start, and now you've lost your entire team. You'll have to rethink the plan and build a brand new team of unproven second choices. There's a recipe for success if I ever heard one. And, as an extra bonus, if I don't steal that painting before it's bought and gone for good, they'll find my body someday at the bottom of the Rio Grande.*

10

Morrow slept on it. That is, he slept for four hours and lay in bed for four more until a plan took shape. Then he put it into action.

Over a lengthy bacon-and-eggs breakfast, with a generous order of hash browns, Morrow picked his new team. It was comprised of a few people he knew and a slew of others referred to him but whom he'd never seen in action. Certainly not the kind of action he had in mind.

Morrow mulled over the situation that was created by the need for new players. *Walter was the key to the original plan. He's a quality actor who could pull off playing the Baltimore mobster. No one else I know can do that. One wrong move, and we're all dead. That changes everything. With time running out, we can't use that plan. We won't get the painting through trickery now—we'll have to steal it. We'll have to get into that safe. I know it's there. LeBlanc showed me the* Sunrise in Siena *piece. It was beautiful but not so great that he's motivated to start every day gazing at it. Gabriel's Steed is in that safe, and we're gonna have to get it ourselves. So now, what do I need to pull that off?*

With only twenty-one days left, Morrow had to hatch a new plan fast. He was fairly certain he knew what he needed. Seven people. Lucky seven: a safecracker, an actor for a minor role, two muscle men, a driver, a lookout, and a woman. The woman would have to be smart and capable of pinch-hitting, playing whatever role might come up. He identified his best shots and started making phone calls.

Two hours and three refusals later, Morrow had five of the seven lined up. It was a start and would have to do.

Wasting no time, Morrow scheduled a meeting at seven o'clock that night at the Park Place Pub. This time, he arrived an hour and a half early. He sat in the rear booth as usual and ordered a dinner salad, a steak medium, and assorted vegetables. As he ate, his penchant for gallows humor emerged. *Look at me. I'm eating healthier food like I might be alive long enough for it to matter.*

Doing his best to dismiss the thought, he made some more notes to himself and considered the elephant in the room—should he tell everyone about his client's propensity of executing anyone who failed? There were some serious pros and cons. For example, nervous, worried con artists screw up more. A con has to flow; it has to be natural. Fear of getting taken out tended to hinder the kind of creativity that a quality con required. On the other hand, not telling them felt wrong and was, it seemed, poor manners. As he finished his meal, he was still undecided on the issue.

The first member of the second team entered the pub at 6:55. Looking around, he spotted the last booth and a man sitting alone, eyes on the door. He walked up to the man in the booth and asked, "You Morrow?"

"You must be Jamal," Morrow replied as he motioned the young Black man to join him in the booth.

Morrow eyed Jamal, a slender man of medium height, dressed totally in black and wearing a black knit cap. In the dark of the bar, it was hard to see where the black seatback ended and Jamal began. Morrow said, "Jesse referred you to me. He said you were the best lookout he knew. Called you something diff—"

"Ghost," Jamal cut him off. "Most people just call me Ghost."

Morrow cocked his head at an angle and said, "Because...you're dead, or supposed to be?"

"No, man, because I'm invisible. No one notices me. I, uh, sorta blend in."

Morrow chuckled. "No shit. I can hardly see you, and you're less than three feet away."

Ghost nodded and said, "Comes in mighty handy when I'm on lookout."

"Well, that's good because that's what I'll need you for."

Morrow looked back toward the door and saw two very large men eyeing him. Two brothers, enforcers, musclemen referred to him by his workmate, Wade. The shorter one stuck his hand out and said, "You must be Morrow. I'm Brady. This is my brother, Shady."

Morrow had to strain his neck to look up to Shady's forehead. He stood six-foot-eight, weighing in at close to three hundred pounds. "Take a seat, guys."

"We didn't think we'd be the first ones here, but it's nice—"

"You're not. Meet Ghost. He's our lookout," an amused Morrow said, pointing to the back of the booth.

"Oh, man, I heard of you," Brady said, sticking his hand out to shake Ghost's.

Again, Ghost just nodded.

"So, Brady," Morrow began, "Ken Westphall said you and your brother were new to the game but very competent. He spoke highly of you."

"Thanks, Morrow. We just like to stay busy, ya know."

Shifting in his seat to look more at the taller brother, Morrow said, "But Ken didn't tell me your brother's name. Shady, that has to be a nickname, right?"

Brady cut in. "He grew so fast. By the time he was ten, he was taller than our dad. Pops started calling him a tree. Then one of my brother's pals made a joke on a hot day, asking him to stand to his left and give him some shade. Next thing you know, everybody's calling him Shady. Brady and Shady, that's us. Kind of a marketing thing now, ya know."

Shaking his head in wonder, Morrow said, "You do all his talking for him?"

Brady glanced at his brother and then replied, "He's mute."

Having no prepared response to that news, Morrow noticed Shady gave his brother a "why'd you have to tell him that?" look, so he said, "Doesn't matter. Brady, Shady, glad to have you aboard."

Standing right there, overhearing it all, was Lucky Lou Scarpelli, the safecracker and bomb builder. Lou was the only player Morrow had met before. Morrow introduced him to everybody as Lou sat down. When he did, he felt like a kid at the grown-up's table.

46

He sunk into his seat and almost seemed to disappear. At five-foot-seven, Lou was diminutive, but his role was likely to be huge.

"Is this everybody?" Lou asked.

"No, we're still waiting on one more. Then what I really need is a woman."

"Jeez, Morrow. I thought this gig was priority one. You gotta curb that appetite of yours," Lou said.

Morrow bounced his head a few times and dryly commented, "I meant I want a woman on the team. A good female player always pays dividends. After we pull this off, then you can make some jokes about me. Meanwhile, this gig has got all my attention. Hey, that might be him now—no, wait, it's a guy and his wife." To Morrow's surprise, the thirty-something couple who just walked in spotted the last booth and made a beeline directly to it.

The man led the way, and he immediately put his hand out and said, "You Morrow?" Not even waiting for an answer, he followed up with, "I'm Tommy Romano, and this is my wife, Connie."

Morrow's eyes went wide as he stood up and whispered, "Tommy, this isn't really the kind of meeting you bring your wife to."

Tommy smiled and said, "I knew you'd say that, but we're a team. We do everything together. Connie's in the know and has lots of connections. She's been a player longer than I have. She won't cost you anything extra, and she can help."

Pointing to the booth, Morrow continued standing until the couple slid in and got comfortable. Morrow gave a nod to Sadie, and she came over to take the first round of orders.

Tommy and Connie seemed to know everyone, so introductions weren't necessary.

"Connie, tell me a little about yourself," Morrow ordered.

"Started being a player when I was fourteen. My old man used to be in the game, and sometimes he'd use me like, you know, a prop. Later I did a few gigs of my own. Met Tommy that way. Now, I mostly do computer stuff and, you know, cameos."

Before Morrow could comment, Tommy added, "She's dynamite, Morrow. She can put a fake website together in an hour for backstories, and she's slick with research too. And a fine actress!"

"Tommy, when she screams 'you're the king' in bed, that's good acting too," Ghost said and chuckled.

"Ghost, you say the rawest things," Connie said with a cackle.

"OK, enough frivolity," Morrow said. "Let's get down to work. Connie, welcome aboard."

For the next hour, Morrow laid out the story, describing his meeting with Almeda. He explained the unique features of *Gabriel's Steed* and how the artist, Bandeaux, must have been divinely inspired since everything else he painted was unimpressive and ordinary. Then he talked about the Ice Queen at LeBlanc's mansion, his one visit there, and the safe.

"So what's the plan?" Lou asked.

"It's a work in progress, Lou," Morrow admitted. "I've already taken some steps. Almeda told me about a painting for sale in a Tucson gallery. I drove down and bought it. It's one of Bandeaux's worthless ones. I used it as my prop when I needed a painting to take into LeBlanc's. I wanted to see how surprised they were and how'd they react to having another Bandeaux painting."

"How'd they do?" Lou asked.

"They were pretty cool about it. Ms. Velloitte danced around it. She knew about the Steed, but I couldn't tell if she knew LeBlanc is dealing it. He sounded really surprised, which makes me think we're on to something."

"Then what are we doing next?" Brady asked.

Morrow admitted they didn't have a solid plan yet but would work it out soon. Looking around at the new team he'd assembled, he made a decision on the fly. He needed to explain why they didn't have a complete plan, which necessitated telling them about the other team.

A bit wide-eyed, Brady said, "Yowza! So we're the B team?"

"Only if you think you are," Morrow replied. "I built the first team with people I knew because it was the path of least resistance. The only one of you I've met before is Lou, and I didn't need him on that team because we had a different plan. Now there isn't enough time to put that plan into motion, so we're going to have to, uh, procure it."

"Why'd the first team quit? They didn't like your plan?" Ghost asked.

Morrow took a deep breath. "They quit because we found out something ugly about our client."

It felt like the silence in the booth was overwhelming the natural din of the pub. Morrow waited a moment to make sure he had everyone's attention.

"Turns out our client has a pattern. Anyone who fails him tends to get some version of the feet-in-the-cement-tub treatment." Morrow looked at each of their faces.

"Is that all?" Connie said. "Shit, in our line of work, you gotta figure you're always up against that."

Morrow tried hard to suppress a grin. He wanted to lean over and plant a wet one on her cheek.

"That's the way we look at it, too," Brady said. Shady nodded his agreement.

Morrow looked in Jamal's direction. "Ghost?"

"They can't kill me if they can't find me. And nobody can find me unless I want 'em to."

Still working hard to suppress a grin, Morrow turned his gaze to Lou. He didn't need to ask.

"Come on, Morrow. You and I both know it's all in the planning. Create a good cool-out, and we'll all be long gone before the competition even knows they're on the bullet train to Chumptown. I know you. I'm fine with it."

Even in the relative darkness of the dim corner booth, Morrow made eye contact with each person at the table, then said, "I was wrong. The first team was the B team. You guys are the A squad."

11

Day twenty before the deadline was spent in meetings. Morrow met with each player individually to discuss their roles and the timing of each action.
The other team members didn't know that the exercise was Morrow's way of fleshing out the plot in his own mind. He still didn't have a good scheme for breaking into the safe, but it was getting to that point that he still had to plan. He trusted that he and Lou would come up with a good safecracking strategy soon.

The next morning found Morrow knocking on the LeBlanc mansion door. Once again, it was the Ice Queen herself, Ms. Velloitte, who responded.

"What do you want now, Mr. Dawes?"

"Well, I'd like to see the repairs you've made to my frame, and I need to talk to Conrad too."

"Mister LeBlanc is out right now," she replied, putting heavy emphasis on the word *mister*.

"Oh, shoot. I had a lead for him. When can I catch him here?"

Ms. Velloitte angled her head to the right and said, "That sounds suspiciously like an appointment. I don't schedule appointments in person. You'll have to call in."

"You're kidding, right? I'm a client now. Clients have privileges, right? And why am I still standing on the porch? Can't you invite me in?"

"I'll tell him you stopped by," she said. "Call me when you want to set up an appointment."

"Now, just a—"

She closed the door in his face.

Morrow turned and walked back to his car, talking to himself every step of the way. "What in the name of Wally Pipp is going on?

This is fuckin' nuts! Nothing is going right here. How am I supposed to get to know LeBlanc if I never get to see him? Who would've expected I would run into the Teutonic Bitch from Hell as his receptionist-guard? She's killing me. I've gotta figure out a way around her—and fast!"

Driving away from this latest humiliating scene, Morrow headed to Sadie's place for some lunch and a quiet thinking booth. He needed time to logic out this newest problem. Parking a half block away in a free spot, Morrow locked up his Toyota and walked to the entrance. Deep in thought, he paid no attention to the two goons walking directly at him. As they got closer, Morrow looked up and instantly knew he was in trouble.

The two Barger musclemen were easy to recognize. He'd last seen them when they were pointing a bazooka at him and Mr. Westcott. They wasted no time picking him up off the ground, each with a hand under his armpits. They escorted him into an alley next to the pub, threw him against the wall, and smiled. They weren't friendly smiles. It was more like the smile you show when you know you're going to win and the other guy isn't.

Without another word, the goon on the right slugged Morrow on the chin. The one on the left gave him a blow to his midsection. Morrow doubled over and coughed out, "What's all this for?"

"Mr. Barger doesn't like you," the goon on the right said. "You're the fancy driver who got Westcott away from us the other day. He wants to let you know we know who you are. It's like a helpful hint. We think you should not be working there anymore. Maybe even get out of town. Think of it as a health tip."

"I take vitamins every morning. I had no idea that Barger was so concerned about my well-being."

The other goon replied, "You got a smart mouth. We don't like smart talkers. Wanna see what we do when we find one?"

"Nah, thanks. I think I saw it already."

"Think of it as our way of saying goodbye." Both goons unleashed on Morrow, landing a series of blows that left him lying on the ground, conscious but wishing he weren't.

An hour later, Morrow had managed to drive himself to a nearby Motel 6, where he got a room. He didn't have the energy to drive himself back to the compound. All he wanted to do was clean up a bit and lie down. Day twenty passed with no further progress.

12

19 days left.

After a three-hour nap, Morrow rose and checked himself out in the mirror. Caked blood on his face and neck. His face looked like it was used as a battering ram. One eye was blackened and partially swollen.

He removed his shirt and gingerly touched the darkest spots on his torso, applying very little pressure and feeling how sensitive they were anyway. More parts of his stomach and chest were discolored than weren't. Taking a deep breath was challenging.

Looking at himself, trying to be objective, he mumbled, "I've seen worse." Armed with that encouraging thought, he took a shower and tried to clean himself up so that his appearance wouldn't scare women and children. When he was finished, it was better, but not by much. Always a hard grader, he gave himself a D+ for his make-up efforts.

This new development put him in a more precarious position. Now he had a client who suggested violence may occur if he wasn't successful and a real enemy who was handing out more than threats and could strike him at any time. As much as he wanted to focus on stealing the painting, he knew that he had to do something about Barger, or Barger's next move could be much worse and would likely foil their plans for *Gabriel's Steed*. There was only one thing he could do—have a drink and plan his move against Barger.

When he entered the Park Place Pub, Sadie looked at him, smiled, and then did a double-take. Morrow approached the bar and took a seat.

"I hope the other guy looks like hell."

"Actually, there were two of them, and no, they look perfectly fine," Morrow quipped.

"Hmmph. Makes sense, I guess. You look like more of a thinker than a fighter."

Morrow nodded. "I tried to tell them we should talk, but, you know, I'm not sure those two guys could fire off a complete sentence. They were pretty good at the violence part, though. How about a Jack and chaser?"

"I'm on it. Your booth is open if you want it."

Straining to get up without causing more pain, Morrow moved over to the dark booth and slipped into it. Sadie followed him with his order.

"You need anything, just holler," she said.

Morrow simply nodded.

He sat in the darkness and nursed his drink. *OK, Morrow, I hate your idea of progress. This morning I was in the frying pan, now I'm in the fire. If it weren't for going backward, I wouldn't move at all. Doesn't take a genius to know what my next move is, but I need to think this through. What questions do I have to ask him?*

I'm going to get one shot at a solution, and it will need to be spot on. I gotta lay low while I do it, and if I fuck it up, they'll be fitting me for cement shoes. Well, no one can say I'm not doing a bang-up job.

After making his list of questions, Morrow finished his drinks and left twelve bucks on the table with the empty glasses. Sadie was in the kitchen, and he wasn't in the mood for conversation anyway. He exited out the front door, walked past the alley where he could still see his blood splattered on the wall, and walked slowly to his car. Thirty minutes later, he was at the gate of Westcott's compound.

To his credit, the guard made no comment about Morrow's appearance. It wasn't like he'd never seen the signs of a tussle on someone's face before. Morrow pulled around to his apartment, cringed as he walked up one flight of stairs, and entered. He immediately sat down on the bed and laid back. He was always amazed how the tiniest bit of exertion would take such a high toll on a bruised body like his. For a brief moment, he flashed back to something his mother told him. She'd said, "When you're sick, your body unleashes millions of little cells that attack the injuries and work furiously trying to take the pain away." It was something a kid could understand, and the vision of it danced in his head now, just as it did when he was nine.

After a few minutes, he went to the bathroom, pulled out his first aid kit, and removed the gauze. Carefully, he wrapped it around his chest where he felt the most pain. He was sure one or more ribs were sprained or maybe even broken. It happened on a few occasions in the past, and he knew how it felt. After binding his chest tightly, he left the apartment and walked over to the Westcott house.

The maid let him in and cast him a long look before she went to find Mr. Westcott. Morrow waited in the foyer, biding his time and reminding himself which questions he needed to ask.

A few minutes later, Morrow was shown into the private den. Westcott sat at his desk, looking at his paperwork. Morrow walked in and stood silently. Westcott looked up and calmly said, "I used to know a tackling dummy that looked better than you."

"I bet he felt better too."

"Take a seat and tell me what happened, as if I can't guess."

Morrow told him about the two Barger goons and their message. He glossed over the gory details. No need to dramatize it more than it was.

When he finished, Westcott rose from his desk and walked over to a picture window, staring out at everything and nothing. Morrow patiently waited for him to come to grips with the news.

"It's not a good sign," Westcott said simply.

"I was thinking the same thing. I'm not aware of how aggressive Barger's been in other areas, but my guess is he's been doing some hit and runs."

Westcott looked over at Morrow, and his tired eyes confirmed that Morrow was right.

"Well, if you're here to inform me, you've done your job. Thank you." Westcott moved back to his desk.

Morrow, stone-faced, said, "That's not why I'm here."

Curious now, Westcott bit. "Why then?"

"This problem with Barger doesn't look like it's going away. They want me to leave town, but I think I have a better idea."

Westcott said nothing, but his eyes said, "I'm listening."

"I had an idea that could turn the tables on him and put him back in his place. It doesn't get rid of him, but it could allow peace for a while. Wanna hear it?"

Morrow laid out the plan and asked his questions. It hinged on knowing where Barger would be at a given time, and Morrow was betting that Westcott knew everything about Barger. He was right.

"Makes sense, I like it," Westcott said. "I can provide some extra men you can use."

"No, it has to be people he doesn't know. If anyone recognizes that any of the men are yours, then the illusion falls apart."

"I just hired four new guys. Two have been vetted. They haven't been out of the compound since they got here. Barger has no idea who they are."

Morrow passed a card to Westcott and said, "Have them call me. I could use two more. Any idea what he'll do next?"

"I know where he'll be on Wednesday night. He's got a little honey stashed away in a condo in Scottsdale. She gets free rent, and he gets a little action every Wednesday night. Usually about ten o'clock." Westcott smiled and continued, "The next spontaneous move Barger makes will be his first. He's predictable, but he's always fully protected. Getting to him won't be easy."

Morrow rose from the chair. "If it were easy, everybody could do it." He headed for the door.

Not one to let someone else have the last word, Westcott called out, "Hey, Morrow. For a guy who likes to lay low, you sure got a high profile."

13

18 days left.

With the new team enlarged, the booth at the pub wasn't big enough anymore. Connie volunteered her house, and the six members of the group met there. Morrow was still looking to add a driver as the seventh.

Morrow spent the first ten minutes explaining how his face came to be in the running for Federal Disaster Funds. Then he explained the new problem and told them that two more men were joining the team just to help resolve the Barger problem.

The knock on the door came early, and, for just a moment, everyone tensed up. They rose and disappeared into the kitchen, out of the line of sight. Connie answered and let the two men in. Morrow led the others out into the living room and said, "Thanks for coming, guys. We can use the help."

The taller one nodded while the other looked around to get his bearings. Tommy emerged from the kitchen last with two beers in his hands. "You guys wanna join us? We're all having a brew."

Before they could sit down, Morrow stepped forward and extended his hand. "I'm Morrow."

"I'm Vic."

The other guy said, "I'm Jayden."

The two accepted their beers and took a seat.

Morrow started right in. "Here's the deal. I imagine Westcott or someone at the compound told you about our little skirmish with Barger and his men."

Vic nodded.

Jayden said, "Yeah, we heard. Sounds like you almost got blown to smithereens. Pretty ballsy of them. Now they're doing hit and runs. Looks like you were one of the hits."

"I should have run, right?"

Everybody except Morrow chuckled.

"So we have a plan for some retaliation that we hope can work," Morrow said. "This is, by the way, a good way for Westcott to see what kind of work you can do. No one, and I mean absolutely no one, can ever learn what we're doing here. We'll all just do it and then keep it to ourselves. You two should never even talk about it when you think you're alone. Got it?"

"Yeah, we got it," Vic said. "Westcott said essentially the same thing."

"OK, so here's the plan. Brady, you're gonna rent a van and put a decal on it that says 'Valley Delivery Service.' Shady, you're going to rent a U-Haul box truck. Pick up a couple pieces of cheap furniture to put in for effect. You got an ID with a different name on it?"

Shady nodded as his brother said, "We both got plenty of IDs and cards that are valid."

"Good," Morrow said. "Keep your receipts. We'll settle up after we win. Lou, you still working with that German guy, the procurer?"

"Yup."

"I have a shopping list here for you. I'll front the money." Morrow handed a list to the safecracker.

Lou looked it over. "Nine bulletproof vests, two one-pound slabs of inert C4, parts for two bombs, four pet tranquilizer guns— what are we gonna do here, Morrow, start some weird war?"

"No, we're just being careful. I don't want anybody hurt." Turning to Connie, he said, "Connie, can you set up your laptop to tap into four or five of the street cameras near Third and Travis? We're gonna need advance warning when Barger is coming and if he's bringing help."

"Hey, I'm the lookout here," Ghost said. "That's my job."

"Not this time. Barger always has extra security coverage. My guess is he'll send one, maybe two sharpshooters to plant themselves in strategic spots to protect him. He's gotta get out of his car and walk thirty yards in the open. This is your chance to use your army sniper training to make sure those fellas never get a shot off."

Morrow took a swig of his beer and continued, "Vic, you and Jayden will be with me. You're gonna take down two of the Barger goons. Wear all black, and black ski masks too. We don't want Barger seeing any faces that work at the Westcott compound. Tommy, same goes for you, but if Ghost sees two shooters, you'll switch over to assist him."

"Got it," Tommy said, nodding.

"Now, listen close," Morrow said. "We have to all work as a team because timing will be critical. I'm going to walk everybody through their actions in order as the whole play will actually go down. We start Wednesday night at eight o'clock getting into positions. Show up with all your gear."

Wednesday night almost came too soon. Lou didn't have the bombs built until seven o'clock, and Tommy had to threaten the poor guy at the print shop with bodily harm to get his fake delivery company sign made on time.

At 8:15, Morrow stood with Ghost, staring at the soon-to-be-demolished apartment building a block away.

"Yeah, that's where I'd be if I were him," Ghost said. "With only a flat parking lot between that dump and the girlfriend's condo, he'd have a clean shot if he had to take it."

"Which floor ya think?" Morrow asked.

Ghost rubbed the stubble on his chin. "It's ten stories. I'm thinkin' he'd want a good angle, so probably the eighth or ninth. Someplace where the window is already broken. I see a few good options there."

"Get in position, and as soon you spot him or them, let me know. If it's two guys, Tommy will get one and you take out the other."

"Uh, Morrow, maybe I misunderstood. You don't want me to *kill* this guy, do ya?"

"No, hell no. We don't do that stuff. You'll get one of the tranquilizer guns. We use this mixture called QuadXX. You shoot him with that anywhere, and he'll turn to mush almost instantly. They lose all muscle function."

"All?" Ghost asked, scrunching up his face.

"Yeah, all. So it may get a little, um, malodorous. Just remove his rifle, tie him up, and leave him there. Barger can get him in the morning. Don't forget to give him the message exactly as I wrote it. That's important."

Ghost chuckled and said, "Man, I've taken out the trash before, but this is a first for me. I got a place picked out. I'll let everyone know on the com when I spot the shooter." With that, he headed over to the parking lot.

Morrow walked over to talk with Brady and Shady and make sure they were ready and understood their roles. He did the same with every member of the team, finally finishing with Connie on her cell phone, parked half a block from the Barger Compound exit. By ten o'clock, he was back in the temporary HQ, a quiet bar on Fourth, to wait for the action to start. As Morrow walked in the door, Ghost called out, "Only one shooter. I got him."

Tommy heard the message and headed to the bar to wait with Morrow.

It was the waiting that was the hard part. Morrow drummed his fingers on the tabletop as Vic, Jayden, and Tommy all sat with him, waiting to hear from Ghost.

Not loving the dead silence, Vic broke it, asking, "So, what's with this guy, Ghost? He's tiny, and you send him to take out the sharpshooter?"

"Ghost has some unique talents. He blends into the dark. He may not look tough, but he makes the most out of his skill set. We should be hearing something soon."

Just then, the radio crackled in Morrow's ear, and all his men could hear it. This time, though, it was Connie. "Morrow, they're getting off the freeway. Should be there in six, maybe seven minutes."

"Thanks, Connie. Go to your designated spot."

"Jeez," Jayden said, "he's almost here. Maybe you should call Ghost,"

"He'll have his radio off. He can't allow the shooter to hear him. Any minute now, Barger's main security man will call his shooter to see if he's in place. That's what Ghost is waiting for."

Ghost sat alone in the darkest corner of what used to be apartment 804. The shooter did not select *his* apartment. He was next door in 806. Ghost had listened to him putting his weapon together and positioning it at the window. Ghost didn't move. A few minutes later, the shooter started making noise again. He was picking up all his things and leaving 806. Ghost knew why. The incentive to move had been planted by him and it took a while for the shooter to realize it.

Old unit 806 had unbroken windows, and Ghost knew that was a problem. The shooter needed an open or broken window to shoot out of, but he didn't want to be the one breaking it. A moment later, the shooter entered 804 and glanced around. He sniffed to see if the aroma in the new apartment was as bad as 806. It wasn't bad at all.

He set up his rifle at the broken window as Ghost watched it all. The shooter's right hand shot up to his headset, and he pressed his talk button. "Yep, all set," he lied into the receiver. He knew Barger was still several minutes out, and he would be set in sixty seconds. He set up his tripod and planted the rifle on it. The view was perfect, and a three-quarter moon gave him more than enough light to see his potential targets.

Still seated, Ghost removed his dart gun from his open bag and aimed it at the shooter. "You're a bad boy, lying to your boss that way."

The shooter turned in the direction of the voice, eyes wide, his right hand reaching for the rifle. Long before he could ever swing it around, his chest presented the target that Ghost wanted. He lined up his shot and pulled the trigger. Instantly a dart loaded with QuadXX struck the shooter's upper chest. The look of surprise on his face amused Ghost as he watched his target grow stiff and then crumble to the floor.

Ghost walked over and kicked the rifle away. He quickly applied ties to the man's wrists and tied his feet together as well. "Can you hear me? Say something."

The shooter was totally conscious, but his muscles betrayed him. Ghost could tell he was trying to move his jaw, but nothing was happening. Ghost reasoned that he wouldn't be able to talk either. Even his tongue wasn't obeying his brain's commands.

"Well, the good news is I won't have to put a gag on you. You'll regain your strength again in four to six hours." Ghost rubbed his nose and said, "You smell that? That, my friend, is the stench of fear. Lots of guys lose it when they're facing death. But today is not your day to die. You just tell Barger not to fucking mess with the Santangelos. We don't like it."

Before Ghost walked out of the room, he bent over and removed the headset and radio from the shooter. As he headed for the stairway of the old apartment building, he turned his radio back on. "Morrow, you copy?"

In the bar, Morrow's headset came alive. "Loud and clear."

"The shooter's down. We're a go."

Vic and Jayden could hear through Morrow's earbud. "Jeez, that little guy did it. Nice! Now what?"

"We stick to plan A," Morrow said. He got on the air and called out to everyone. "Shooter is down. Proceed with plan A. Lou, Shady, you're up."

Lucky Lou once worked as a make-up man for an acting group. He applied those skills he learned to change his appearance—to look older than he was, slower than he was, and poorer than he was.

Dressed as a homeless person in a long dingy overcoat, Lou started a slow walk in front of the Sands Place Condos. He stalled at the trash can as he rifled through it, appearing to look as though he were searching for food.

A black town car turned the corner a block away. Morrow called out, "They're here. Shady, start backing in."

The box truck, double-parked on the street now, began a slow maneuver to back up and parallel park in a space just ahead of the passenger load zone. They knew that was where Barger's driver would aim to stop. By being there prior to Barger's car showing up, it appeared to the guards that this was a coincidental happening and certainly no threat. Shady was three-quarters of the way into the parking spot when Barger's driver came to a stop in the middle of the passenger load zone. Behind them was fifteen more feet to the corner—not nearly enough space to legally park in.

The guards looked around the area. The old homeless man was all they saw moving, other than the backing truck. The back door was up, clearly displaying a table and sofa inside the truck, giving the appearance of a routine household delivery. The guard in the front seat called on the radio to the shooter. "Anything?" he asked.

Just as succinctly, Ghost did his best to mimic the shooter, whispering, "Clear."

Barger's driver exited the car first and walked up toward the cab of the truck Shady was driving. As he did, Brady's white delivery van pulled around the corner, slowed, and then parked in the illegal spot, leaving three inches between his front bumper and Barger's rear fender.

He shut off the engine and instantly jumped out with a small box under his arm. Barger's driver turned around and waved his hands in the air at Brady, screaming, "You can't be there! Gotta move!"

Brady screamed back, "I'll only be a minute!" Then he continued running down the side of the condo building toward some other destination.

Lou was now only ten feet away from Barger's car, stumbling and appearing drunk. He leaned over to pick up something shiny on the sidewalk. Both of the other guards got out of the car, reminding Barger to stay in the locked vehicle. One went toward Lou and the other moved toward the van to check it out. When the driver turned to look back at the truck, it was fully parked and backing up, less than two feet from the front of Barger's town car.

"No, no!" the driver screamed. "You have to leave us room to get out."

The truck continued to move slowly backward, stopping a mere six inches from the front bumper. Shady parked and shut off the engine. Exiting the cab, he spotted the driver/guard approaching him. He stopped, quickly pulled out his loaded dart gun, and calmly shot the man in the leg.

Tommy stepped out of a shadow and shot a dose of QuadXX into the leg of the guard near the delivery van. Vic, always hidden by Shady's truck, walked out into the open and shot the other guard in the rear, aiming for areas that would not be protected by a bulletproof vest, just as Morrow had coached them.

All three guards were down within five seconds of each other. Lou leaped up and attached one of his bombs to the windshield of Barger's car and another to the passenger side rear window where Barger sat, staring wide-eyed from the events of the last few seconds.

The car was bulletproof and locked. He could stay there, and no one could get to him. No one had ever gotten to him. But now he stared at the digital display of each synchronized bomb ticking down. 30...29...28...

Barger yelled to no one and practically squealed, "You bastards!"

The keys were still in the ignition, but the car remained trapped between a van and the box truck. Even if he could rapidly get to the front seat and start the car, there was nowhere to go. 22...21...20...

In a childish gesture, he flipped his middle finger at the homeless man and swore at him. 16...15...14...

Looking more closely at the bombs, he could see they both appeared to have about a pound of C4, and he knew the explosion would disintegrate everything for ten yards around. 9...8...7...

With no choice left, he unlocked his door and darted out of it, past the homeless man who was—wait! Why wasn't he running?

Dressed head to toe in black and sporting full ski masks, Tommy and Vic grabbed Barger's arms and dragged him over to the van. They threw him in, and Shady joined him and began to tie him up.

"Who—who the fuck are you?" Barger screamed.

Of course, Shady said nothing. Brady and Vic got into the front, backed the van up, and pulled onto the street. Morrow and Tommy followed in Morrow's car.

"Fuck me. Fuck me," Barger said. "They weren't even bombs. I didn't have to get out. You fuckers, you set this up and—"

Barger stopped talking when Shady gave him a look that would have stopped a charging elephant. Shady placed a dark blue pillow cover over his head and pushed his torso down so he was lying flat. Not another word was spoken for the rest of the fifteen-minute ride.

Barger was still steaming as he sat silently on a stool. His hands were bound, and his ankles were tied together.

Dressed all in black with a ski mask covering his face, Morrow checked to see if everybody was in position. Tommy, Vic, and Jaden were stationed in an arc facing their quarry.

Barger didn't know it yet, but he was seated in the middle of a large warehouse. No lights were on, but the roof was filled with skylights, and the moon shined brightly tonight. Enough light came through so everyone could see clearly.

Morrow approached him and removed the pillowcase cover. Immediately, he earned a snarl and a nasty stare from Barger.

Barger spit on the floor next to him. "You're a dead man. You know that? No one does this to me. No one."

Morrow didn't reply. Instead, he sat down on another stool, about fifteen feet from Barger—close enough so Barger could hear every word he said without raising his voice, but distant enough from the three guards so they may have some difficulty hearing much of anything.

Not as true for Barger, who was near the end of an obscenity-laced diatribe, screaming out his curses at all of them. Morrow waited for him to finish.

"Who are you, anyway? Do you know that I run this town? What do you want with me, you piece of shit?"

Again, Morrow made no comment. Only when Barger stopped for air did he ask, "Are you done? If not, I'll come back later."

Barger stared at him, then spit to the side again. Reluctantly, he remained quiet.

Morrow stood up. "I want to ask you why you are stealing from us."

"I'm not stealing anything. I don't even know who you are," Barger blurted out.

"We don't like what you tried to do. You tried to kill one of our assets. We own him, and we get to decide if he lives or dies, not you."

Barger froze. Now he knew who had abducted him, and it caused his stomach to twist inside out.

"You're from Santan—"

Morrow cut him off. "No names! Shut the fuck up and listen."

Barger let his sentence end early and tried to assume a straighter posture.

"We put you and the other fella in charge of this town. We have a plan for both of you. Taking him out without authority would fuck up that plan. That would be like stealing from us."

Morrow paused to let that sink in. Then, he continued, "Use your imagination and guess what it is we do to people who steal from us. The day your target got away was your lucky day. Otherwise, you'd be six feet under by now."

"We, uh, were just trying to scare him. It was, um, in fun, but it got out of hand," Barger tried.

"Shut up. When I want to hear from you, I'll let you know. I'm leaving tonight. You may be alive when I get on that plane going east, or you may not. It depends on what you decide to do. Let me tell you what we want you to do."

Morrow turned around and motioned the three guards to come in closer. Each of them held an assault rifle across their chest.

"First, we want you to cease and desist all actions against our asset to the south. And no more attacks on his men, either. Second, we want you to give back whatever areas you took from the south. Third, everything should go back to normal, but we want 5 percent more than you've been paying. That's your penalty. Or you can spit again, and then I'm leaving, and my boys can have some target practice."

Barger swallowed hard as if he had been saving up for another act of bravado.

Morrow stepped closer to Barger and whispered, "This is where you say, 'Yes, sir.' Any other answer is unacceptable."

Barger stared back at his captor, trying but failing to hide the rage he felt inside. He snarled a muted, "Yes, sir."

Perhaps enjoying the moment a bit too much, Morrow replied, "I can't hear you. I'll have to assume you don't want to cooperate."

Before he was into his second step toward the door, Barger bellowed, "I said yes, sir!"

Morrow turned to his guards. "Did you hear something?"

Tommy replied, "I heard something, but I couldn't quite make it out. Maybe he needs to say it really loud."

Morrow turned his face to Barger and whispered, "I want them to be able to hear you in Baltimore. Last chance, Barger."

His fear now clear on his face, Barger called out at the top of his lungs, "Yes, sir!"

Morrow looked at his guard crew and nodded with his head toward the exit. As they prepared to leave, Morrow told Vic to go back and untie Barger's ankles. As Vic headed toward their captive, Morrow called out, "Barger, you do what we say and never discuss this episode with us again, or with anyone else for that matter. This never happened, got it?"

"I got it," Barger said, a healthy dose of loathing dripping from every word.

"One other thing," Morrow said. "We rented this place, and I told the owner we'd clean up after ourselves. You spit on his floor. I want you to clean it up. Wipe it up with your suitcoat sleeve. My guard will stay behind to make sure you do a good job." He nodded to Tommy and winked.

Forty minutes later, Morrow was back at his new apartment in the city. He poured himself a bourbon and sat down on the lone couch. It came furnished, but the cigarette burns in the couch arms were, apparently, part of the décor. He assumed the scratches on the coffee table were freely thrown into the deal as well. It didn't matter to him. It was a convenient place to sleep. He didn't plan on inviting any company in, so he was the only one to be offended. In light of some of the places he'd called home, he wasn't offended in the least.

Dialing Westcott on his cell, he got through to the man immediately.

"Morrow, how'd it go?"

For the next ten minutes, Morrow told every detail of the story to his former boss, working overtime to keep the emotion out of it. When he finished, he wrapped it up, saying, "I felt certain that he got the message and that he was clear it was from your mutual boss."

Morrow could almost hear the relief in Westcott's voice.

"That's really good news, Morrow. I wish you weren't leaving. I asked my lieutenants to come up with some ideas of how to stop this war. They had nothing. You came up with a plan in a few days."

"His two goons helped to incentivize me," Morrow said dryly.

"I imagine. Anyway, I owe you. We never discussed what you'd like for doing this."

"I appreciated the manpower you loaned me. They both handled themselves well, but I did this for myself as well as you. I valued my time at the compound. How about I may ask you for a favor someday, and if you can help, that would be great. And if not, we're still even in my book."

"Fair enough," Westcott said. "Try not to get yourself killed, OK? I may need a favor someday too."

"There's a goal I can get behind." With nothing more that needed to be said, Morrow broke the connection and set his phone on the coffee table. He poured one more shot of bourbon for himself and put his feet up on the table. In his mind, this escapade was an unwelcome diversion but a necessary one. Now it was over. He turned his attention back to *Gabriel's Steed*. He had seventeen days left.

14

The following morning, Morrow showed up at the LeBlanc mansion and knocked on the door. It was a few minutes after eight.

Ms. Velloitte opened the door. "Now what?"

Morrow was in no mood to play games. He pushed back on the door and squeezed his way into the foyer.

"I'm not aware of any appointment you have, Mr. Dawes."

"Screw the appointment," Dawes said. "I don't have time for that nonsense. I want to see my painting and how it looks with the new frame on it."

"It's not fixed yet. Probably sometime next week. I'll let you know—"

"Not fixed?" Morrow cried out, trying to play the disappointed client. "I need to see LeBlanc right now. I've got some leads on people who will want to see it. I'd like to get this show on the road."

"Mr. LeBlanc is not available," she said. Then she paused to look more closely at Morrow's face. "What happened to you?"

"I'm clumsy, remember. I ran into a door."

"Uh-huh. Whatever it was, I'm sure you deserved it."

"You're probably right," Dawes said. "Now that we have that out of the way, could you please tell me why you thwart my every effort to see Mr. LeBlanc?"

"I have no idea what you're talking about. I think you should leave."

"You *always* think I should leave. Maybe I should tell Mr. LeBlanc how rude you are and suggest he get a new secretary."

Ms. Velloitte cocked her head and smiled. "Really? That's the best you can come up with? OK, knock yourself out. Tell him. But, you see, I'm not his secretary. I'm his office manager, and he has made more money since I joined the operation than ever before. All because of what I've done. So, you do your worst. See if I care."

Dawes pulled his phone out and quickly snapped a picture of LeBlanc's office manager. "That isn't all I got. I'm just getting started, Ms. Velloitte. Something isn't right here, and I'm going to find out what it is. Or you can make an appointment for me this afternoon with LeBlanc."

With daggers flying out of her eyes, Ms. Velloitte said, "I've told you before, Mr. Dawes. I don't make appointments in person."

Dawes turned around and headed for the exit. Over his shoulder, he called out, "I suggest you make an exception this time. I think I've got your number now, and you aren't going to like what I'm going to do next."

The moment he was in his car, he called Tommy's number.

"Morrow, what's up? You need me?" Tommy asked.

"No, I need Connie. Is she there?"

He handed the phone to his wife.

"What do you need, Morrow?"

"I'm sending you a picture of a—oh shit, I don't know her first name. Well, her last name is Velloitte, and I need to find out more about her."

"Morrow, I'll do all I can, but without a first name, it's pretty tough. OK, I'm seeing the picture now. How old is she?"

"I don't know," Morrow admitted. Flustered now, he added, "She looks young. Twenty-five, maybe?"

"You're guessing?" Connie asked. "Great, well, how do you spell her last name? Just like it sounds? One L or two?"

Morrow put his head into his hands.

Connie could imagine what he was doing. Graciously, she pushed him no further.

After another thirty seconds, Morrow said, "Connie, forget it. I have no idea how to spell it. I'll have to go at her a different way. I'll get back to you when I have more." He hung up.

His next call was to Ghost. He sent a copy of the picture to him too and ordered his lookout to watch for when Ms. Velloitte left the LeBlanc mansion. "Follow her without being seen and tell me what she does, where she goes, and where she lives. Then call me anytime tonight, no matter how late."

Never one to waste time, Jamal replied, "On it."

Morrow headed home. *Another wasted day. Too few left. I wonder what it feels like to stand in a cement bucket.*

Jamal called at 10:45 that evening.

Morrow recognized his number and wasted no time with niceties. "What did you find out about her?"

"Some things I doubt you expected. She left work at 6:45. She was carrying what might have been a painting inside a leather case. She placed it in the trunk of her car, which was parked in the lot to the north of LeBlanc's mansion. It's a Honda Fit, a little subcompact. Pulled out of the lot, went south on North 44th to Thomas Road. Took a right, as though she'd done it a million times, drove another mile, and slipped into a tiny parking spot on the street. She drives fast, by the way."

"She lives up there, on Thomas Road?"

"No, but there's an Irish bar across the street from where she parked. She didn't go into it like it was a new experience. She was driving right for it."

Morrow listened quietly without comment, but Jamal thought he could hear the wheels in Morrow's head turning.

"I went in about ten minutes later. As you can imagine, no one hardly looked at me. I ordered a beer at the bar and took it to a table off to the side of where Ms. Velloitte was sitting—on a stool at the bar, yakking it up with the bartender. I mean, talkin' like she'd known him all her life."

"You're right, Jamal. I wouldn't have guessed this. Miss Prim and Proper hanging out in an Irish bar."

"It's called Mickey's Mash House, and it looks like a hole in the wall kinda place, but it's pretty classy inside," Ghost added.

"Curiouser and curiouser," Morrow muttered under his breath.

"I just watched her. The way you described her, I was beginning to wonder if this was the same person. She hung out there for three hours or so, talking to different people and nibbling on some dishes. Probably too soon to say, but I certainly got the feeling this was a ritual. I'd bet she goes there more than a few times a week."

"Amazing. She seemed more likely to go to a library or straight home. So, where *is* home?"

"Just off Dobson Road near West Ray: Donnen Plaza. Looks like a nice apartment complex. Not too pricey, but not cheap either. It's a secure building, so I couldn't follow her in. No idea which unit number."

"Doesn't matter," Morrow replied. "Nice work, Jamal."

"What are we gonna do?"

"Plan to follow her again tomorrow night. Wherever she goes, I'm going too. I'm going to chat her up and get her to go to dinner with me."

"You wanna date her?" Jamal asked.

"No, I believe all differences can be settled over a meal. I'm going to make Ms. Velloitte an offer she can't refuse. She's either going to join us or get out of our way."

At 8:20 the next morning, Morrow made his phone call to the LeBlanc mansion. Ms. Velloitte answered immediately, and Morrow calmly said, "This is Chuck Dawes. I'd like to make an appointment to see Mr. LeBlanc today."

A frosty silence iced its way through the phone lines. Then, in an equally cool and indifferent way, Ms. Velloitte said, "Let me check his schedule."

Morrow waited. She tried his patience as he listened to dead air for forty seconds.

"Mr. LeBlanc is completely booked up today, but he has some openings next week. How does Tuesday at four p.m. sound?"

"Like an eternity from now. Unacceptable. I need to see him today."

"As I said, he's booked up. Feel free to call me next week, and I'll see what I can do."

As Morrow prepared to fire off his next salvo, the line went dead. "That witch just hung up on me!" he said to himself.

Setting his phone down on the coffee table, Morrow leaned back in his seat and rethought his strategy. It was full-court press time, and he knew it.

15

16 days left.

"She's at Mickey's again, Morrow."

Ghost's words were what he expected. Morrow was parked three blocks away on a side street from Mickey's Mash House. His research had revealed that it was an Irish Pub and Brewery. It looked like a dive bar, but that was part of the décor. Further research indicated it was one of the more popular singles hangouts in the city.

Morrow texted Nate Slaton. YOU IN PLACE?

Morrow inhaled deeply, then exhaled, then repeated the process again just as he always did to relax before a performance. It was his job to play Chuck Dawes, an unaware, gregarious slob of a man nearly the polar opposite of what Morrow was. Psyching himself up for the role was mandatory. *If this plan doesn't work, we'll need to do something more extreme.*

Nate texted back. READY

Morrow met Nate four years ago when he first moved into town. He'd lived down the hall in an apartment building in Mesa. Nate had a gig going and needed a driver. It was one of Morrow's first jobs in Phoenix, and he met a slew of talented individuals on that job. Nate was an amateur magician who learned to use his sleight of hand for various gray-area activities. Over the years, they only worked together a few more times, but they stayed in touch, and Morrow had come to count on Nate as a good friend, perhaps his best friend. One he could always count on.

One more inhale and exhale, extra deep this time, and Morrow turned on the engine. He drove two blocks north and found a parking spot near the corner. Leaving the car, he reminded himself again that he was Chuck Dawes. The big difference was that he dressed in more normal and subdued clothing: jeans and a blue button-down shirt. No mismatching outfit this time.

He entered the pub and glanced around. The main room was dominated by a very lengthy L-shaped bar. It was manned by four very busy bartenders with one enormous old-fashioned cash register in the center of the bar, an oversized relic from the early 1900s. The interior was rustic, and it was packed. Morrow spotted Ms. Velloitte, perfectly coifed, seated near the far end of the long bar, chatting with a dapper man to her right. *Competition, I love it,* Morrow thought.

Morrow took the open stool to her left and ordered a Kilkenny Ale.

Hearing the familiar voice, Ms. Velloitte turned his way and said, "You following me?"

"Maybe. I don't have an appointment if that's what you mean."

"I'm on my own time here and, quite honestly, Chuck," she paused as she mockingly drawled his name. "I don't care to spend it with you."

"That's part of your problem," Chuck said. "You're so timid. You need to just say what you mean. Don't hold anything back." He smiled briefly at his own sarcasm.

For a fleeting second, Morrow thought he saw the start of a smile being returned, but if he did, it disappeared immediately. She simply turned away from him and renewed her conversation with the guy on her right.

Morrow sipped his beer silently. One of the bartenders working their end of the lengthy bar looked at him and said, "You want something to eat?"

"No, this'll do me. I have reservations at Le Crepe in thirty minutes."

Feeling a bit dissed and trying hard to ignore the crass name-dropping that the new face pulled, the bartender walked away.

Morrow resumed drinking his beer. Softly he nudged Ms. Velloitte, and she looked back at him icily. "Do you know how hard it is to get a reservation for two at Le Crepe? Most popular French restaurant for five hundred miles. But I have one for tonight. It's my way of apologizing for getting off on the wrong foot with you. I'm sorry. I thought if we went to dinner—"

"Forget it. I don't do dinner with clients." She turned away again.

Continuing to talk as though she were looking right at him, Morrow said, "My mother often said that two good people could always settle their differences over a fine meal. So I got the fine meal part set up; now I just have to get you to come along."

"What part of NO do you not understand, Chuck? Leave me alone."

Chuck nodded as though he understood. His words denied it. "I didn't hear the word *no*. I heard forget it, but how could I forget reservations for two? Especially when they're ready a mere twenty-five minutes from now?"

Chuck waited until he had Ms. Velloitte's attention once again.

She sighed and began to talk, but Chuck cut her off.

"I did hear that you want me to leave you alone. I understand, but the problem is I can't get an appointment with Mr. LeBlanc, so I think I'll just hang out here with you until you reconsider and decide to enjoy an outstanding meal at Le Crepe with me."

"Listen to me, Chuck. There is nothing in this world that will get me to go to dinner with you. Tonight, tomorrow, next week, next lifetime, next anytime. Got it?"

"Could you clarify that for me? I'm not sure I got it. Did you mean you don't *think* there is anything that could compel you, or did you mean there is *solid scientific proof* that there is nothing?"

Ms. Velloitte pursed her lips and struggled to keep her composure. "I meant that if you don't leave me alone, I will have you thrown out of here."

"Hmmm, so if I got thrown out, then would you go to dinner with me?"

Again, the smile almost broke out on her face.

Before she could reply, Chuck smiled disarmingly and said, "See, I think we could get along better, and that would mean more business for your employer. That would be a good thing. And on top of that, I was planning on telling you all about how you can get a cut of all the profits on the paintings I bring in. All that and an awesome meal to boot. What do you say?"

Ms. Velloitte smiled for real and said, "No. I admire your tenacity, but no, I won't go to dinner with you."

How about if we make a bet? If I win, we go to dinner together. If you win, I'll leave you alone."

"No," Ms. Velloitte said and turned away from Morrow again.

"Wait! You haven't heard the bet yet. The odds are all in your favor."

"I don't care. Please go away," she said.

"See, that's the thing. If I lose, I will go away. Don't you want to hear what the bet is?"

Allowing her eyes to close for a moment, surrendering, she replied, "OK, I'll listen if it will make you go away faster."

"Great. This is what I'm going to do. I'm going to get the bartender to write a secret word on a hundred-dollar bill. Then, long story short, I will burn it in front of your eyes, and it will magically reappear inside that giant cash register over there." Morrow pointed to the register about thirty feet away.

Ms. Velloitte stared at Morrow and asked, "After you burn it, it will appear in the cash register? How long after?"

"Immediately."

"And if it doesn't, then you'll leave and not bother me anymore?"

"Absolutely. But if I do it, then we have to leave right away to keep the reservation. Le Crepe is only four minutes from here."

Shaking her head, the object of Chuck's affections once again said, "I don't believe you. You're certifiable."

"Trust me; it's only four minutes away."

That said, Chuck immediately stood up and announced in a booming voice for the entire room to hear, "Ladies and gentlemen! Your attention, please! I have reservations for two at seven thirty tonight at Le Crepe, one of the world's finest French restaurants. I'm here to ask my work associate if she will join me there, even though I have been unbearable to work with. I've admitted it is all my fault, and I have apologized, so she has now given me her word that she will go to dinner with me if, and only if, I can perform a feat of magic so amazing, so entertaining, so awe-inspiring, and so impossible that she will know that time itself has stood still before her very eyes. Are you ready to see it?"

The bar quieted as Morrow spoke, then gave out a chorus of yeses in response to his question.

Standing up, Ms. Velloitte said, "No, no, no. I did not give my word. He is making that up."

Ignoring her, Morrow pulled out a hundred-dollar bill from his pocket and opened it up, holding it high above his head for all to see.

"This hundred-dollar bill was going to pay for my lonely beer over there," Morrow said, working the crowd into a more sympathetic mood. "Instead, I'm going to ask the bartender to write a single word on this bill. He won't tell us what it is until later." Morrow walked back to the bar and handed the hundred to the bartender.

The barkeep wrote something on the front of the bill and looked up. "Now what?"

"Place the bill on the counter and cover it up with a paper napkin," Morrow said. "I'll stand to the side and will not even touch it."

Morrow checked the crowd and made sure he had their full attention. "I need a volunteer." He looked around the room and saw the many hands of eager participants raised. Sweeping the audience with his eyes, he said, "Put your hands down. I want someone who has no interest in this. You, sir, the one reading the book, can you help me out?"

A man in a gray sweater closed his novel and shook his head. "Not me. Pick someone else, please."

Morrow swiftly walked to his table and said, "That's precisely why I need you. It'll just take a second." He put his hand underneath the man's arm, helped him up, and escorted him over to the stage.

"What's your name?"

The man looked around nervously and mumbled, "Ben."

"OK, Ben. All I need you to do is peek under the napkin and touch it to confirm that the hundred-dollar bill is still there."

"That's it?" Ben asked.

"That's all."

Ben lifted the napkin, peeked at it, and touched it. "Yeah, it's there. I mean, I could see it and feel it."

"Thank you, Ben. Now pick up the napkin with the bill and scrunch it up into a little ball."

Ben did as told while Morrow took an empty plate from the bar and said, "Put it on this plate and take a bow. You're done, thank you."

Ben put it on the plate, made a crooked smile, and slightly bowed as he walked back to his table where his book lay next to his finished dinner plate and a near-empty beer.

Morrow raised the plate with the scrunched-up napkin and hundred-dollar bill and said, "Now I'm going to light a match and let my coworker burn this bill and napkin up. Then, the magic will happen. That same hundred-dollar bill, with the unknown word on it, will magically reappear." Morrow looked around at everyone to make sure they were listening. "Oh, I forgot to mention one thing. It will reappear in the closed cash register!"

Now the room was full of guffaws and chatter. Many in the crowd expressed grave doubts. Ms. Velloitte was watching, mildly amused as she shook her head.

Morrow called on Ms. Velloitte to take the match and set the napkin and bill on fire. As she passed him, she whispered, "Looking forward to you being gone."

It burned brightly for a few seconds, and then it was over. Morrow made a big show of letting it finish. Then he asked her, "Is it gone? Up in smoke?"

She pushed the ashes around with her finger and said, "I see a few tiny green pieces still here, but yes, it is gone. It's toast."

Morrow turned to the bartender and said, "Please, sir, tell everyone now, what is it you wrote on the bill?"

"I wrote the word *bullshit*, and I added a little curly-Q to the end of the T so it can't be copied," he said, crowing a bit.

"Whoa!" Morrow said, still milking all the drama he could get out of it. "I think, technically, that might be two words. Well, that may stop the magic from working."

Groans and dismissive waves came from the audience. Ms. Velloitte snickered.

"Just kidding. I have confidence in magic, but there's only one way to find out for sure. Open up the cash register."

A man in the crowd cleared his throat. That was the only sound anyone could hear as the room grew eerily quiet. The bartender opened the register and picked up the tray to look underneath where the fifties and hundred-dollar bills were stowed. There was only one hundred in the bin. He pulled it out, turned it face up, and looked at it. He cried out, "Bullshit! It's the hundred I wrote on!"

He showed it all around. The crowd applauded and cheered, and a few of the women in the crowd started chanting, "Le Crepe. Le Crepe. Le Crepe!"

Standing up, Ms. Velloitte declared, "I never gave my word. He made that part up."

The crowd booed.

She shook her head as Chuck walked up to her and said, "If you go with me, I'll tell you how I did the trick."

She stared at him. Then looked back at the crowd.

"Yes! Yes! Yes!" they were all chanting.

"Oh, God. I can't believe I'm doing this," she said. "Well, I guess I am kinda hungry. One time only, OK?"

"Agreed. We'll have to hustle to get there on time." Chuck slapped a fifty-dollar bill on the bar to cover his and her drinks. It did more than that.

Morrow led her out the front door, making eye contact with the gray-sweatered Nate and brushing his nose in the universal victory sign of the con-world.

They placed their orders, and Ms. Velloitte stared across the table at him. "That was some performance back there. How'd you do it?"

"Wow, right to business. If I told you, you might leave, so I'll tell you when we have dessert."

"Very sneaky."

"Thanks. Now, I have a question for you. What's your first name?"

"Tara," she said. "But I'm still Ms. Velloitte to you, got it?"

Nodding, Chuck said, "Got it. Thank you, Tara."

80

Tara rolled her eyes. "I bet you never did anything your parents told you to do, did you?"

"You think so little of me. Maybe I was a good kid who got straight A's."

"I doubt it. You were probably hell on wheels."

The two of them traded barbs over dinner and learned more about each other. Chuck told stories about some of the jobs he'd had while Tara told about her education in Europe and all her travels to art museums around the world. It was clear as the meal wrapped up that they had absolutely nothing in common other than, perhaps, an appreciation for fine French food.

When the desserts were served, Morrow was ready to get to his point. "Do you like working for LeBlanc?"

"He's interesting."

"How's the pay?" Chuck asked.

"I don't discuss things like that," Tara said.

"Whatever he is paying you, I'd pay you three times that amount."

"To do what?"

"I need a buyer who really knows art," Chuck began. "I'd finance your trips all over the world to find good deals, buy the paintings, and let me find a buyer who will pay double what we paid. Wouldn't that be a dream job for you?"

"I'd hate to leave Mr. LeBlanc shorthanded. I think I'm better off right where I am. It, um, fits my long-term plan better."

"I think you should reconsider. Tell me what you need, and I'll make it happen."

"Like magic?"

"Sort of. I'm pressed for time, though. I'd want you to start right away. Tomorrow?"

"Who would handle Mr. LeBlanc's affairs then? I don't think—"

"I've got someone that can step right in for you," Chuck said, cutting her off.

Tara laughed. "Oh, God, and, let me guess, she'd give you free access to Mr. LeBlanc. No appointment delays ever. Right?"

"Well, I guess. That certainly isn't the—"

Tara laughed. "Oh, Chuck, or whatever your name is, give it a rest. I know who you are and what you are, and your act hasn't fooled me for one minute."

"What? What do you mean by that?"

"You aren't dealing with Mr. LeBlanc so you can sell that cheap painting. You're trying to get into his safe and steal his prize painting. You're nothing but a thief."

Morrow choked on his last morsel of dessert and took a moment to regain his composure. "I'm what? A thief?"

"Oh, stop it. I saw you coming before I even opened the door. I know what you are. It's plain as day. When the idiot guard clobbered you, you blew it. You didn't do what a normal person would have done. Normal people sue for violence like that. No, I know what you're up to, and it's no good. I want you to leave me alone. I'll give you your stupid painting back, and then I don't want to see you again."

Morrow shook his head. "You have this all wrong. You hardly know me. How can you be so sure?"

Tara finished her wine and locked eyes with Morrow. "I'm sure. Please come by and pick up your painting. We won't be doing business with you anymore."

She left the table and exited the restaurant.

PART TWO

16

15 days left.

There are days in our lives when time flies by at breakneck speed. And there are times when the pace of the day is outrun by the slowest glacier. Morrow knew that this day, fifteen days before he would disappoint Dr. Almeda, was the latter.

Last night, he stayed at Le Crepe for an extra hour downing more bourbon than he could afford. The drinks at the high-class restaurant were priced almost triple what he would pay at Sadie's. He didn't care. After three more bourbons, he paid the bill and caught a taxi home.

How did she know? What did I do that made it so obvious? Shit, I may not be very good at this whole con game after all. I may need a new line of work. I may also need to change my name and move away from here. On the other hand, I may be getting a long bath with my feet set in concrete two weeks from now.

Now it was early morning when Morrow rose from his seat on his couch and poured himself his first drink of the day. "It's gotta be five o'clock somewhere in this world, so it's not too early," he mumbled to himself. Looking at his watch, he noted it was only 7:15 in the morning. He shook it, certain it was wrong, and checked his phone. It *was* wrong. It was 7:17. Morrow accepted the revelation for the minuscule victory that it was and put the drink to his lips.

Pausing for a moment, he placed it back on the counter. *I need to come up with a new plan, or I'm a dead man.*

Morrow walked into the kitchen and poured himself a glass of water. Then it was back to the couch. *Get a grip, Morrow. You've been in tough spots before. Just sit here and come up with a plan that'll work.*

Mentally, he threw out everything he'd done and started over, trying to dream up a strategy that resolved his dilemma. By the time noon rolled around, he had walked himself through four different scenarios, and every one of them had the same problem. Tara Velloitte blocked every path he could conceive.

Recognizing Tara as the source of resistance, Morrow realized that he had to attack that problem first.

He called Ghost and got an answer on the first ring.

"Morrow, what's up?"

"My dinner with Ms. Velloitte did not go well. She seems to be onto us somehow. Maybe a good guess or I—I don't know. Maybe I blew it and did something that tipped her off. She's not going to do business with me anymore. I won't even be able to get in the door."

"Shit! Now what are we gonna do?"

"I've got a new plan. Today, while she's working, I need you to get into her apartment building and into her unit. Think you can do that?"

Ghost was silent for a moment, then said, "I don't know her unit number, but I know how to figure it out. How soon do you need me inside?"

"Before she gets home," Morrow said. "I'll put Tommy on lookout to let us know when she leaves work and if and when she's coming home. I'd say get in before six and spend the time looking around. See if you can find out anything about her that we don't already know."

"Should be easy. I don't know nothin'. I'll be in and out in no time."

"No, I don't want you to leave. I'm coming by, arriving just before she does. I'll need you to buzz me in. We're going to wait for her and ambush her in her own place."

Another long silence. "Rough stuff?" Ghost asked.

"No, sorry, poor choice of words. I meant 'ambush her with questions.' I need to know if she told LeBlanc anything. Then I'm gonna start in on helping her rethink her position. It'd be a hell of a lot easier if she were working with us instead of against us."

"Got that right. OK, I'll call you when I'm in." Ghost hung up.

Morrow looked at the phone and thought, *OK, I think I was done anyway. Gotta like his style. Never a wasted moment, even saying goodbye.*

The next call was to Tommy. He answered on the second ring.

"This is Tommy," he said simply.

"Tommy, Morrow. You available?"

Tommy chuckled. "I'm at your beck and call. Whatchya got?"

"I had to pull Ghost off the tail. He's doing something else for us. I need you to go to the LeBlanc mansion, park strategically so you won't be seen, and watch the front door and the parking lot. I need to know when Ms. Velloitte leaves the office and where she's going after that. Could take a while. She's not totally who we thought she was. She likes to hit the bars at night."

"Wow. Not something I would expect from the way you described her. OK, I can do that. Connie and I are heading there now."

"No. Not Connie. I need to talk to her next. I have another job for her." Having a woman with him tonight would reduce Tara's immediate fear level.

Tommy handed his phone to his wife, and she jumped on the call. "You got something for me, Morrow?"

"Yeah, you and I are going to pay Ms. Velloitte a little visit."

The first call back to Morrow came from Ghost at four o'clock. "I'm in. Had to pretend to be delivering a package for Ms. Velloitte to get her unit number from the concierge. First, he told me that my unit number on the package label was wrong, then he didn't want to say what the correct number was. I told him we don't care, that this was one of hundreds we're delivering today, but dispatch needs to fix our records so that we don't have this same problem every time. He bought it. She's in unit 624."

"Nice work. Did the concierge see your car?"

"Morrow, I know we haven't worked together for very long, but don't ask me questions like that. I pride myself on being impossible to find. No one knows what my car looks like or if I even have one. I don't fuck up that kind of stuff. Chill, OK?"

Morrow laughed. A real laugh this time, and he realized how tense he was. Ghost snapped him out of it. *Doing something, hell, doing anything is feeling good too.*

"OK, sorry, Jamal. I should have known. I'll make a note: Ghost needs no micromanagement."

"I'll be here to buzz you in when you get here," Ghost said, then rang off.

Tommy called when Tara left the office at 5:45. Then again at six when she stopped and parked across from Mickey's Mash House.

"Damn!" Morrow said. "She must really like that place. Every night. Well, call me when she leaves. If she's going home from there, it'll take her close to forty minutes to get there. Plenty of time for us to meet her there."

Nearly three hours passed before Tommy called again. "She's on the move. Looks like she's heading home."

"Thanks, Tommy. Tail her from a distance anyway to make sure."

Tommy agreed and pulled out into traffic.

Morrow met up with Connie at a pub near Tara's apartment complex and walked the three blocks to the entrance. Ghost buzzed them in and greeted them at unit 624.

"So, what's the plan?" he asked.

Morrow took a good look around the unit and said, "Find a place where she won't see you but stay in hearing distance. I don't want her to know you're here until the time is right. Connie and I are going to ask some questions, and I want her off-balance and nervous. Harder to lie well in those conditions."

Ghost just nodded and immediately picked the hallway as his hangout. Connie and Morrow each took a chair on one side of the coffee table. The couch was on the other side. They moved the chairs back about eighteen inches, so they weren't in Tara's line of sight when she entered the apartment. It was important that their mark would be shocked and frightened when she saw the intruders.

"Ghost, be watching. I'll scratch my chest when I want you to speak up. We'll be talking about severe steps, and I'll want you to comment out of the blue about what you think we should do with her. It'll shake her up to know you've been there all along."

Ghost nodded his agreement.

Morrow looked to Connie and asked, "What name do you want to go by?"

"I'll be Renee," Connie replied. "You going by Chuck Dawes or Dan Thompkins?"

"Neither. It doesn't matter now. Almeda is connected. He'll know who I really am, so I'm just going to be Morrow. I'll need to gain some credibility with Tara if I'm going to have any chance to convince her to join us."

"Seems like a longshot to me, Morrow," Ghost weighed in.

Morrow checked his watch. His phone rang. "Tommy, what's up?"

"She just pulled into the building parking lot. Should be up there in a few minutes."

"Thanks, Tommy. Nice work. That's all we need tonight."

Morrow put his phone on silent and reminded the others to do the same.

"Mine's always on silent," Ghost said, chuckling.

"I believe you. OK, no more talking now. We don't want Tara hearing us before she unlocks the door."

They sat stone-faced for another six minutes. The lock clicked, and Tara entered, flipping on the hallway light. The living room and the rest of the apartment were in shadows and darkness.

Tara set her purse and keys on the hallway table and casually walked into the living room as she perused her mail. "Junk, junk, bill. That's all I ever—"

Suddenly she stood straight as a board as she spotted two figures in the shadows, seated in the chairs along the west wall. "Hey! Who—what...?"

"It's me, Chuck Dawes," Morrow said quietly.

Connie chimed in. "And I'm Renee, Chuck's associate."

"Jesus! How'd you get in here? What the fuck are you doing here?"

Morrow stood up and motioned Tara toward her couch. "Leave the lights off and sit down. We need to talk."

"No fuckin' way. I'm calling the cops right now," Tara said, reaching for her phone in her vest pocket.

"Tara, sit down," Connie said so forcefully that Tara froze for a moment. "Put the phone down and relax. We're only here to talk."

Considering her options, Tara agreed and took a seat on the couch.

With her back to him, Ghost took advantage of the moment and silently seated himself in a living room chair in a dark corner.

"What do you want?" Tara asked.

"First of all, you're perceptive; I am a thief and a conman. I've been hired to steal *Gabriel's Steed*."

Both Connie and Morrow watched her closely, trying to judge her reaction. There was a flicker of recognition and then an awkward attempt to conceal it.

"I know of the painting you're talking about. I don't believe LeBlanc has it. It's been missing for, what, six or eight years now. I think I'd know if he was dealing it."

"We have it on high authority that the painting is being held by LeBlanc for a purchase two weeks from now," Morrow said. "Dr. Jacob Almeda and his family owned the painting, and it was stolen from him. We are simply trying to right a wrong and return the painting to its rightful owner."

Tara shook her head. "Really? Out of the goodness of your heart? I know the story about the Steed. It may have been stolen from him, but he wasn't the rightful owner. He stole it from someone else. He's no better than any of them."

"Perhaps," Morrow admitted. "But here's the problem. We didn't know that when we accepted the job. That was my mistake; however, now, a lot of people working with me will face the wrath of Almeda if we don't produce the painting for him before it's purchased again. We didn't know he was connected. But now we know, and we also know what will happen to us. It's, um, a rather permanent punishment for failure."

"Yeah, I've heard," Tara said. "His kind do revenge like it's the national pastime. You'll get offed in some alley or fitted for cement overshoes."

"Bingo. I figure it'll be the latter," Morrow said, with a tinge of gallows humor.

"Well, hell, he'll be looking for Chuck Dawes, right? You didn't use your real name, did you?"

Morrow shook his head. "Doesn't matter. Not only will they have pictures of me, but he's connected, and I'm sure he already knows who I am."

Tara's meager smile disappeared. "And who are you?"

"My name is Morrow."

"Just Morrow?" Tara asked. "What, are you like Madonna or Prince? So famous you only need one name?"

"I'm no rock star. That's just how people know me. If I don't bring that painting home to him, I'm dead. And so is Sylvia and—oh, shit, I mean Renee, and everyone else."

Connie knew how to play along. She put her hand on Morrow's and said, "It's OK, Morrow. We're all in this thing now. Aliases don't mean shit."

All three of them sat quietly for a moment. Tara broke the silence. "So, sounds like you failed to do your homework, saw all the big dollar signs, and got yourself into this jam. What do you want from me?"

Morrow gazed up at the ceiling and collected his thoughts. Making eye contact with the mark one more time, he said, "I was hoping that, under the circumstances, you would help us out. We'd like you to join us and share in the profits."

"Seriously?" Tara asked.

"Our take is six hundred K, Tara," Connie said. "We'd spiff you a healthy cut if you would work with us."

"Well, let's see. My choice is to report you all to Mr. LeBlanc and/or the police or join you and get a share of zero dollars and then, as a team member on the losing team, get a death sentence from Almeda." She let that hang in the air for a few seconds, then added,

"Wow, that's a tough one. Keep my job and probably get a bonus or join you and become fish food at the bottom of some river."

Morrow smiled. "Well, when you put it that way, it doesn't sound very appealing."

"No shit!" Tara said. "I'm no lawbreaker. My answer is no. I work for Mr. LeBlanc, and that will never change."

Connie nudged Morrow, and he nodded to her. "Actually, there is an upside to joining us. When we steal the painting, there's a good hundred thousand in it for you."

Tara started to speak, but Morrow held his traffic cop hand up to silence her. "I'm not finished. Not joining us also means we will have to take more severe measures to get you out of our way." He scratched his chest.

Tara's eyes widened. She found she had no snappy retort.

Suddenly, from behind her, another voice piped up. "Say the word, Morrow, and I can finish her right here."

Tara leaped up and turned around. "Where...how did...who are you?"

"That's Ghost, Tara. He works with me."

"Oh fuck! Can just anybody get into my apartment? Anybody else lurking around? You're saying you're going to—to—"

"No. Relax, Tara. We aren't going to kill you. Ghost, I've thought about it, and it could cause more problems than it solves. Not exactly our style either."

Ghost jumped in again. "We could break both her legs. Then she couldn't work, and we could get someone else in there that doesn't get in our way."

Connie turned to Morrow and said, "I think that has some real merit, Morrow. She wouldn't tell anyone either because she knows we could always get to her and take more drastic action."

Tara watched the conversation smoothly flowing as though they were talking about where to go for dinner.

Morrow suddenly stood up. He shook his head. "No. Too drastic. Not right now anyway. I'll think on it some more."

Staring at Tara, he added, "You have to admire her. She's a straight shooter. Tells you what she thinks. Loyal to her boss, even if he is a low-life law-breaking fence. Doesn't seem fair to penalize her. She's just trying to stay on the right side of the law. Let's go."

"Morrow, this is bullshit," Ghost said. "With her out of the way, we can get it. We've got a good plan. We can win this one and make some great cash. I still think we should off her. I mean, I got three littles. Sylvia has a husband and two kids. We've got a lot of lives to protect here."

Connie seconded him. "Morrow, I gotta tell ya, I'm starting to get a little nervous on this one. We only have a few weeks left."

Morrow exchanged glances with both of them and nodded. "You both have good points. We'll keep all our options open, and I'll put something in motion by the end of the week."

Looking directly at Tara, Morrow closed out the meeting. "Ms. Velloitte, you have my admiration. For what it's worth, I'm sorry you got involved in this. Sleep well."

17

14 days left.

Back at the Park Place Pub for a debriefing, Ghost, Connie, and Morrow were joined by Tommy. He'd waited outside the apartment complex for his wife.

Seated in their usual booth, the pub was quiet on this late weeknight. They ordered one round, and Connie brought her husband up to date, filling him in on how the meeting with LeBlanc's receptionist went.

When she finished, Ghost started in. "I don't get it, Morrow. I'm not sure we achieved anything tonight. Now she knows more about us than we know about her. Why didn't we just take some action?"

"Like what?" Morrow asked.

"Like, I don't know, get her to come over to our side somehow."

Connie jumped in. "I agree, Morrow. We haven't got time left to fool around. At the very least, I think you should have given her an ultimatum. You know, help us or else. Something that would make her change her mind."

"It's a good point. Tommy, you got thoughts?"

Tommy started in as well. For the next twenty minutes, they bandied around multiple ideas for getting Tara Velloitte out of the picture—breaking her legs, kidnapping her, faking her death, sending her on a world cruise, every wacky idea that they could come up with during the brainstorming session.

Morrow just listened. When they ran out of suggestions, the three of them turned to Morrow and waited for his response.

"I think we all agree that some of those ideas are undoable, and some will only make things worse. So, my plan is to do nothing and wait."

Tommy's jaw dropped, Connie went wide-eyed, and Ghost put his head in his hands.

"Morrow, we've got fourteen days left to pull this off, and we're worse off than when we started. We can't wait. We have to take action," Tommy said.

Again Connie and Ghost chimed in, and the back-and-forth patter continued for another eight minutes as Morrow listened quietly.

Feeling that their confidence in his leadership was probably at an all-time low, Morrow let them finish a second time.

"I get it. Everybody is scared. I am, too, a bit, but I have a plan, and I'm sticking to it. We'll do nothing."

"Oh, God," Connie groaned. "Ya know, maybe Tommy and I are out now. I mean, you should have insisted that she agree to work with us. Instead, you complimented her on her loyalty to LeBlanc and told her to sleep well or something."

"Listen to me," Morrow said, "This is how a con works. Right now, she's the mark. If she's gonna work with us, it *has* to be *her* idea. She'll phone me tomorrow and ask for a meeting."

"Oh, really?" Ghost said. "Just like that? Tomorrow she'll call and say she's had a change of heart? You're living in Neverland, Morrow. You can't just pretend that everything is OK and will work out. You have to *make* it happen."

Tommy jumped in. "Morrow, Connie may be right. I mean, you *do* have experience running a full-fledged con before, right?"

"Not exactly," Morrow replied.

Now, Ghost's eyes went so wide they looked like two flashlight beams coming from the darkest corner of the booth.

"Oh, this is great," Connie said, looking at her husband.

Morrow finished his comment. "I've done some smaller jobs, sort of like projects, like the game we played on Barger a few days ago. This is my first, you know, extended play like this."

"We're out," Tommy declared as he started to slide out of the booth, his hand on Connie's.

"Stay seated," Morrow said firmly. "Let me tell you what's going to happen."

Connie and her husband stopped moving and nodded to Morrow.

"First of all, let me ask you, what's the scariest thing you could face?"

"What do you mean? I can think of hundreds of things that would scare the shit out of me," Ghost said.

"Me too," Connie and Tommy said at almost the same time.

Morrow locked eyes with all of them. "You said I didn't give an ultimatum or a threat. But I did. I challenged her to sleep well. I can guarantee you she won't sleep well tonight. We invaded her space and broke in easily. Ghost, I had you stay in the background and emerge forty minutes into the meeting. That scared the hell out of her. To know that someone could be lurking in the darkest corners of her apartment every night when she comes home. Now, that's scary."

Morrow took a sip of his beer while his partners pondered that.

"So, I actually did threaten her. There is nothing more disconcerting and fear-inducing than uncertainty. Believe me, she's going to go to work tomorrow and realize she doesn't want to go home. Now, she'll be fearful that someone like Ghost will be waiting for her in the dark to kill her or hurt her. She won't know what she's supposed to do. Uncertainty about what the next hour may bring is the scariest thing of all. She'll call me. My guess is somewhere around five o'clock."

Silence filled the booth.

"This may be my first full-fledged con," Morrow continued, "but I guarantee you it won't be my last. I have many faults, but I know people, and I know how they will react to certain stimuli. If I'm wrong and she doesn't call me, you can all quit then, but she will, and she'll join us, and then we'll have all the edge we need. Someone on the inside and a bonus too."

"What's the bonus?" Ghost asked.

"Like I said, I know human nature. She's smart, super smart. I think her IQ is off the charts. I sense that she knows what we don't know. She is one fast-thinking woman, and she will be the lynchpin to pulling this all off. I think we'll have the painting in our hands within a week."

18

13 days left.

Morrow forced himself to sleep in as long as he could the next morning. Today was for waiting, and he dreaded the thought.

He purposely took his time making an elaborate breakfast for himself. He fried four slices of bacon in a pan on the stove and prepped two eggs with seasoning and finely cut onion and green pepper pieces. He scrambled them and placed the finished, slightly burnt product on a piece of wheat bread, perfectly buttered. His mother used to call it a Royal Egg Sandwich. For a moment, he remembered back to those days when he felt safe and had no cares in the world. Sharing one of her special sandwiches was one of those happy memories that never went away. That was a good thing, in light of the way life would turn out. He could count the happy moments of his life on one hand and still have three fingers left over for the days that were missing.

Morrow shook off the thought, retrieved his newspaper from in front of the apartment door, and sat down to read it and eat. He gulped down the meal and devoured the newspaper. When he read, he read everything. *Everything.* No article was too small or of too little interest. Some that amused him he'd read twice. Today, an article in the sports section spoke of a female high school basketball player who joined the team as a walk-on and became its star player. He read it twice. He always read the stories of underdogs twice. Just as he always rooted for the weaker teams to win.

It was noon when he finished the paper. His phone was on, but it emitted not a single sound. He picked up a deck of cards. He played a game he'd invented: Texas Hold 'Em solitaire. He dealt four hands of two cards down, peaked at his own, and either placed a bet or folded. He'd do the same with all the players' cards. The flop of three cards would be revealed, and he'd repeat the process of betting or folding until there was a winner. After each hand, he'd analyze it, trying to figure out if it was played correctly.

Hold 'Em was his favorite when he lived in Las Vegas for a while. It wasn't luck. Every hand, from an Ace-King to a deuce-7, was a potential winner if played right. He educated himself a lot during his time in Vegas. Most of what he learned was about human nature. He would read the players, watching for subtleties: a head scratch, a sly smile, too straight a face, twitches or tics, anything that might help him read the players' intentions. That process became second nature to him, and reading people in ordinary life was very much the same.

By one o'clock, he knew he still had more time to kill. He did some push-ups and sit-ups, took a shower, read a few chapters in a mystery book that wasn't grabbing him, and checked the clock again. 2:45.

He drummed his fingers on his knee. *Gawd, this is boring.*

Morrow didn't have a TV. He used to have one at the compound, but after checking all the shows on cable and all the local stations, he remembered why he didn't bother to have one. He was fairly certain that TV was a dastardly plot by evil people to dumb the populace down. It felt like millions of brain cells took their last breath during each hour of the invention's spewings.

By four o'clock, he stopped making any pretense of killing time. He sat on the couch staring at the crooked picture of an Arizona sunset. Morrow walked himself, for the hundredth time, through the current play, thinking about each step toward stealing *Gabriel's Steed*. He tried not to think about how his team would react if he was wrong—if Ms. Velloitte did not call him as he expected. He shook that negative thought from his brain.

He stared at the sunset again and wondered if it was trying to tell him something.

Five o'clock passed. As did five thirty. Morrow mimicked the picture on the wall. He didn't move.

Tara's call came in at 5:37 that evening. She asked to meet Morrow at any bar across town and out of the line of sight of people she was likely to know. Morrow gave her the address of Sadie's place, knowing it fit the bill perfectly.

It was six thirty when Tara showed up. Sadie noticed her first as she did any new face. She pointed to the back corner booth where Morrow was already seated. She noticed that Tara took a deep breath as though she were preparing to charge into battle.

Tara stood at the booth and looked at Morrow. She glanced around the room and nodded her head. It was dark and out of sight. "This works."

Morrow slid to his right toward the back of the U-shaped booth and motioned Tara to sit where he had been. That placed her back against the room and kept her even farther out of sight.

"Been here long?" she asked, glancing at the two empty bottles on the table.

"I was just waiting for your call," Morrow replied.

"Well, congratulations. You win the bully of the year contest."

Morrow didn't smile or respond.

Tara sat down, gathered herself, and seconds later, Sadie came to the booth. "What can I get you?"

She glanced at the half-full shot glass of bourbon and the bottle of Corona in front of Morrow and said, "That looks pretty good."

Sadie disappeared.

"You said you wanted to talk about our, uh, predicament," Morrow started.

"After she serves my drink, I'll tell you why," Tara said, trying hard to regain control of the conversation. "In the meantime, though, you can tell me how you did that stupid trick at the bar the other night."

Morrow chuckled to himself. "Admit it, that was kinda fun, wasn't it?"

"How'd you do it?"

"OK, first off, this trick is called the Eddie Fields Switch. To pull it off, I enlisted a friend of mine who specializes in a fine art: sleight of hand."

"Mr. Gray Sweater," Tara acknowledged, nodding to herself as the lightbulb went on.

"He had his own hundred-dollar bill. When he looked under the napkin and reached in to feel it, he palmed the one that the bartender wrote on and left his there."

Tara mulled that over and said, "Great, so then you burned the napkin and a perfectly fine hundred dollars too, but how did the bill get back into the cash register?"

"This is actually a really simple trick that's easy to do at any bar where there are multiple bartenders. Mr. Gray Sweater, as you call him, went around the corner of the L-shaped bar and, out of sight of most of the patrons, paid for his dinner with the hundred-dollar bill. It wasn't unusual because he had been there for a while and had run up a bar and food bill of over seventy dollars. He paid the bartender, got his change, and walked out. The bartender came over and put it in the bottom of the register, which they always do with fifties and hundreds. No one noticed because that was when everyone was watching the napkin and hundred burn up."

"Humph. Too easy," Tara said. "I was impressed at the moment, but now I know it was just classic misdirection."

Morrow smiled briefly. "Ah, misdirection. A conman's best friend."

They locked eyes.

Sadie delivered the shot glass and beer and departed.

Back to the subject at hand, Morrow looked at the mark and said, "Did you sleep well?"

Tara shook her head. "You know I didn't."

Morrow, ever patient for a mark to get to the point, sat silently.

"Damn you, Morrow. You really fucked things up. You don't even know what you did, do you?"

Not following this line of reasoning, Morrow sought Tara's eyes to see if they would lend a clue as to what she was talking about. He got nothing.

Before he could say anything, Tara continued, "You know how I knew you were a conman?"

"How?"

Tara downed half the shot and said, "'Cuz it takes one to know one. I've been working a long con for nearly six months now."

It was as if George Washington had just told Morrow that he was an English spy. The very last thing Morrow expected to hear was delivered by Tara with nary a hint of inflection.

"You—you are a—"

"Yes, I'm a conman," Tara said. "Or conwoman, as the case may be."

"What were you—how were—"

Tara chuckled. "You can't even get a full sentence out, can you? Yeah, I've been after *Gabriel's Steed* for the last eight months. I read a story about it, and then I got lucky. I held my head to the train rails until I heard some rumors that the painting was headed to Phoenix. I did some research and identified the only fence in town who was wealthy enough to handle the transaction. Then his, um, secretary had good fortune and landed a higher paying job. I was the temp who the agency hired to send to cover for her while interviews were happening."

Morrow shook his head. "I'm still trying to get my head around this. You've been doing a long con for months, working for LeBlanc for what? To somehow intercept *Gabriel's Steed* before he sold it?"

"I convinced him to hire me full time by showing him that I knew far more about art than he did. Then I worked on gaining his trust. I was hoping he'd trust me with the combination to the safe, but I overestimated my female charms."

"You were going to seduce him?"

"That was the plan, or at least part of it. I wasn't successful. It's, um, very troubling and not much of a confidence builder either. Beyond making me doubt my feminine wiles, it also made me switch to plan B. Ever had to do that?" Tara asked snidely. She knew full well that Morrow was already deep into plan C, flirting with plans D and E.

Ignoring her question, Morrow said, "Let me guess. You helped his old secretary get that new job, right?"

"I can neither confirm nor deny it," Tara said. "Look, the real problem here is that my pops was right. Never do a long con. Too many things can go wrong. I was almost there. Then you came along, and you wanted the same thing I did. I mean, it's gonna be hard enough to steal that sucker without having to look over my shoulder and watch you. I had high hopes I could retire off the four mil I expected to net from its sale."

"Retire?" Morrow asked. "You're kidding, right? What are you, sixteen? You look a little too young to be thinking about retiring."

"I'm twenty-two. Well, almost. Yeah, I guess I'm young, but I feel a lot older. My pops has been in the game all his life, and I grew up in it. Now I'm on my own, and I decided to go for one big score and bail. And like I said, then you came along and screwed everything up."

Morrow put his hand on his chin, shook his head, and failed to suppress his amusement with the situation.

"It's not funny, Morrow."

"No, no, of course not," Morrow said, "but, actually, it sort of *is*. And, oh boy, does it ever change things."

The two of them looked at each other for a moment before Tara asked, "So now what?"

Morrow thought for a moment and said, "Tell me what your roadblock is. How come you haven't stolen it yet?"

Tara sighed. "I've been working this heist up for so long and so carefully. Do you know that every night for the last three months, I put one of his reject paintings into my custom-made, one-of-a-kind portfolio case, which I bought in Milan, by the way, and take it home with me? I swap out the frames—a cheap one for the better one—and I do it so everyone gets used to me walking out with my portfolio case. The plan was to walk out one night with the Steed, and no one would think anything of it. But he doesn't trust anybody. He's never gonna tell me the safe combination."

"Yeah, I saw the keypad. It requires his thumbprint and a five-digit code. I think I know the first digit, though."

Tara smiled. "So do I. It's one. I'm sure of it. He tries to hide what numbers he pushes on the pad, but I can tell from the angle of his arm what the first one is. And I already solved the thumbprint issue. I got him to hold my coffee cup once when he wasn't wearing gloves, which isn't very often. After he left the room, I used a large roll of tape to capture every print on the cup. It wasn't hard to recognize the one from his thumb. I affixed it to a small piece of plastic I cut to resemble a thumb, and all I need now are the last four digits."

"Very well done. With the first number known, we only need to pick from ten thousand possible combinations," Morrow said with a tone of optimism.

"What's this 'we' business?" Tara said. "I didn't sign any partnership agreement."

"I assumed that's why we're here. I can help you. We're far better off working together than separately."

"Thanks, I'll pass. I can do this myself."

Morrow shook his head. "That's not an option. I have the lives of the people who work for me to protect, not to mention my own, which I'm fairly fond of, by the way."

"Sounds like a personal problem to me. I was just informing you so that you'd get out of my way. Call it professional courtesy," Tara said, suddenly feeling she was in a better position than Morrow.

"Oh, shucks, that's too bad. It'd be so easy. See, I can get the combination for you. We could open the safe together. Take the painting and be out of there in a few days. But, if you insist on going it alone, I get it. Ghost will simply have to pay you a visit some night this week."

"Oh, fuck, I forgot about that," Tara drawled out sullenly. "Damn you, Morrow. You really ruin everything, don't you?"

19

After Tara left the pub, Morrow called the rest of the team and told them to meet him at their favorite booth at eight o'clock tomorrow night. With the shocking news about Tara Velloitte being willing to work with them, Morrow felt immediately unburdened. He was so giddy he almost wanted to smile.

What he had viewed as a roadblock had suddenly morphed into his redemption. As badly as the con had started, it now appeared it would end well and in plenty of time. All they had to do was break into the safe, steal the Steed, and deliver it to Almeda. Everyone would get their split of six hundred thousand and be happy. *Well, except Tara, that is. She'll get maybe a hundred thou—probably a big disappointment compared to the four mil she wanted. Maybe—maybe there's a way I can turn this into something more. I'll have to think on that.*

Morrow arrived back at the Park Place Pub at 7:40 and settled into the booth he'd asked Sadie to reserve for him. One by one, his team showed up. Ghost arrived first, as usual, followed by Brady and Shady three minutes later. Lucky Lou joined next. Connie and Tommy walked in at eight o'clock on the dot.

When all were seated with a drink in their hands, Morrow filled them in. "So, it looks like we finally got a break. As I told you on the phone, Tara has agreed to join us."

A few hopeful glances were shared between the team. Tommy spoke first. "Looks like you were right, Morrow. Maybe we jumped the gun a bit."

"Can we trust her?" Ghost asked, verbalizing what everyone else was thinking.

"No. Hell, can we trust anybody?" Morrow said. "But it's more than that. I didn't tell you the bombshell she dropped, and it'll knock your socks off." He paused to take a sip of his drink, and when he was sure everyone was on the edge of their seats, he continued, "You see, Tara is like us. In many ways. Turns out, she's been running a con game herself—a long con. She's also after the Steed."

Lou's mouth fell open. Brady and Shady looked at each other wide-eyed. Ghost shook his head in disbelief. Only Connie and Tommy didn't appear surprised.

"I told Tommy something didn't seem right when we ambushed her two days ago. She handled it too well. She shoulda been way more scared," Connie said.

"I agree," Morrow said. "But, honestly, I never thought she was running her own con. I just thought she was composed and damn smart. Anyway, having her on our team is a huge plus. Now we have someone on the inside."

Ghost nodded and said, "Morrow, I'll give you that one. I thought you were way too optimistic about her joining us without more, uh, incentive. But you read her right. I guess that fact alone makes me feel more comfortable with this whole thing. Who knows, we may actually not get killed."

"Now that's the kind of positive thinking I appreciate," Lou said, smirking.

Connie butted in to ask, "Morrow, she goes by Tara, but what's her real name?"

"I, uh, well—"

"You didn't ask her, did you," Connie said. It wasn't a question.

"No, I didn't. I was going to, but Tara dropped the bit about running a long con, and I just, I don't know, fell off-track, I guess. Anyway, the important thing is that she's now part of our team, and that's good news."

"So if she's on the team, how come she's not here?" Brady asked.

Morrow took a swallow of his seltzer water and replied, "I wanted to meet with all of you first to tell you her backstory. She's going to be here at eight thirty, and you can meet her then. Here's what I want from each of you. Accept her wholeheartedly. Smile a lot.

Make her feel needed and appreciated—because she's both. We need to get her defenses down, and we need her to underestimate us. Got it?"

Morrow looked around the table to make sure everyone understood. The look in Brady's eyes made Morrow stop and stare at him. "Problem?"

"Uh, well, I don't quite get it. Don't we want her to feel comfortable working with us? Why do we want her to underestimate us?"

Morrow glanced at the veteran Lou and then Ghost, knowing that they knew. Connie and Tommy were already wise.

"Brady, she's smart. Too smart, probably, for her own good. And she's young. We need her, but we can't trust her fully. We *do* want her to be comfortable with us, and allowing her to underestimate us will make her even more comfortable." He stopped talking, hoping that Brady could put the rest together himself.

Shady nudged his brother and subtly shook his head.

"OK," Brady said, hesitating. "OK, so, sorry, guess I'm still not seeing why we want her to underestimate us."

"She wants the Steed for herself, Brady. If she thinks we're not playing at her level, she'll let her guard down. We want that. I suspect it's likely she'll help us get the painting and then make a move to, uh, liberate us from the burden of ownership."

"You think she'll try to steal it from us?" Brady asked. Shady was with him, asking it with his eyes.

"Brady, Shady, let me ask you. When you were kids, did you ever agree to play a ballgame with a team you knew you could beat?"

The brothers looked at each other. Brady said, "Yeah, of course. So you think she agreed to join us so she can use us and then slip out with the painting?"

"Exactly," Morrow said. "And that's why we have you with us. We'll be expecting it, and I'll need you two to take out the goons she hires to protect her."

"Oh, shit! That's slick. So we kinda act like we think we have our act together, but she'll think we don't, but we really will. And we'll be ready for her. This is cool, Morrow. I guess I see now why you're heading up this thing. I would never have thought of that."

"You would've," Morrow assured him. "Sooner or later, we all learn these things."

Everyone nodded. Morrow continued filling them in with what he knew about her. Tara walked into the pub at 8:25 and strolled straight to the dark booth in the corner.

Morrow rose from his seat on the end and motioned for Tara to slide in. "Everyone, this is Tara Velloitte." Morrow introduced all of the players, starting with Lou, Brady and Shady, Ghost, and then Tommy and Connie.

Seated next to Connie, Tara tried to smile and said, "Of course, I had the pleasure of already meeting Ghost and also Renee. Or Sylvia or Connie. Which one is it?"

Connie rolled her eyes a bit and said, "Well, I was going to say Sylvia, after both Morrow and I worked so hard to convince you that's what it was, but my real name is Connie, and now that you're on the team, maybe you can share your real name too."

"Good idea. I'll pass. Probably best you all call me Tara for now."

Trying hard to defuse the impending fireworks that Connie had started, Morrow said, "Let's get to it. A few things have changed in the plan."

"First of all, we don't need to do any elaborate con now on LeBlanc. Tara already has a makeshift thumbprint we can use to get into the safe. Based on our observations, we both agree that the number one is the first of the five digits he enters into the keypad. With Lucky Lou's help, I'm confident we go the brute strength route and just break into the safe and get the painting."

"He's got guards there all day, right?" Lou asked.

"There are five thousand ways I know to get around the guards," Morrow said.

"Yowza! Like what?" Brady asked.

"Like, uh, whatever it is I'm going to come up with," Morrow replied. "Are you asking do I have one now? No, I don't, but that isn't the hard part. I'll divert their attention, or we'll come up with something."

"I just lost that comfortable feeling I was telling you all about thirty minutes ago," Ghost clowned.

Morrow chuckled. "I get it. All of us would like a foolproof plan laid out step-by-step from the get-go. I got news for ya. That's only in the movies. In real life, a con is like a military skirmish. The battle plan never survives the first shot. It begins evolving before it ever gets put into play. The key to victory is reacting fast enough to solve each problem as it comes up. That's what we're doing."

"I like the movie version better," Ghost said, showing off his pearly whites as he smiled.

Morrow looked to Tara. "I'm assuming you can get me in now to have a meeting with LeBlanc?"

"I'll set it up for nine in the morning. He's not an early riser. You better have something worth his time, or he'll start wondering about you."

"It's pretty straightforward. I'll talk to him about expanding our relationship with a boatload of more paintings. We'll talk about that and then, as like an after-thought, I'll say I want to see my painting. Did you fix the damaged frame yet?"

Tara shook her head. "It wasn't high on my to-do list before. Now it is. I'll fix it tonight."

"OK, good. I need to see LeBlanc open the safe again, so make sure my painting is back in it. Make him think I'm coming to discuss some new business. Then I'll casually ask to see how the new frame looks so I can watch him open the safe again. Maybe I can figure out the second number."

Tara nodded. "OK, I'll set it up. Let's move the meeting up to ten o'clock. That will give me time to catch him and ask him to place it back in the safe."

Lou jumped in. "Tara, can you tell me what the safe brand name is?"

"It's a German safe maker. Gehrstreyer. Ever heard of them?"

Lou shook his head. "No. That's not good. I'll go online and do some research tonight. I'd like to know more about them before I say if I can crack it or not."

Morrow continued on, discussing the plan and making the last few steps seem easy. The team broke up at ten that night, and one by one, they departed until only Tara and Morrow remained. By this time, they both had a shot of bourbon and a half-finished beer remaining in front of them.

"I know this is probably the wrong attitude, but I always feel it's like slapping the universe in the face to leave a drink without finishing it. Not to mention bad luck," Morrow said in almost a whisper.

"Sounds like you're superstitious. My pops always disliked working with superstitious people," Tara said.

"And you?"

"I'm like him. I try not to be, but I've never seen him make a mistake. I was going to prove him wrong. Run one long con and score big. Instead, I have to admit he was right. I'm never going to do a long con again. Pops was right. Something or someone always comes along to ruin your perfect plan."

They both sat beside each other, nursing their drinks.

"And I have you to thank for that, Morrow," she added.

20

12 days left.

Morrow pushed the doorbell at the LeBlanc mansion. He was sure that Tara already knew he was there. LeBlanc would have a camera at the front door, among other safety protocols.

Tara opened the door, smiled sarcastically, and said, "Mr. Dawes! You're right on time. Please come in."

Morrow took a seat in Tara's office and decided to stick to the script. For all he knew, LeBlanc could be listening in or watching everything. "Is Mr. LeBlanc ready to see me?"

"He's running a few minutes late, but he knows you're here and should be down in a few minutes. Would you like some coffee?"

Morrow was certain that offering coffee to him was not something Tara really wanted to do. The imp in him immediately said, "Yes. That'd be great. Black is fine."

Tara shot him a "you were supposed to say no" look and left her office. She walked the fifteen feet to the kitchenette and drew some hot coffee from the urn. Handing it to Morrow, she said, "Black, as you ordered."

"You know, actually, I think I'd like one sugar cube with it," Morrow said, testing Tara's patience.

"Oh, I'm sorry. We don't stock sugar cubes. Sugar is so bad for you. It's our way of taking good care of our clients." Tara smiled and batted her eyes coquettishly.

OK, one to one. Tie ballgame, Morrow thought.

LeBlanc entered the room. "Chuck! Good to see you. What can I do for you?"

Setting his coffee on the table, Chuck bounced to his feet and extended his hand. They shook, and Chuck said, "I'm glad you have some time for me, Mr. LeBlanc. Maybe we could take a short walk and see some art, so I could tell you all about something exciting that I have cooking."

"Of course, let's wander a little bit." LeBlanc guided his new client down a hallway they had not ventured into last time. It led to another large room, not as big as the dance ballroom he saw on his first visit but impressive nonetheless.

Having achieved his goal of getting away from Tara, he started in on his prepared spiel. "I, uh, I'm working on a new project. I like this idea of finding well-heeled buyers and selling paintings that I bought, um, you know, economically. So while I was doing some research, I sort of stumbled across a source of, well, quite a steady stream of those kinds of paintings."

LeBlanc studied Chuck's face for a moment, then in a quieter voice said, "Naturally, you would be getting a true and accurate receipt from the seller, correct?"

"Oh, yeah. That, uh, that's a must," Chuck said unconvincingly. "Anyway, I think I could bring ten or fifteen paintings every month to you. We could both do really well, and I was wondering what kind of a rate I could work out with you."

"Chuck, that would be very exciting indeed, but finding buyers for, um, exceptional paintings is laborious work. I'm afraid I don't really do volume discounts."

"Oh, wow. So I was hoping to get a rate that, you know, was maybe a little less than this first painting. I thought you could quote me a rate for all of them, so I know how much to pay and how to set a price that makes it worthwhile."

LeBlanc led Chuck down another hall to what appeared to be a den. More of a man cave than a den. On the walls were all sorts of sports photos and paintings. The far wall, at the end of the room, was completely covered by a huge white screen for viewing games via a projector. The wall on the other end featured a whole section devoted to the Chicago Bears and, in particular, to Walter Payton, the Bears' famous running back.

"Oh, hey, this is cool," Chuck said. "Big Bears fan, huh?"

"Oh, yes," LeBlanc said, seizing the opportunity to change the subject. "Grew up in Chicago as a kid and idolized Payton. Incredible running back. I don't know if anyone holds a candle to him."

Chuck moved closer to a full-size painting of Payton frozen in time on LeBlanc's wall. His hips were in mid-swivel as he stiff-armed an imaginary tackler. His career statistics were engraved on a plaque below the painting. Chuck pretended to examine it.

"Well, I knew you'd appreciate all this, Chuck. I'll give you a quote you can count on to be consistent. Won't be much different than what we've done with your current painting, but I suppose I could shave a bit off. Just for the goodwill, right?"

"That would be super, Mr. LeBlanc. You won't regret it."

They started to walk back to the entrance when Chuck suddenly stopped. "Oh, wait! One other thing. I was hoping to see my painting and how the new frame looks. Maybe I could take a picture of it. I got a guy who's interested, and it would be good to show it to him."

LeBlanc looked at his watch and said, "I'm a little short on time, Chuck. I, uh, well, we'd have to make it quick."

"I'm all for quick. I really need to see how it looks now with the new frame."

"Of course. Follow me."

Once again, they stopped at the top of the stairs leading to the basement. Just like last time, LeBlanc called for the guard to wait for the two of them at the top of the stairs. "We'll be brief. It should only be five minutes or so," he said.

Morrow knew that was the polite way of saying, "If we're not back in five or six minutes, call in help and come on down, armed."

LeBlanc placed a black bag over Chuck's head. He led him down the stairs and around the maze. He unlocked the door, guided Chuck in, and then closed the door. Flipping on a light, he removed Chuck's hood and said, "Sorry, but you know why I have to be careful. After all, I'm protecting all these paintings, including your own. You wouldn't want me to be sloppy, would you?"

They walked together through the storage closet and then arrived at the dead end. LeBlanc pointed to Chuck's feet and said, "Watch out for that paint can on the side." Morrow glanced down and then heard the whirring of the mechanism that opened the wall to display the safe.

Morrow chastised himself for being manipulated so easily. *He's smooth. He doesn't want me to see how he opens the wall. He did something like that last time too.*

"I'll have to ask you to turn around, Chuck, while I get this thing open."

"No problem. I'll just snap my one pic of the painting, and we can leave."

Morrow turned around but raised his phone high as though he were testing it to get the camera set up properly. In truth, he was looking over his shoulder, hoping to make a video of LeBlanc's motions as he entered the five-digit combination. As LeBlanc completed the action and started to turn around, Chuck pulled the phone down and out of sight. "Can I turn around now?" he asked.

"You bet," LeBlanc said as he entered the small walk-in safe. His phone beeped, and LeBlanc ignored it. Bending over and searching for the painting marked *DAWES 120*, he located it on the second shelf. "Here we go," he said.

Carefully, he removed the brown wrapping paper and held the painting in front of his face for Chuck to take his picture.

"Got it!" Chuck said, as if taking a picture with his phone was an impressive feat of skill and dexterity. He beamed at LeBlanc. "The frame looks nice. I don't remember what the original one looked like, but it must have been a lot like this one, right?"

"Tara—um, Ms. Velloitte always tries her best to match the old frame. She does good work."

"I'll be sure to thank her," Chuck said as the dark hood was placed over his head once again.

A few minutes later, Morrow was shown out. As he stood at the front door with Tara, he said, "Take a look at this great picture I got of my painting."

He held up his phone close to Tara's face. It wasn't a picture of his painting. It was a shot Morrow had taken much earlier—a notepad with the words *Park Place Pub – tonight, 7 p.m.*

"Oh, you did a good job getting such good lighting. Nice work, Chuck."

"Thanks. And thanks for the good work on the frame. It looks super!" Mimicking the oaf that Chuck was, he flashed a thumbs up at her and smiled broadly. He waved and headed back to his car, the mission accomplished.

21

Wasting no time, Morrow approached his Toyota. About three car lengths behind his car, two men exited their vehicle and started walking toward him. One of them held up a badge.

"Excuse us. We're with the PPD. I wonder if you can help us."

Trying to appear unconcerned, Morrow shrugged, flashed a helpful smile, and said, "Sure, what do ya need?"

"You came out of the LeBlanc mansion, didn't you?"

"I'm sorry, I didn't catch your name," Morrow said, buying time.

The lead man wore an ill-fitting suit. He was close to fifty but had a full unruly head of red hair on his head. He pulled his wallet out again and showed his badge up close. "I'm Detective Fuller. This is Morgan Sawyer, my, um, assistant," he said, pointing to the shorter man.

Again, playing the rube, Morrow said, "What's up?"

"Your name?" Fuller asked.

"I'm Chuck Dawes."

"And your business inside with LeBlanc?"

"Why? Am I breaking some kind of law when I make a sales call?"

Fuller and Sawyer glanced at each other. Fuller replied, "Actually, the way this works is that we get to ask the questions, and you get to answer."

Chuck rubbed his chin. "I don't know. Don't you need a warrant or something?"

Fuller pulled handcuffs out of his back pocket and said, "Let's finish this down at the station. Turn around and spread your legs. Put your hands on the hood of the car."

To assist, Fuller swiveled Chuck around facing the car and pushed on his back to lower him while simultaneously kicking at one of his feet to spread his legs more and reduce his leverage. Morrow could tell he'd done this far too many times before. Going to the police station now was not on his list of things to do. On the other hand, he knew if he cooperated, his visit would be short. With no further comments, he allowed himself to be placed in Fuller's back seat. They headed to the precinct in silence.

Arriving twelve minutes later, Fuller guided Morrow into the building. As they entered, the three of them noticed quite a few officers rushing out of the building in a hurry.

Fuller glanced back at Sawyer and muttered, "I'm going to get my partner to sit with this character while you and I have a little talk."

Sawyer nodded.

As Fuller approached his office, another detective headed past him in the hallway, stopping long enough to say, "Riot of some kind down on the south side. Chief says anyone not otherwise engaged needs to make a beeline for it. They need bodies. You coming?"

Fuller shook his head. "No, I've got a POI here. I was hoping you could hold him for a few minutes while I—"

Cutting him off, his partner said, "No way. I'm not missing this. Put him in a cell for a while." With that, he moved on past them down the hallway.

"Great," Fuller said under his breath before returning to Morrow. "Mr. Dawes, you're going to have to wait in a cell for a brief time. We'll get back to you shortly."

"I have other appointments," Morrow tried. "How long you gonna hold me? And what for?"

Red Fuller didn't answer him. He turned around and led his person of interest down a different hall to a series of holding cells. He picked an empty one and lightly pressed on Morrow's back, easing him inside. He unlocked the cuffs and gave him another gentle shove. Then he locked the door behind him.

Morrow sat down on a bench and checked out his surroundings. There were six cells all facing the hallway. He was in the first one. The others were holding one to three guests. No one looked happy to be there. Morrow knew what was happening. *The cops were watching LeBlanc's mansion for who knows what reason. They were camped out and, lucky me, I just happened to walk out while they were there. The two geniuses decided they might learn something from anyone coming out, so they grabbed me. Fastest way for me to get out of here is to give them a good but unprovable story and play dumb. If I'm lucky, I'm out of here in less than an hour, and maybe I'll learn something about LeBlanc I can use.*

Ten minutes after arriving, a uniformed officer walked a large, handcuffed man and a scrawny kid down the hall. He stopped at cell number one, Morrow's cell, and told them to go inside. Once inside, he closed the cell door and unlocked the big man's cuffs from the other side of the bars. Morrow watched until the guard was out of sight.

The kid looked like he was seventeen. He sported a wacky haircut with a wild mop of black hair on the top and closely shaved sides. He sat down on a bench next to Morrow's and looked like he was ready to unload enough tears to fill Lake Mead.

The big guy grumbled to himself. He was no piece of art. Morrow suspected he tested positive for ugly and stupid. A second after that thought ran through his mind, the big guy confirmed it. With his face scrunched up into an ugly scowl, he turned to the kid and screamed, "What you lookin' at?"

The kid averted his eyes instantly and shook his head. "Nothing. I—I was just looking, I guess."

The big fellow took two steps closer and formed two fists. "I don't like you!" He screamed at the kid. "How would you like it if I showed you—"

"Hey, cut the kid some slack. He's no threat," Morrow called out to him.

Mr. Big and Ugly turned to Morrow and looked him up and down. Morrow remained seated, staring back at him. Big and Ugly walked over the four steps to stand right beside Morrow. He glared at him for a moment, saying nothing.

Morrow broke the eye contact and looked away, hoping to defuse the incident. A second later, Big and Ugly's right fist smashed into Morrow's temple, knocking him completely off the bench and onto the floor.

The boy screamed as Big and Ugly walked over and kicked Morrow in the stomach and then tried with his left foot to hammer Morrow again in the head. Moving as swiftly as he could, Morrow rolled out of the way, grabbed his attacker's left foot on the upswing, and violently pushed it higher. The big man lost his balance and fell on his back, making a thud that brought the guard rushing back to the cells.

With the big fellow on his back moaning, the guard flipped him over and handcuffed him again. He nodded to Morrow and the kid and said, "Follow me. I've got a different cell for you two."

It was at that moment that Detective Fuller returned and called out, "Just take the kid. I'm ready for Mr. Dawes here."

Morrow turned to the detective and dryly said, "A little earlier would've been nice."

Fuller took one look at Morrow's face and grimaced. "Nice shiner. What'd ya do? Get the big guy riled up?"

"Worse than that. I looked in his general direction," Morrow deadpanned.

"Well, I'm sorry, Mr. Dawes. This stuff happens now and then. We just have a few questions for ya."

Morrow could think of a thousand retorts to that, but he held his tongue and grunted instead. Fuller led him into an interrogation room, and Sawyer followed. They sat at a small white table with both Fuller and Sawyer opposite Morrow, and Fuller opened the discussion.

"Look, Mr. Dawes, I'm sorry that happened to you. I don't think you're dangerous, so I'm not gonna cuff ya."

"I'm supposed to be happy about that, right?" Morrow asked, not expecting an answer.

"We'd like to know what your business was at the LeBlanc mansion," Fuller started.

"None of your business, Fuller," Morrow said.

A soft *tsk* escaped Fuller's lips, and he replied, "Mr. Dawes, you're right, of course, but humor me. We're investigating a case, and we believe Mr. LeBlanc is involved. We have no reason to believe you are. We're only looking for some information on the mansion owner."

Morrow stared back at him for a moment, then said, "I heard a rumor that his mansion might be for sale. I thought maybe I could find out and pretend to be the kinda guy who could buy it."

"Why would you do that?" Sawyer asked, getting himself a harsh stare from Fuller in return.

Morrow watched the exchange and realized Sawyer probably wasn't a cop. Fuller allowed him to be there, but he wasn't supposed to speak.

"I, you know, was trying to make a buck. I know some real estate people. If I could verify that the mansion was for sale, then it was an easy step to find a realtor who could bring in a buyer and make an offer. The commission they could get would be monstrous. I get spiffed a few thousand for connecting them. It's not a crime—it's called marketing."

Morrow could tell by the downcast look on Fuller's face that he bought it. And, more importantly, that he knew he was not going to get anything of substance from Chuck Dawes.

Sawyer spoke up again. "Did you see any paintings on the walls? Anything special?"

Now, Morrow's antenna shot up about ten feet. He decided to throw Sawyer a bone and see how much he gnawed at it. "Oh, yeah, he was proud of the place. He showed me around, and I saw some huge rooms with all kinds of paintings hanging there."

Reminding Morrow of one of Pavlov's dogs, Sawyer bit and followed it up. "Did you—did you see any, uh, paintings that featured an angel and a white horse?"

Fuller intervened. Looking at Sawyer, he said, "Uh, Morgan, I think you've asked enough now. Why don't you wait in the other room for me."

"Not till he answers," Sawyer blurted out. "The angel and the steed? Did you see it?"

"Steed? Oh, you mean a horse. No, I can't say I saw anything like that, but, you know, frankly, I don't know squat about art. I wasn't really paying attention anyway."

Sawyer looked at Fuller and said, "This is a waste of time. He's an idiot."

Fuller closed his eyes and forced himself to stay calm. "Mr. Dawes, I appreciate your time. Sorry, again, about the cell incident. I think we're done here. Are you going to, uh, you know—"

"Complain to someone about the customer service here?" Morrow finished his sentence for him.

"Yeah," Fuller said quietly.

Morrow rose from his seat. "I got a better idea, Fuller. You wasted my time with this idiot"—he pointed to Sawyer—"and I got a shiner to boot. How about you just let me outta here, and maybe someday I'll need a favor, and maybe you'll do me a solid if you can."

Fuller looked into Morrow's eyes and guessed he saw a glimmer of more smarts than Chuck Dawes ever displayed.

He mulled that over for ten seconds, then nodded and said, "You can go. I hope not to see you around."

Morrow nodded back and left the precinct.

22

O nce home, Morrow tried to clean himself up, but there was only so much he could do. All the while he was in custody, he couldn't think of anything else except the short video he made of LeBlanc entering digits into the keypad.

After wiping the blood off his head and rebandaging his lower chest to quell the pain from the one good kick his attacker got in, he sat down on the couch. Pulling his phone out and going quickly to the gallery, he clicked on the six-second video and watched it intently. Then he watched it again another dozen times.

He rehashed the possibilities in his mind. The first digit seemed certain to be one. The other four could be one of two, he was guessing. "Two to the fourth power," he mumbled to himself. He did the math again and was certain he was right. With his opinion formed, he sent a text blast out to the team.

PARK PLACE PUB 7 P.M.

Tonight was different. Morrow let everyone arrive first. Watching from a café across the street, he observed their entrance and looked around to see if anyone was tailed. Seeing no evidence of that, he joined them.

"It's not like you to be late, boss," Lou said. "Jeez, nice shiner."

"Yeah, did I miss the memo?" Tommy asked. "Is this National Beat up on Morrow Month or something?"

Ignoring their questions, Morrow said, "I was across the street watching for tails. Besides, I knew I'd get some smartass comments about my appearance, and I didn't want to have to tell the story more than once."

"What happened?" Tara asked, sounding as if she actually cared.

"I was having a cup of joe at another bar. Miss America was sitting three stools away from me, and the rest of the bar was filled with Hell's Angels bikers having a reunion."

Sadie appeared with Morrow's customary seltzer while everyone at the table grinned and nudged each other with their elbows.

"Well, you can guess the rest. Someone said something untoward to Miss America, and I defended her and took on all sixty-five of the bikers with just my bare fists. Of course, I took them all down, but one of them got a lucky punch in. When our meeting is over, I'm meeting Miss America at her place to get what she called a *very* special thank-you."

Smiles and chortles permeated the air. Morrow kept a straight face.

"Right. What really happened?" Tara asked.

"Cops picked me up, and some oaf in the holding cell sucker punched me."

The smiles disappeared.

"Why'd they pick you up?" Brady asked.

"This is the bad news. They were on stake-out half a block down the street, watching LeBlanc's place. It seems everybody wants that damn painting."

"They know about it?" Connie asked.

"Yeah. The cop had someone with him, someone not a cop. I don't know what he was exactly, but he asked me very specifically if I saw a painting with an angel and a horse in it."

"What was the cop's name?" Ghost asked.

"Fuller. Detective Fuller. Red hair. You know him?"

"We've run into each other a few times," Ghost said. "He's a good cop. Smart, but plays kinda dumb. You're right, Morrow. This isn't good news."

Connie spoke up. "Who do you think the other guy was?"

Morrow shook his head. "No idea. I was thinking maybe he was an art expert on the case. Or maybe from some other government agency."

"Doesn't matter," Tommy said. "I mean, is there anybody in this town that isn't after *Gabriel's Steed*? Ghost is right, this is very bad news."

"It's the nature of what we do," Morrow said. "It's just one more hurdle. They're probably parked out there every day for a few hours. They'd mix it up, at different times, in different cars. I'll figure out some way to make that work for us."

"Like how?" Brady asked.

Before Morrow could respond, Lou said, "Brady, relax. Morrow doesn't know yet, but he'll figure something out and get them out of our hair. You don't need to know everything."

Making eye contact with Lou, Brady said, "I know. I just, you know, me and Shady, this is all kinda new to us, so we get nervous when there's no plan in place."

Lou looked at Morrow. "Boss, when did you have that little caper we pulled with you-know-who in the warehouse all figured out?"

"About six minutes before it began. Everyone did a very fine job, by the way."

Tara looked around at the faces at the table. "When was this? He told me he just met you guys two weeks ago."

"It was sort of impromptu last Friday night. Now let's get back to A) not talking about that caper ever again and B) planning the safe break-in. How many days we got left?" Morrow asked even though he knew the answer.

"Eleven," Connie said.

Morrow turned to Lou. "Tell me about the safe. What did you learn about the Gehrstreyer?"

Lou gave a full description of the company and their products. He talked about the features and raved about the security system. When he finished twelve minutes later, everyone felt less confident than before.

Tommy jumped in. "So, the safe sounds impenetrable. I mean, you don't have any tools that will detect the sound of the tumbler mechanism, right? So when you start to enter a number into the keypad, you can't get any feedback. We'd only get three tries, and then it freezes us out. You can't drill through it. We can't blow it up.

EARL JAMES

We'd have to have his thumbprint and then guess the five digits correctly, right?"

Lou nodded. "That about sums it up. Actually, there's one other thing. Anytime the safe is opened, the owner gets a text message telling him the safe is open."

"Ah," Morrow said. "That's the reason LeBlanc's phone beeped both times as we entered."

Glances were traded between the players. Then, almost simultaneously, they all looked to Morrow.

"Jeez, a little adversity and you guys get all nervous," Morrow said. "Relax. Tara has the thumbprint problem solved, and that just leaves the five-digit combination for us to figure out. Both Tara and I are pretty sure we know the first digit is one. We'll figure it out."

They spent the next hour discussing what the remaining four digits could be. Everyone put in their two cents. For virtually every suggestion of a birthdate, a social security number, a tattoo on LeBlanc's chest, a phone number, an address, a zip code, a word spelled out on a telephone pad—Tara blew it off.

"Guys, I've already tried everything you mentioned and more," Tara said. "I mean, I've been at this for months. I think it's a good thing, though. We've eliminated a ton of possibilities. And I didn't know about the text to LeBlanc if it opened. If I did get it open, he woulda caught me, so it's good I failed. Morrow and I will figure it out."

Silence reigned. After a few quiet moments, Ghost said, "Maybe it's a random number."

Everyone nodded and agreed that was possible.

"It's not random," Morrow stated.

"Why? It could be," Brady said.

"Nope. People don't use random numbers for something that important. They use a number they can never forget. And it's a number they're sure no one else would ever figure out. But we'll come up with it in a few days. We'll break in this weekend."

"Just like that?" Tommy asked.

Morrow started getting up from the table. "Yup. Just like that."

23

10 days left.

Morrow met with Tara at the Park Place Pub again the next night. He invited her for dinner. Tara suggested some nicer restaurants, but Morrow reminded her that the goal was not to be seen together. "The food is good. They have steak salads and stuff. You'll like it," he promised. She showed up at 6:15, complaining about the traffic.

"Did you remove a painting from the premises again as usual?" Morrow asked as she sat down.

"You know I did. I've been doing it for months, every night, treating it casually, placing it in the trunk."

Morrow nodded. "You're establishing a pattern, so when you walk out with the Steed, no one will even think to question you."

"Duh," Tara said.

"I'm just thinking out loud here," Morrow said, crossing his arms over his chest.

"We have to get into the safe first," Tara reminded him. "Walking out with it is the easy part, thanks to me, by the way."

Sadie came by and took their order. She eyed Morrow with a secret smile as if she knew what he was doing. Morrow knew she didn't. He had no strong feelings for Tara other than getting down to business.

Tara took advantage of the break to needle Morrow some more. "So your shiner looks even brighter tonight. You know, I can't even remember you without half your face smashed in."

"I've had worse."

"Now that I can believe. You aren't much of a fighter, are you, Morrow?"

"Fighting solves nothing. The only winner in a fight is violence."

"Hmmph," Tara muttered. "So this guy in the cell just comes up to you and sucker punches you for no reason? You didn't say anything to spur him on?"

"He was bugging some young kid who was scared to death. I told him to give the kid a break. That's all."

"Then he punched you?" Tara asked, finding the story almost as unbelievable as his Miss America version.

"No. If you must know, he stood next to me and glared at me. I turned away, and then he let me have it."

"He didn't say anything first?"

"I don't think he was a Mensa candidate. You know what they say: violence is the first resort of the inarticulate."

"Wow, have you ever, I mean, *ever* won a fight?"

Morrow sipped his seltzer water. "I took down Buster Harlow once. Barehanded. Just me. So, yeah, I've won a fight before."

"What was that about?"

Glancing around uneasily, Morrow mumbled, "He and I both liked the same girl."

"Ah! Finally, something interesting. You still with her?" Tara said, taking a sip of her martini.

"No. We were in the third grade."

Tara lurched forward, nearly spitting her mouthful out as she tried to regain composure. "Gawd, Morrow. You're pathetic. That was the last fight you won?"

Morrow allowed himself a brief smile. His reward was a revival of the pain in his jaw. "*Last* one? It was the *only* one."

"Jeez, remind me not to count on you coming to my rescue."

"You keep damaging my self-respect, and I can assure you won't have to worry about that. You're rapidly falling to the bottom of my list of people I want to save."

Still smiling, Tara nodded and said, "OK, got it. Back to business. How are you going to deal with the cops, distract the guard, and figure out the combination to the safe?"

"You're smarter than I am. I assumed you'd do all that, and I'd watch."

Flashing angry eyes at Morrow, she rebutted, "I already did a ton of work. I've cased the place, I got his thumbprint, I tested out dozens of combinations, I set up the—"

Morrow had a strange mini-smile on his face. Tara stopped talking and eyed him.

"I was just kidding, Tara."

Tara crossed her arms over her chest and said, "I know that. I was just thinking out loud." Then she shook her head and chuckled. "I'm on edge, sorry."

"No harm. So we have the first digit. We agree it has to be a one. Four more to go. Take a look at this video I made." Morrow handed his phone to her.

Tara watched. Then she did it again, watching more closely. Seven times she replayed it as Morrow watched her.

She furrowed her brow and squinted her eyes, and her head moved back and forth as she seemed to be trying to mimic LeBlanc's movements.

"This is good," Tara said under her breath.

"I have my own opinions of what I think it tells us. I want to hear yours."

"It's all conjecture. I mean, we can't really see anything."

"Go on," Morrow whispered.

"OK, he positions himself dead center, but he's right-handed, and he clearly is moving his arm up and to the far left, which coincides with both of our thoughts that he's punching the one. Then you can see his arm move back a bit, down ever so slightly and to the right. I'd say that means he's hitting the five or six key. If he were hitting four, he wouldn't show any movement to the right."

"Keep going," Morrow said. "I like your thinking."

Tara ran the video again. "OK, on the third number, his head's direction seemed to go to the left, maybe down, maybe not, but definitely not up. So I'd say he hit four or maybe seven. The fourth number feels like a guess. Somewhere in the center. I'm thinking either two or five. Then he clearly moves back to the right, and the last one looks like it's on the right side of the keypad. Six or nine, I'd say."

Morrow looked at his dinner partner and eyed her with more respect. "That's very close to what I saw, and I've got a few years on you. You're very observant."

For a moment, Tara acted like she hadn't had a compliment since Clinton was president, but she quickly recovered, giving Morrow a small nod.

"I was thinking essentially the same thing," Morrow said. "So, now, assuming we're right, the combination could be one, then five or six, then maybe four or seven, then back to two or five, and then maybe six or nine. If we're right, we could pencil out all those possible outcomes and be down to a handful."

A bit more optimistic now, Tara said, "I could try out a few between now and the time we're ready to do it so we could eliminate more."

"Nope, can't. Suppose you stumbled on the right one before we're ready. Then LeBlanc would get the text on his phone, and we'd be dead meat."

"Shit! I keep forgetting that."

Morrow finished his dinner and downed his last seltzer water. He waved to Sadie and mouthed, "My usual."

Sadie, adept at reading lips and minds amid the clatter of a noisy bar, nodded and served a shot of Jack and an IPA to him one minute later.

Morrow leaned closer to Tara and said, "Tell me about LeBlanc. I want to know everything you know about him. Somewhere in his past is the answer to our problem."

Tara talked for twenty minutes about her boss. Morrow interrupted a few times with follow-up questions, but he had learned long ago that it's best to let marks and teammates ramble on. It's in the rambling that little secrets raise their heads and beg to be noticed.

Morrow had always been a good listener. Near the end, he listened to his mother tell him stories about her past and his too. Listening meant he didn't have to talk, and that seemed more natural to him. It also gave him time to think so when he did speak, it was worth hearing.

Morrow found he was enjoying himself. Tara was smart, beautiful, and probably way too young for him, but he reveled in watching her and hearing her melodic voice. For a very brief time, he imagined a lifetime of being with someone as interesting and challenging as she was. As quickly as the thought arose, he squashed it. That kind of life was for someone who deserved it. Knowing what he'd done automatically made him the first cut from the field of nominees.

"Morrow! Morrow, you still there?" Tara asked.

"Uh, what?"

"You looked like you were a million miles away. Getting tired or something?"

Morrow nodded. "Something. You were talking about his social habits. I, uh, missed that last part."

Tara gave him an odd look and continued, "I was saying there is no lady in his life. But I know what he does that he doesn't talk about. Every Friday night, he goes to the Jaguar Club."

Morrow sat up straighter. "The Gentlemen's Club? On Indian School Road?"

Now Tara looked at him a whole different way. "You perv. You probably go there too."

"I hate to burst your bubble, but I'm not sure there's a single male over twenty-one in Phoenix who hasn't gone to the Jaguar Club at least once."

"Well, he goes *every* Friday night. And he stays there for three or four hours, spending time and money with different girls. But that's it when it comes to socializing. No girlfriend. No guys he hangs out with. Just his paintings, his man cave, and that giant screen TV so he can watch sports."

"That solves the phone texting problem," Morrow said, almost talking to himself.

"It does? How?"

Ignoring her question, Morrow downed the remainder of his Jack Daniels and polished off his beer in one swig. "I've gotta go. We're doing the heist this Friday. I know how to do it now and not get caught. I'll get the bill. Be here tomorrow night at eight. I'll walk everyone through the plan step-by-step."

Morrow left the booth and headed over to Sadie to pay the bill.

Tara joined him. "Morrow," she whispered. "We still don't have the combination. What about that?"

"We'll figure it out before Friday night. Good meeting, Tara. Thanks. I got it from here."

He laid some cash on the bar and waved to Sadie. Then he was gone.

Sadie looked at the shocked expression on Tara's face and nodded toward the door. "That was a fast exit."

"Yeah, I'll say," Tara replied.

Sadie eyed her and said, "Sit down. I think you need the cocktail of the day."

"I need more than that," Tara mumbled.

Sadie nodded her agreement. "I know. I think you need an easy ear to bend. Lucky for you, I'm here. Ain't no ears easier than these two."

Tara gave the bartender a soft smile and sat down.

Sadie served her the Rum Party Special and said, "Morrow's an interesting guy, isn't he?"

Tara didn't answer.

That didn't bother Sadie. "Let Auntie Sadie fill you in. He doesn't say much, but I can read him like a book. And let me tell ya, he's a page-turner. And for a guy with new damage to his face every day, he's not too bad lookin', either."

24

The Park Place Pub was in Morrow's rearview mirror seconds after he left. He had learned long ago not to fight his instincts or his intuition during a con. His mind was full of steps, plans, and backup plans, so when something clicked and he realized it was important enough to change everything, he'd learned to embrace it. That's what happened when Tara told him about LeBlanc's Friday night routine at the Jaguar. On this Thursday night, he estimated his arrival time at his current destination to be twenty-five minutes.

Paying the cover fee of ten bucks at the Hot Tail Club, Morrow got semi-escorted into the main room where dancers were on the stage and at the tables nearly everywhere. He got a beer at the bar, then leaned over to the bartender and asked, "Is Lexy working tonight?"

The guy nodded and pointed to the left. "Last time I saw her, she was on Stage Three over there."

Morrow knew that meant she could be anywhere, but at least she was in the building. He wandered around, nursing his beer until he spotted her doing a table dance for a half-drunk customer. He sat down at an open table along the walkway that he knew she'd be taking sooner or later. It was later. The half-drunk patron was working his way toward fully drunk one table dance at a time. He liked Lexy and kept paying her to stay with him. Lexy was no fool. She was happy to stay where the money was flowing freely.

About six songs later, the drunk, apparently running low on cash, realized he could spend his remaining money on beers or on one more table dance. He chose beer.

Lexy turned around and started walking back to the center of the room, glancing left and right, looking for a new lonely face she

EARL JAMES

could entertain. She stopped walking when she saw Morrow.

"Morrow! Haven't seen you in—in, I don't know, way too long. How are you?"

Morrow motioned for her to take the seat across from him. "I've been busy. How are you, Lex?"

"Better than you, I think. You look like a sparring partner who forgot his head gear. You OK?"

"And you look gorgeous as usual."

Lexy eyed him and said, "This is business, not pleasure, right?"

"As always, you're very observant. I, um, I need a favor."

"Name it."

"You're a, um, still a free agent, right?" Morrow asked.

"I'm an independent contractor," she replied.

"Right, and so you can work anywhere you want. I mean anywhere that will have you, right?"

"Yeah," Lexy said, dragging out the one syllable word into the next minute.

"I know you said you used to work at the Jaguar before here. Did you leave on good terms?"

"Morrow, just spit it out. What do you need?"

Morrow moved a bit closer to the table and leaned in. "I was wondering if I could talk you into working tomorrow night at the Jaguar. Just one night. There's a guy coming in that spends a lot of dough on the girls and I need him to be, um, occupied and distracted. I thought that maybe some serious beauty could do that for me."

"How distracted?"

"Oh, I don't know. So distracted that if his phone beeped with an important message, he wouldn't hear it or take time to respond to it if he did."

"You mean like being 'extra entertained' in one of the private rooms?"

Morrow nodded. "That might be one way. Another might be a soft mickey in his drink at a certain time. The key is if he hears his phone and he's thinking clearly, he'll answer it. I don't want him to."

"This guy dangerous?"

"Could be. Probably best if you used a brand-new name. You

131

could be the new girl who he wants to meet. I'd make it worth your while. Say a grand."

"You insult me! I thought—"

"I'm sorry," Morrow cut her off. "I could do twenty-five hundred."

"Morrow! Stop it. Are you kidding me? I owe *you*. You don't have to pay me. You got rid of the creep who was stalking me. I don't know how you did it, but you did. Since that last time, when he got out of control, I haven't seen him again. He scared me big time, and you saw that and did what no one else had been able to do. I can't thank you enough. You don't need to pay me nothin'."

"It wasn't that hard to do. I'm glad he's not bothering you anymore."

Lexy shook her head. "You're hard to figure. Tell me what you need."

Morrow spent the next fifteen minutes explaining what he needed, offering suggestions, and emphasizing that his prey was no dumb pigeon. When he finished, he looked her in the eye and said, "If you're not comfortable doing this, it's OK. I have a million other backup plans."

"Liar. You've got nothing, or you wouldn't be here," Lexy said, smiling. "I can do it. And I like it. Now, I'm saving you and your crew!"

Morrow allowed himself a laugh. It wasn't real. A real laugh was something that was shared and had to be earned. This laugh was for Lexy's sake because she expected it. No, because she needed it. He knew Lexy had too few laughs in her life.

He said his thanks and reminded her to check her phone and keep it on high volume after nine o'clock. It would be a disaster if she didn't hear it when he texted her.

He kissed her on the cheek and turned to leave.

Lexy called out to him. "Morrow, don't forget, I offered you free table dances any time you came in here for helping me out. You've never taken me up on that."

"I, um, I'm saving them all up for a rainy day."

"When this is all over, stop by and tell me how it turned out, OK?"

Morrow nodded and disappeared into the crowd.

25

9 days left.

The gang all assembled at Sadie's place at four that afternoon as instructed. Morrow forced them all to have non-alcoholic drinks as they discussed the game plan for that evening.

"Did you figure out the combination yet?" Brady asked before Morrow was even situated in his seat.

Lou cringed.

"We'll get to that, Brady," Morrow replied as he glanced at Tara, making eye contact. "First, I need to get brought up to date. Lou, you were going to talk to someone about the Gehrstreyer safe."

"I did. I learned a lot, but none of it really helpful. It's well built. Bottom line is I don't see any way we can get in without the thumbprint and the combination."

"I kinda figured," Morrow said. "It's still good to know we aren't missing something, though."

He readied himself to move on, but Lou interrupted. "Morrow, I don't feel like I'm pulling my weight here. I wish I could do more. It's fine if you cut me to half share or something."

"Not happening," Morrow stated. "Everybody gets a full share. Each of you has special contributions to make. Hell, Lou, you should get a full share just on the basis of playing the old homeless dude on the Mr. B caper. Now, everyone, listen up."

He paused to make sure he had their attention.

"I'm going to go through the steps and the roles. Ghost, you are lookout, as usual. Find a good spot with a perfect view of the LeBlanc mansion and the roadways leading to and from it. You need to report anything unusual via the coms. Speaking of which, here they are. Earplug usage is mandatory. We don't need anyone else hearing in by accident."

Morrow handed out small radio units with a range of three hundred feet. They clipped to the belt and used wireless earbuds.

"Brady and Tommy, you're our distraction of the night. You'll both play drunks. Two minutes after I give the signal, you two walk down the street arguing and talking loudly. Make the discussion about a woman. When you get to the LeBlanc mansion, I want you to walk onto the lawn like you're taking a shortcut to the street behind it. When you get on the side of the building, you two should get into a shoving match. Make a lot of noise. Pound the wall of the building so the guard will hear and check it out."

"You think he'll come out?" Brady asked.

"I doubt it. He'll probably yell at you from the upper windows. Feel free to say whatever comes to mind that might spur him to do something as stupid as coming out to shut you up. If he does, keep him busy, but I doubt he will. He'll probably call the cops."

"What then?" Brady asked.

"Just keep making noise until Ghost lets you know the cops are on the way. If they are, skedaddle."

Brady and Tommy glanced at each other, smiling. They had plenty of ideas on how to keep the guard busy.

Morrow looked at Brady's brother and said, "Shady, you're the backup and the getaway car driver. I want you parked nearby so you can see your brother and Tommy mixing it up. If the guard does come out, you go over and make sure he doesn't hurt them, OK?"

Shady nodded.

"I should clarify. Make sure he doesn't hurt *them*, but do not *kill him*. Got it?"

Again Shady nodded.

"Good. Later, when we come out of the building with the painting, unlock the trunk so we can place the painting there, and then we'll get in the back seat, and you'll leave at a very normal speed and safely drive us to Connie's house where we will check the painting out and celebrate a bit."

Morrow took a sip of his seltzer water and looked at Connie. Growing weary of jawing, he gave her his one-question query. "Anything?"

"Morrow, late this morning, you asked me to do an online search of any five-digit numbers starting with one and using the various combinations of two, four, five, six, seven, and nine for the remaining four. You wanted to see if anything jumped out as a date or dollar amount or address or statistic or anything quasi-important on a frequent basis. You told me to look for things in Arizona, Chicago, or France, or anything that could somehow be connected to LeBlanc."

"And?" Morrow said, his facial expression growing hopeful.

"I got zip. Zilch. Nada. I found some zip codes that matched in Pennsylvania and other states, but there was no connection. I found a slew of addresses in Arizona that matched many of the numbers of houses there, but LeBlanc had nothing to do with them. I checked public records to see what houses were owned in Arizona by anyone with the name LeBlanc. There were a few, but only two that Conrad LeBlanc owned. One was the mansion, and the other was a rambler in Mesa, but the address for that one didn't even come close to the numbers we were searching on. You told me to check the Chicago area too. That was harder, but I checked census records and found where his family lived. No connection to any of the numbers. Now and then, some other obscure item would come up, but I followed your directions and checked them out, and they really had no significance, nor did they have anything I could connect to LeBlanc. I'm sorry."

Tara gulped. They were less than four hours away from executing the break-in.

Morrow shuffled in his seat. "It's OK; it was a long shot, anyway. Thanks for making the effort. Tara and I got this anyway."

"What about the detective and his buddy?" Lou asked. "What if they show up when we're pulling this off?"

"Oh, yeah, that was Connie's job too. What you'd find out, Con?" Morrow asked.

"Public records show that Detective Fuller was not the detective on the case to find the stolen painting. It was an older guy, Detective MacElhany. He retired and ate a bullet three years ago."

"Jeez, keep the cheery details to yourself next time, Con," Ghost said.

"Well, just trying to be thorough," Connie said. "Maybe the fact that he killed himself might mean something."

"Yeah, it means being a cop takes a toll on people," Morrow said. "Otherwise, I'm not sure there's any relevance. OK, back to the plan. Tara is going to show up at the office around 8:50 tonight. She'll exchange pleasantries with the guard, who is used to seeing her drop by at all times of the night. She set this up long ago so that she could come and go without suspicion. She has a workshop downstairs where she does repairs. The guard is used to seeing her go down there.

"Brady and Tommy will start their distraction around nine. When Tara is sure the guard is engaged, she'll let me in the front door. We'll go downstairs, open the safe, get the painting, and exit."

Morrow signaled Sadie with a twirling of his finger. She returned three minutes later with eight Corona beers.

Morrow held his beer up and said, "This is the start of a tradition. This is us. A solid team. A team that takes care of each other. A team that leaves no one behind. A team that gets the job done. Here's to our success."

Everyone raised their glass in a toast to themselves and took a long swallow. Smiles abounded on seven faces. Only Morrow didn't smile. Smiling was something he did after he'd won.

"OK, it's really pretty straightforward. Any questions?"

Ghost spoke up. "What time you want us in position, Morrow?"

Morrow thought for a moment and said, "Ghost, you should—"

"How about a picture of all of you? Sounds like you're celebrating," a college-age kid with a Nikon D750 and a mounted light interrupted. "Only ten bucks!"

Morrow immediately said, "No thanks, we—"

Before he could finish, the kid took the shot and swiftly headed down the hall and out the back door into the alley. Morrow rose and ran down the hall after him. A large fellow, moving slowly, exited the men's room and filled the hallway with his oversized frame. Morrow struggled to get past him, but he lost valuable seconds. By the time he got to the alley, no one was in sight.

Upon his return to the booth, Lou looked up at him. "What the fuck? Was that what I think it was?"

Seconds later, Tommy walked in the front door and reported, "I checked out front. I saw the kid jump into a car with another guy. They took off like the Concord leaving Paris."

"Great," Lou said.

"Folks," Morrow began slowly, "I think we have to assume that was our client getting our mug shots, so he knows who to kill if we fail him."

No one spoke.

"Fucking shit," Ghost finally said.

"Anybody here a sports fan?" Morrow asked. No one responded, so he continued, "This gives new meaning to a few good phrases, like 'do or die' and 'there's no tomorrow.' Sorry, just a little gallows humor to lighten things up. Come on, let's get out of here and go do our job. Ghost, be in position by 8:45. Everybody else within ten minutes of that. Keep your coms on."

26

The team left, leaving Tara and Morrow. Morrow paid the bill and took hold of Tara's elbow, leading her out of the bar.

"Where are we going?" Tara asked.

"We're going to my place. It's walking distance."

The night had grown cooler. That is, cooler by Phoenix standards. It felt like it might be in the mid-seventies. Humidity was very low, and it made for a pleasant evening stroll. If their lives hadn't been hanging by a slender thread, it may even have felt romantic.

As they walked, Morrow decided to share one of his fears with Tara. "One of the things I'm a bit worried about is the painting itself. How would we know if it's real? I mean, I don't know jack about art. What if LeBlanc made up the whole thing about having the Steed, and all he has is a really good fake?"

Tara eyed him and said, "You think he would try to pawn off a fake to a mobster?"

Time to go fishing now, Morrow, he thought to himself. *She's been hooked, now let's see if I can bring her in. I need to know what I'm sure she knows.*

"I don't know. Maybe not," Morrow mused. "Maybe *he* got conned. Maybe he thinks it's real, but it isn't. The problem is, how would we know?"

They continued their walk in silence. *Come on, Tara, give me something.*

Finally, she spoke. "He has a tell."

"What? A tell? We're talking about art here, not poker," Morrow replied.

"Not LeBlanc. It's Bandeaux, the artist, who has a tell. When I was researching Bandeaux, I traveled all over Europe, visiting the museums where they displayed his lesser works. I studied the hell out of them. Lo and behold, I found a tell."

"What was it?"

"I've never told anyone. Why should I tell you?"

Morrow said nothing for half a block. *Patience now, Morrow. Wait for it. She wants to tell someone.*

"I mean, you of all people," Tara said. "First of all, I hate you for screwing my plan up, and second, you don't even appreciate art. It's wasted on your tiny little pea-sized art brain. It's all pointless."

"I get it. But, if you're going to earn your cut, you have to be with me when I present the painting to Almeda. He, above all, will know if it's fake or not. I just think that if we knew in advance that it was the real deal or a fake, that information may prolong our lives."

Now it was Tara's turn to be silent as she pondered that reality. After a few moments, she said, "This sucks. I worked so hard to study, plan, and protect my secret, and now the guy I have to tell it to is an art moron."

"Sticks and stones."

"Oh, shut up, Morrow. Gawd, you're irritating. His tell is that right under his signature, he always hides something in the painting."

Morrow pondered that for a moment. "What do you mean, he hides something?"

"In all his other paintings, he added a tiny, out of place object in the picture. He blended it in, color-wise, and made it kind of, you know, Where's Waldo–like."

"Give me an example," Morrow said.

"Well, in one painting of Madonna and Child, surrounded by angels, Bandeaux signed it near the bottom, under an angel's toes. Below his signature, well-hidden and very small, was a silver piano Like a toy. To the casual eye, it was so small it wasn't even recognized. But if you looked really closely, you could see it was a tiny piano with the lid propped up. About the size for a flea to play *Moonlight Serenade* on."

"That's weird. How is it you spotted that and no one else has over the last five hundred years?"

"Because hard work is rewarded, that's why. Because everybody fawned over the Steed, but they dismissed all his other paintings as prosaic."

Morrow smiled to himself. "Nice word, *prosaic*. *Ordinary* works fine for most folks. I haven't heard someone ever use that word in a conversation."

"That's it? That's all you have to say? I just told you an art secret that no one else in the world knows, and your response is to applaud my vocabulary? Maybe you should've been a grammarian instead of a conman."

Morrow found himself chuckling. Something he rarely did. "You're right; what you did was terrific detective work. It'll come in handy. So we should be able to look at *Gabriel's Steed* and find the anomaly under his signature, right? And that would tell us if it's the original or not?"

"That's it, Sherlock. Congratulations on figuring out the obvious."

Morrow pointed to the right, ignoring her comment, and said, "This is my place."

They entered Morrow's humble apartment complex, and he led her into the elevator and up to his unit.

"Morrow, what are we doing here? You really live here, or is this your safe house?"

"I'm not here much. Just to sleep, most of the time."

"It's kinda dark and gloomy," Tara said.

"That's what light bulbs are for. Turn on the lamp next to the sofa. I'll turn on the ceiling light." He flipped the switch as she turned on the lamp. "There. Better?"

"It's lighter, but it's still kinda gloomy."

"Everybody's a critic," Morrow mumbled.

Tara turned around and looked at the living room's west wall. A white board hung there where his sunset painting used to be. She moved closer.

"What's this?"

POSSIBLE COMBINATIONS				
1ST	**2nd**	**3rd**	**4th**	**5th**
1	5 OR 6	4 OR 7	2 OR 5	6 OR 9
1	5	4	2	6
1	5	4	2	9
1	5	4	5	6
1	5	4	5	9
1	5	7	2	6
1	5	7	2	9
1	5	7	5	6
1	5	7	5	9
1	6	4	2	6
1	6	4	2	9
1	6	4	5	6
1	6	4	5	9
1	6	7	2	6
1	6	7	2	9
1	6	7	5	6
1	6	7	5	9

"It's our choices," Morrow said. "If we believe what we think we saw on the video, then his combination is one of these sixteen possibilities. Two to the fourth power."

"Huh?" Tara asked. "Two to what?"

"Two to the fourth," Morrow said. "Sixteen possible choices. I came to the same conclusions you did. That means either we're correct or we're both wrong in the same way. I'd say with time running out, we need to believe in ourselves. One of those sixteen lines is the correct combination. I need you to look closely at them and see if you have a good feeling about any of them."

"You—you mean we should get to the safe and then...guess?"

Morrow poured himself a shot of Jack. "You got a better idea?"

27

Tara and Morrow sat in his car as darkness began to envelope the scene before them. It was 8:48, and they were both on edge. Back at Morrow's apartment, they had dissected the list of possible combinations and eliminated five. Making the assumption that the combination was handpicked by LeBlanc for a reason unknown, Tara felt strongly that some of the combinations with similar numbers would not be easy ones to remember, so she crossed off three on the list: 15456, 15756, and 16456.

Morrow had a nagging feeling that he was missing something. He felt strongly that the numbers weren't random. It didn't mean they were hard to remember because of repetitive numbers, as Tara suggested, but having no other ideas, he agreed they had to pare down the totals somehow. He eliminated two other numbers only because they didn't *feel* like they might represent something. Those were 16459 and 16756.

"It's 8:51. I think I should go in now," Tara said.

"Just a minute," Morrow said, sounding distracted.

This is just like Edwin described it. Years ago, when I was still learning the trade. I didn't get it then, but now I do. He was right. These are the moments—like the calm before the storm. Look around. Nothing's happening. It's a routine evening in the suburbs. One woman out walking her dog. A guy on his front lawn, coiling up the hose to put it away. No one else may notice anything tonight, but for us, every minute will feel like eternity. Every action we take has been planned to the nth degree. Every decision we make will upset this calm atmosphere, and the storm will begin. Once she gets out of the car, walks back to her car, and drives it into the parking lot, it will set off a series of events that will race to a conclusion. It could end in great victory or despair and death. Edwin, I get it now. It sounded like the ramblings of an old man, but I was too clueless to understand. Now, in a moment, I'll decide when the storm begins. I'll be all-powerful and all vulnerable at the same time.

"Morrow, I think I should go," Tara repeated.

It was 8:54.

"OK, let's make it happen," he said.

Tara opened the car door and looked back one more time at him. For a brief second, their eyes met, and Morrow immediately sensed her lack of confidence in the plan.

"Go. We've got this," he said in a calm but firm voice.

Tara nodded and left the car. Morrow watched her drive into the parking lot next to the mansion and park in her usual space.

"Don't rush now. Easy does it. This is like any other late-night visit," Morrow mumbled under his breath, watching as she removed a painting from the trunk and walked at a normal pace up to the porch and inside.

Morrow picked up his radio and said, "Time for a drunken excursion, boys."

Half a block away, Tommy and Brady began a slow meandering walk in the general direction of the mansion. Morrow had choreographed this play with them and told them to take it slow. He didn't want it happening too close to the same time that Tara showed up inside.

The two of them talked loudly and nearly yelled at each other a few times before they were even in sight of the LeBlanc mansion. Morrow hoped that the guard might hear some of it before he could actually see them. A large bank of trees obscured the view, except for immediately straight ahead of the front of the building. Slowly, the pair worked their way into view.

Inside, Tara nonchalantly said hi to the guard and told her she wouldn't be long. She cited a few last-minute tasks she needed to finish prior to tomorrow morning. The guard pretended to be interested, but it was clear he wasn't. He returned to the main room and sat down.

143

Tommy and Brady moved ever closer. Finally, still screaming at each other and now talking about some woman named Helen, they came into view of the front windows of the mansion. On this quiet night, their discussions could be heard quite clearly.

The guard rose and walked over to the windows. He could see the liquor bottles in the two men's hands and watched in mild amusement as they yelled and pushed at each other. The shorter one took a long swig of what looked like vodka and started walking on the lawn toward the mansion.

Brady stopped about ten feet onto the lawn and yelled at Tommy, "I'm tellin' ya. Stay away from her. She's mine."

"Fuck you!" Tommy slurred back. "You can't tell me what to do!"

As this little opera was playing out, Morrow left his car and began to angle in toward the property. He cut through some trees to minimize his time in the open, but as the sun had set and he was dressed in all black, he was barely visible anyway.

The argument escalated. Brady started to run away but stumbled three times, as an inebriated person was likely to do. Not faring too much better, Tommy came after him, catching up with him on the side of the house and pushing him hard into the side panels. Brady hit them with a thud.

The guard left the front windows and moved over to the side to look down at the two who were now rolling on the grass. He opened a window and yelled down, "This is private property. You two go fight somewhere else, or I'll be calling the police."

As the guard was distracted, Tara quietly opened the front door, and Morrow, at the ready, slipped on in. They both immediately went down the stairs to where the safe was waiting for them.

Without a black bag on his head, Morrow saw the open area where he had been led as though they were going through a long maze. His suspicion confirmed, he thought of how LeBlanc felt it was important to mislead Morrow. He remembered the way LeBlanc led him, abruptly turning and changing directions like a running back, cutting his way across the gridiron on the way to a touchdown.

Instead, it was wide open, and there were five doors, A through E, looking like closet doors. Without hesitating, Tara went straight to Door B and unlocked it.

"You have a key!" Morrow said. "You didn't tell me that. I brought my tools for picking the lock."

"I know a lot you don't, and don't forget that when we split up the take," she replied.

Tara opened the door and led him in. It wasn't a closet. Morrow assumed that meant the other four were.

"LeBlanc wanted any thieves to waste a bunch of time trying to figure out which door led to the safe," Morrow muttered, half to himself.

"That's what I figured too," Tara said, looking back at Morrow. "This way."

She led him back to where the hallway turned to the right, then another left, and then ended. She flipped all the light switches on as she passed.

"This is where he took me, and somehow, he opened the sliding wall to reveal the safe," Morrow said.

"I know. When I first came here, he did the same to me. Then, one day, about forty days into the job, he didn't. He left the bag off and told me it was time I learned where the safe was. But it took me another two weeks to figure out how he opened it. It's on this wall." She pointed to the wood-paneled wall on her right.

"A button hidden somewhere?" Morrow guessed.

"Don't touch, just look. Can you find it?"

Morrow stared at it. He stepped closer. He saw nothing. "It's not on the wall. He had a clicker in his pocket or something."

"Look out," Tara said, pushing him gently to the side. She placed her finger on a dark knot in the wood panel. The sliding door moved to the left and out of view. The safe stood before them.

"Slick. LeBlanc's no dummy," Morrow said.

Looking directly at him, she said, "All this was easy. Now we have to do the hard part: open the fucking safe. Got our cheat sheet in your pocket?"

Morrow pulled out a notecard and handed it to her. "Wait, I have to text Lexy."

"Who's Lexy?"

"She's the professional distraction at the Jaguar. She has to slip the mickey into LeBlanc's drink right now."

"Oh, that's how you're doing it. Lexy, huh? Someone you hang out with a lot?"

"What? You don't think a pretty girl could like me?"

"Not the way you look. I've seen battering rams prettier than you."

Morrow's lip twitched as he finished his texting. "Eyes on the prize. We need to make our first pick. What do you like?"

Tara looked at the card. Two rows of five-digit numbers with five crossed out. "This is nuts. This list is based on so many flimsy guesses. The odds are way higher that the combination's not even on this list."

Morrow looked at his watch. It showed 9:13. He shook it. Turning to his cell phone, he checked the time displayed. 9:16. "Tara, we had this discussion in spades back at my apartment. It's all we've got. Pick a number."

Tara looked over the list. After inhaling deeply and exhaling dramatically, she said, "I'm going with 15729. It, um, it seems easy to remember."

She turned to the keypad and positioned her wooden thumb above it.

"Wait," Morrow said.

"Wait for what? We have to get this show on the road."

"I want to make sure Lexy has enough time. Your first try could open the safe, and she has to be ready."

"Time? For the mickey to take effect?"

"Yeah, that, and if we get it open, she has to get his phone while he's in sleepy land and delete the text. Otherwise, he'd see it later, and the jig would be up."

"This is pointless anyway. We get three lousy tries. We had sixteen possibilities, and arbitrarily, on a fucking whim, we deleted five. Now we got three shots out of eleven. What is that? Less than 35 percent or something?"

"27.3 percent," Morrow said.

"See, even you know it's pointless. When did you figure that out, back at the apartment?"

Morrow shook his head. "Just now. Three tries out of eleven is always 27.3 percent."

"You figured that out in your head just now?"

"Tara, any schoolboy knows if you get three hits in eleven at-bats, you're batting .273. Now let's get on with it. Focus and type slowly and carefully."

"Yes, Dad. Damn, you are one weird dude, Morrow."

Tara placed the thumb on the imprint pad, and the numerical pad lit up. Without skipping a beat, Tara punched in one, five, seven, two, and nine. The next second lasted for eternity, and then they both exhaled. Nothing. No noise, no gears grinding. No door opening.

"Well, surprise, surprise. First guess wasted. You want the second one?"

Morrow nodded. "Yeah. I'll go with 16426. It's the only one of the sixteen that is all even numbers."

"Because you think that's significant?" Tara asked, hopefully.

"No, because I'm guessing, and I need to have a reason for the guess."

"Great," Tara said, "that's a real confidence builder. Remind me never to work with you again."

"Remind me never to hire you. You're all doom and gloom."

Ignoring him, she used the thumb again to punch in the numbers.

Nothing.

"Shit, we're so fucked. This is the stupidest plan ever," Tara mumbled.

She looked back to Morrow and said, "Might as well pick the next number too. I'm not picking it. I only got one suggestion left."

"What's that?"

"Pick something with a seven in it. Sevens are lucky. And he's a big football fan, so seven points for a touchdown might be something he'd like."

Morrow shook his head. "Actually, a touchdown is worth six points. Gotta get the seventh with a—with a—um, hang on a minute."

Morrow pressed his eyes closed and tried to transport himself back in time. His nagging thought that he was exposed to the answer kept returning to him. *Big football fan. Loves Walter Payton. Has the picture on the wall. A monument to the Bears and Payton. All his stats on the plaque and—oh, boy, that's it!*

"Tara, you're on to something. When he showed me around, he proudly showed off his man cave with the sports posters and that giant painting of Walter Payton. He was his boyhood hero. He'd know everything about him. It's—it's a stat—something with five digits."

"Number of touchdowns he scored?"

"No, no, that would only be two or three digits. What else? What else? Think, Morrow," he said, talking to himself.

"Morrow, don't we have to hurry? How long can Lexy keep LeBlanc out?"

"Yes, yes, it has to be now." Morrow pulled his phone out and connected to the web. He typed in career football records. After forty seconds, he said, "*Yes*! This might do it. Is 16,726 on our list?"

"Sixteen thousand? Um, oh, one, six, sev—yes! 16726. It's on our list."

"That's it. It's the number of yards Walter Payton ran for. Second most in history. He'd know it. Try it. Try it now!"

Her hand shaking, Tara placed the thumb on the reader. Nothing happened.

"Do it again," Morrow said.

She tried again. This time she pressed a bit harder, and the keypad lit up. "Got it! What numbers again?"

Morrow walked her through them. The second she entered the final six, the door creaked, the gears rolled, and it opened.

Tara wanted to scream, but the guard was still upstairs, so she let loose with a wide grin and led the way inside. One glance at the paintings hanging on the walls in glass frames told her *Gabriel's Steed* was not among them.

"It's one of these on the shelves or floor with the paper wrapped around them. Open the paper very slowly and carefully, one at a time, and just peak in. Don't unwrap it completely. If you think you might have it, stop and tell me."

Realizing Tara was in her realm now, Morrow was fine with following her lead. One by one, they peaked inside at the paintings on the floor and shelves. As time was slipping by, she suggested he shouldn't waste time with anything that didn't appear to be two feet by three feet. That was the Steed's size.

Six minutes later, Morrow's phone beeped. It was a text from Lexy. SUBJECT COMING TO. DELETED THE TEXT.

Morrow put the phone back in his pocket, saying a silent prayer of thanks to the stripper who saved the day, and reached for another piece of art of the right size.

Tara reached for the same painting at the same time. She looked at him and said, "Bad news, Morrow."

"What?"

"This is the last one to check. If this isn't it, all this was for nothing."

Morrow gulped and tried to sound positive. "Then this has to be it."

Tara started to roll her eyes but realized she wanted to believe it too. She took it from Morrow and slowly peeled back part of the paper. She glanced under it and said nothing. She just held it there in front of her face.

Unable to stand it any longer, Morrow said, "Well?"

Tara locked eyes with him and said, "It's not it. The Steed isn't here."

28

The lights burned late at Tommy and Connie's house. The team retreated there as planned, but the celebration they expected to have wafted away on the evening breeze.

"Now what do we do?" Brady asked, his voice rising a few octaves as he spoke.

"This gig is cursed," Tommy added. "It's living proof of Murphy's law. If it can go wrong, it will."

"I doubted we'd even get into the safe," Lou said, "but, Morrow, you pulled a rabbit out of your hat on that one."

"Tara provided the inspiration. I just had a hunch on the stat." Morrow took another sip of beer and continued, "We got lucky. And if you're looking for a silver lining, it's the fact that we aren't wasting our time trying again to break into that damn safe."

"Small consolation," Connie said quietly.

"OK," Morrow said as he clapped his hands to get their attention. "Obviously, the painting is somewhere else. Time to brainstorm. Shout out where you think it could be. Let's hear some ideas."

The next three minutes were filled with a flurry of ideas ranging from LeBlanc's car to a secret home to a cluttered closet in the mansion. Then, as suddenly as the stream of ideas poured out of their mouths, they ended. In the silence that followed, Morrow looked to Tara and said, "I didn't hear from you."

Quietly, she said, "I think it's in his bedroom."

"Why do you think that?" Morrow asked.

"A few reasons. One, he made it clear from day one when I started there that his bedroom was off-limits. Two, the guards never leave the main room. I mean, they don't go downstairs to check on

150

the safe or anything else for that matter. The main room has the only stairway to the second level, where all the bedrooms are. I've tried several times to think of a job-related reason why I should go up there, but I have none. And he knows that. And three, I think he loves that painting, and he likes waking up and seeing it on the wall every morning. He's kinda sentimental that way."

Morrow weighed that and said, "I agree. First time we met, he spoke of one favorite painting and said it's the first thing he loves to look at each morning. He tried to tell me it was some sunrise painting in the safe, but if he loved it so much, why wasn't it hanging on the wall to see instead of wrapped up on a shelf? I think you're right, Tara."

"There are other possibilities, Morrow," Ghost said. "Maybe he hasn't got it yet. Maybe it's being delivered to him sometime before next Saturday."

"Yowza, he's right. He may not have it yet," Brady blurted out.

"Actually, I hate to be a spoilsport, but there are all kinds of other possibilities," Tommy said. "Maybe the rumors are wrong. He's not the dealer."

"Or maybe there *is* no deal. It's all conjecture," Lou suggested.

"We could be way off, Morrow. What if the client is playing us? Maybe there is no painting, and he has a whole different agenda," Connie said. "Maybe we're just an elaborate misdirection, and he's the one running the con."

"Oh, jeez! Anything's possible," Brady said.

Morrow looked at each of them and said, "Maybe aliens beamed the painting up from the safe and took it to their home planet."

Glumly, Tara shook her head. "Occam's Razor," she muttered under her breath.

"What? What'd you say, Tara?" Connie asked.

Morrow answered for her. "She said Occam's Razor."

"What's that?" Brady asked.

Morrow reached for his beer and replied, "It's a scientific and philosophical rule that states that the simplest of competing theories is preferred to the more complicated ones."

Brady rubbed his chin, "Sorry, I must be dense. I'm still not quite getting it."

Morrow finished off his beer and said, "The simplest explanation is usually right."

"Oh, I get it now."

"Morrow, I don't think we can discount the other possibilities completely," Connie said.

"We won't. But for now, we shouldn't make assumptions we have no proof of." Morrow turned to Tara. "What ideas do you have about getting into the master bedroom?"

"Well, I told you about one of those plans and how I felt when I realized it would never happen."

Morrow flashed back to their conversation about her inability to seduce LeBlanc. "I remember. OK, that's out. Maybe we just find a way to take the guard down and break in. Thoughts?"

Lou was in his element now. "Morrow, I'd advise against it. Unlike the safe escapade, failing to find the painting there would be known. Tara would lose her job, and we'd lose the only edge we've got. Based on what you told us about LeBlanc's subterfuge regarding the safe security, I'd say you'd have to assume he has his bedroom wired too. Maybe even monitored. With the safe, we knew in advance about the text warnings and the other features. We know nothing about how he might be protecting valuables in his own bedroom."

Morrow nodded, considering the sage advice. "All good points, Lou. Besides, breaking in sounds violent. People could get hurt." He leaned back into the short couch and took on the expression he showed when his mind was going a mile a minute.

Tommy got up from his seat and said, "I'm getting another beer. Anyone else?"

Everyone except Tara and Morrow raised their hand.

Morrow continued to sit there, a mere eighteen inches from Tara and yet miles away from her and the others. Before Tommy could return with the beers, Morrow stood up and appeared to be reorienting himself, almost as if he were surprised to be where he was.

"I gotta go," he said.

"Morrow!" Connie called to him as he reached the door.

He stopped and turned back to her, saying nothing.

Her voice quivering a bit, Connie said, "Morrow, should we, I mean, should all of us go too? You know, get out of town while we can?"

"Oh, um, no. I didn't mean it that way. Everyone, meet me at the pub at six tomorrow night. I'm buying dinner, and then I'll tell you all about our new plan."

"We aren't going to break in?" Brady asked.

"No, my plan is much simpler."

"Yowza! How are we going to get it?"

Morrow turned the handle on the door and stepped out onto the porch. Before closing the door, he said, "LeBlanc's just going to give it to us."

29

8 days left.

Morrow drove home, continuing to plan on the way. It was after midnight when he arrived. He showered, made a list on paper of everyone he needed to call in the morning, and went directly to bed.

Getting up at six sharp, he walked to the Sunrise Café, three blocks from his apartment. He ordered his usual scrambled eggs, hash browns, and bacon. As he ate, he added two more people to his call list.

Normally, Morrow would relax over breakfast, read the paper, study the baseball box scores, and enjoy the moment. This time was different. He walked himself through the plan and fought the urge to smile at the end. No celebrating till it was over.

After arriving back home, he made all his calls, restructured the plan based on who agreed to help, and walked himself through the plan one more time. Then he called Tara.

She answered his call instantly. "Morrow, are you OK?"

"Yeah, I'm fine. You worried about me? You starting to like me?"

"Oh, please, don't flatter yourself. I still hate you for screwing up my play, but now I need you to get the painting for me. That's all."

"For you? Aren't you forgetting that I'm getting the painting for our client, and then we get some money?"

"I didn't forget. But he's *your* client, not mine."

Morrow didn't respond.

After too long a silence, Tara said, "*You* called *me*. Why?"

"I have some questions for you about LeBlanc."

"Fire away."

"He, um, seems like an educated man and, I don't know, kind of a straightforward guy. He's friendly and seemed genuine while he was showing me around. So, my question is, is that who he is? A nice guy who works in the gray area of the law?"

"Morrow, he's an ass. He's not a nice guy. He acts like one, but he hates women and most of his clients too."

"Not the impression I got. Lexy said he was a bit rough around the edges, but he appeared to genuinely like women very much."

"Oh, he does. He does—until he doesn't. Once he gets the women to go out with him, you know, away from the club, he gets pretty rough. Just in the four months I've been with him, he had to settle out of court with two women who accused him of rape."

"A lot of rich guys get accused. Chicks after his money and stuff. You think they were legit?"

"Morrow, I saw the last one, and she was marked up bad. She said he did it to her. If he didn't, why is he paying them cash to settle? He's not a nice guy."

"He seemed nice enough about helping me out," Morrow countered.

"Boy, for a conman, you sure miss a lot. Do you know why I was giving you the bum's rush that first day?"

"You didn't want me to screw up your plan," Morrow said. "Right?"

"Wrong. I had no idea that first day that you might mess things up for me. I was trying to get you out of there before LeBlanc got his hands on you. You see, it's guys like you, clients he figures are small-time players, that he screws every day of the week. He tells them he has a buyer, and then the deal falls through, and he points to section six, paragraph five of the contract you signed. In deep legalese, it says he has the right to sell the painting to anyone of his choosing if the first attempt goes awry."

"I didn't see that in there," Morrow said defensively.

"Neither does anyone else. He sells them to an underground dealer for whatever he can get, takes his minimum fixed rate cut, and tells the client to take a hike because there's nothing left for him or her. He explains the language in the contract and then reminds them that he has muscle that will take them out if they cause any trouble. That's what he was going to do with you."

Morrow thought on it for a moment and said, "So while he's working on big sales, like the Steed, where he makes a huge commission, he supplements his income by screwing the small-time players like me, right?"

"Exactly. So, see, I was trying to help you and keep you from getting flimflammed," Tara said, almost triumphantly.

"Did he ever use his muscle? You know, get rough with any of these guys?"

"There was one I know of for sure. That guy spent time in the hospital with a concussion and two broken legs. I overheard LeBlanc laughing about it on the phone with one of his thugs. Now do you believe me?"

"Yes, I guess that's what I wanted to hear. Thank you."

"That's it? You called to get a review of my employer?" Tara asked.

"He's not your employer; he's your mark. And I asked because when we are successful and get our hands on *Gabriel's Steed*, it seems likely that some unhealthy things may happen to him. I was just trying to find out if I should care or not. See you at six at the pub."

Again, Morrow waited across the street, nursing a coffee and watching for tails or anyone showing too much interest in one of his team members. Ever since the hustling photographer episode, it was obvious that someone, most likely Almeda, was watching them, and that wasn't good. New security procedures would have to be put in place.

When everyone had arrived at the pub, and Morrow was certain the coast was clear, he entered and joined them. The expectant looks on their faces did nothing to belie their fears.

Morrow slipped into the booth at the end, and Sadie delivered a seltzer water to him four seconds later. He flashed her an appreciative nod.

"Got a brand new plan for us?" Brady asked.

"I do, but first a little housekeeping. Someone is tracking us and followed one of you here before the photographer came in and snapped our picture. Security has to be tighter. All future meetings will be at Tommy and Connie's house, if that's OK?" Morrow looked at Connie to gauge her willingness.

"Fine by us," she said.

"Everyone needs to make sure they aren't being tailed. Double up security. Ghost, when our meeting is over tonight, I want you to leave in your car…" Morrow hesitated. Realizing he'd never seen Ghost except on foot, he asked, "You do have a car, right?"

"Maybe I do," Ghost said.

Morrow looked at everyone else at the table and said, "I love how Ghost tells me to mind my own business so nicely."

Everyone nodded, chuckled, or both.

"Anyway, I want you to leave in your car or Batmobile or Lear jet or whatever, and then circle back and get into position to watch everybody else leave. I've been watching each of you when you arrive and seen nothing out of the ordinary. Now we have to start watching when we leave too. Ghost, if you see someone being tailed, let them know first and then me."

"Got it."

Sadie showed up with her order pad in hand. "Too soon to order food?"

"No, not at all," Morrow said. "Place your orders. I'm buying for everyone, but please feel free to select any entrée on the menu under three dollars."

More laughter. "Morrow, you always were a big spender," Lou said.

Morrow mentally checked the box next to "loosen everyone up with a little levity" on his to-do list. He was fearful that a few of them were on the edge of quitting and leaving town. Just as Edwin had done so many years ago, he'd crack a few jokes and try to lower the tension. When the younger Morrow had asked later why he made jokes when the team was in trouble, Edwin had said, "It's rule number seven: keep the team loose. They need to let some of the tension out of their body so they can think straight. Every action for a purpose, Morrow."

Sadie left with all their orders. She didn't need to ask Morrow. He'd flashed two fingers at her earlier, signifying his number two favorite meal: Caesar salad with chicken and an order of onion rings.

Left alone once again, Morrow started right in. "We're going to do a little something called the Big Boss Shuffle."

Lou immediately let out a quiet but knowing "yes!" and everyone looked at him. He just smiled.

"We know the mob man is coming into town on Saturday to buy the painting. He'll fly into the Phoenix Goodyear Airport sometime early in the afternoon. The intel I have says he will be coming directly to LeBlanc's to see and buy the painting. Our plan is to slow him down at the airport and on the road so he'll be about twenty minutes late. Instead, we will show up with an actor playing Mr. Mob."

"And how do we pay six million dollars or whatever it is?" Tommy asked.

"That's the rub. We don't. Now, I mentioned to some of you that my former teammate and computer wizard had a program she developed, something she called the Dream Stealer. An assistant outside in a car would run the program. All she had to do was get her homemade remote gadget within five feet of LeBlanc's laptop. Then it would connect with his laptop and display his bank account screen. The mob guy would pay him via a money transfer that would show up in his account. Except it was all fantasy. It was like watching a cartoon. The numbers would roll in on the screen, he'd think he was receiving the money into his account, and it would still be showing in his account for as long as the remote was within five feet. By the time it wasn't, the mob man and his painting would be gone."

"Wow, that's slick," Brady said.

"I thought you said she didn't want to be involved?" Connie asked.

"She didn't, and she still doesn't."

Brady scratched his head. "So, how are we—"

"Brady, be patient," Lou cut him off. "Morrow will get to it."

A few of the easier meals came. Morrow got his salad and dug in as Lou told a short story about a safecracking con he was involved in.

After, Morrow continued, "We don't have the program, but we're going to do something different. We'll arrive when Leblanc's expecting the Big Boss to. Our best intel says he's never met Santangelo, but he's probably heard descriptions of him. He's in his late fifties, about five-eleven and carrying more weight than he should. I reached out to the actor on the first team, who can make himself look like that, and he's interested now. I sweetened the pot a bit for him. He's mulling it over and will give me an answer tomorrow. I think he's in. He's a good actor, and he's going to *need* to be one."

Morrow stalled a moment as his onion rings arrived along with the other meals. When the server left, he continued. "Our Big Boss is going to ask to see the painting, and after he's confirmed that it's there, he's going to inform LeBlanc that he's decided not to pay for it. He's simply going to take it instead."

"Oh, man! We gonna need guns?" Brady asked, displaying a lack of patience once again.

"We'll be ready. With Tara on the inside, we'll know how much security he has. He usually has one guard there at all times. Our guess is he'll have two, possibly three, but not more. We'll have four, and before our Big Boss states that he's stealing it, we'll be disarming his guards. I don't want any shots fired. We'll just take the painting and leave. LeBlanc isn't foolish enough to challenge a mob boss."

No one said anything.

"These are just the broad strokes. There's much more each of you will have to do to speed things along. We need to get in and out of the mansion in less than eighteen minutes. That's about all the time we'll have before the real Santangelo shows up."

"I don't think we've got enough people, Morrow," Tommy said.

Morrow nodded. "More are on the way. We'll need four more for sure, maybe six. I've got my feelers out."

"More mouths to feed," Tara said. She wasn't talking about dinner.

"I know. I'm working on ways to make this a little more lucrative. I won't be decreasing your expected shares. The new guys will have minor roles, so they won't get much."

"Maybe you won't either," Lou said.

"Don't worry about the money. I won't pay myself until each of you gets what you expect."

Tara fought the urge to comment, but she resisted. She knew now she would never get what she had planned—or anything close to it.

For the next two hours, the team discussed individual duties and the precise timing needed to pull it off. Morrow walked through it several times to make sure they all understood how their specific roles impacted everyone else. The tab topped four hundred as the last few rounds were all alcoholic.

At 9:15, Morrow nodded to Ghost. "You ready for your gig tonight?"

Ghost just nodded. Everyone on one side of the U-shaped booth got out so Ghost, seated in the middle, could too. He left out the back door, noting the time.

"Tommy, Connie, you two are next at 9:25. We'll give Ghost time to get into position, and then I want everyone to leave in about five-minute intervals. Remember to keep your phones on so you can hear from Ghost if you're being tailed."

"And if we are?" Connie asked.

"Then lose 'em," Morrow replied.

Tommy smiled. "I'm driving, babe. This'll be fun."

To Morrow's great relief, everyone else at the table was smiling too. There was no lack of confidence on this team.

One by one, they all left. By ten o'clock, only Tara and Morrow remained.

Tara felt the need to say what was on her mind. She knew she shouldn't, but she couldn't stop herself. "We're doing this on Saturday. One day before we're supposed to hand over the painting to Almeda."

Morrow nodded with a straight face.

"No time left for a plan B. This *has* to work, Morrow. It *has* to."

"It will," Morrow whispered.

"Your bold confidence isn't impressing me." Tara got up from her seat and readied herself to leave.

This time it was Morrow who threw caution to the wind and said what Edwin always taught him never to say: never, ever promise anything. "Tara, I know this hasn't been easy. I appreciate what you add to the team. I promise you, this will work. And you'll be paid well—no matter what. I promise."

30

7 days left.

Morrow hustled out of the Park Place Pub and drove to Scottsdale, where his friend, Nate Slaton, was waiting for him. Twenty minutes later, he found a parking place and entered the Arrowhead Bar and spotted Nate in a back booth. Morrow needed more help, and Nate was the man who could give it to him.

Ghost reported in to Morrow ten minutes before the Slaton meeting began. "Morrow, everybody left the pub without being tailed. We're fine for tonight, but it's a good idea to be extra careful after every meeting."

Morrow wasn't surprised, but it did give him greater peace of mind knowing their every move wasn't being watched. Morrow started to thank Ghost for his diligent efforts, but the line went dead. He nodded to himself and muttered, "That's Ghost for ya."

Brady, always good with the ladies, and Shady, the epitome of the strong, silent type, left the meeting after hearing Morrow's new plan. They were back to feeling young and invincible. They headed to Scottsdale to hit a few of the nightclubs. They were both large, muscled, attractive men, and finding women to spend some time with was not a difficult task.

Lou drove home and cruised past his rented home without even slowing down. He parked on a side street and walked his usual route on the neighboring avenue. Cutting through a dead-end alley and a neighbor's backyard, he reached the back of his house and checked the door. The loose pebble he'd placed in the door crack was still there. He unlocked it and entered. There were people in Phoenix who would love to know where he lived so they could make it where he died too. *Vigilance is the price of freedom*, he reminded himself as he entered the small rambler and settled in for the night.

Tara's cell phone rang just as she got into her car. She didn't recognize the number. "Hello," she said in a monotone.

"I'm coming to Phoenix," the voice said.

"Pops! How did you find me?"

"I've got my ways. You in trouble?"

"No. Well, yeah, kinda, but I got it under control."

"I'm coming anyway. Let's have dinner together tomorrow night. You can tell me all about what you got cookin'. Pick a nice spot for us. A steak house would be good."

The line went dead.

"Bye, Pops," Tara mumbled to herself. *Some things never change.*

Tommy turned off Main Street and onto South Stapley Drive, nearing their home in Mesa. "I like Morrow's plan. It's actually kinda simple. All we have to do is see the painting when we're there and then remove the guards from the equation."

"That's all we have to do, huh?" Connie said, shooting holes in her husband's analysis. "Perhaps you're forgetting that Lou has to get into the secure airport area and convince the pilots and Santangelo that he's with the TSA doing a spot inspection. Then we have to delay them at the main gate and, later, get his drivers to go the wrong way and miss their first turn."

"You're always so negative. The first thing you think about is what could go wrong," Tommy countered.

"That's because everything else has gone wrong on this con. Going wrong is the norm for this play. And then there's that one other deal-breaker that Morrow glossed over."

"What's that?"

"Morrow's plan hinges on the belief that LeBlanc has never met or seen Santangelo up close. If he has, he'll blow the whole con immediately."

Tommy grimaced as he pulled into their driveway. "Ugh. I didn't think of that."

"Tommy, we should be ready to move out if—" Connie froze and stopped talking.

Tommy twisted around to see four large men approaching their car, two on each side. Their car blocked the driveway behind them. "Don't say anything. I've got it."

He slowly exited the vehicle as Connie did the same. She came around to the driver's side to stand by her husband.

"Are you guys lost? Need directions?" Tommy asked.

Not wasting any time on formalities, the lead thug said, "We want to know what Morrow's up to."

Tommy scratched his head. "I—uh—knew a guy named Sorrow once but—"

A giant fist interrupted his sentence, smashing into his right cheek and knocking him to the ground. Connie wanted to scream but knew better. She bit her lip instead.

Tommy got back up. "You didn't tell me who I have the pleasure of talking to."

This time, speaking more quickly, he finished the whole sentence before the thug on the right decked him again.

"What is he up to?" the lead man repeated.

Recognizing the bad hand he was playing, running short on cheekbones and not wanting another broken, Tommy remained on the ground, looking up at the men. "OK, OK, Morrow has a heist going. We're supposed to help, but he's playing it close to his vest. We don't even know what the target is or what our take is gonna be."

The lead man looked at the brute to his left, like a baseball manager summons the lefty from the bullpen. "Rudy, help him understand why that answer isn't cutting it for us."

Rudy stepped forward, leaned over, and pulled Tommy back up on his feet.

"OK! Alright!" Tommy called out just a bit too loud. He knew no neighbors were going to come to his rescue. He and Connie had a low profile in the neighborhood, and no one was going to assist or even call the police. But he also knew that the four thugs didn't know that.

"Tell him, Tommy. Morrow's probably gonna fail anyway," Connie said.

Tommy rubbed his chin and slowly said, "OK, what is it you wanna know?"

Morrow joined Nate in his booth and said, "I know it was short notice. Thanks for meeting me."

"What's up?" Nate asked as he twirled his finger at the barmaid, implying two more.

"I need two guys. Pretty serious guys who can play a role and pull it off. I jotted down the description." Morrow handed over a notepad sheet.

"Jeez, this is, uh, challenging."

"To say the least," Morrow agreed. "I know what I'm asking, but it's for a good cause."

"Hmmm. The Griffith Morrow Retirement Plan?"

Morrow chuckled. "No. Actually, it's more like the No Cement Overshoes for Morrow Plan. And my team is sort of sweating bricks right now too."

"Did you mess up?" Nate asked without smiling.

"Let me put it this way, I'm working on backup plan D. Your guys, if you can find them, are needed in plan E."

"Are *you* sweating bricks?"

"Maybe little ones," Morrow said as the beers arrived, and he downed half of his in one swallow.

"How much could I tell these guys they'd get?"

"If plan D goes well and I don't need them, I'll still pay them five large just for being ready to play."

Nate considered that and then asked the inevitable. "And if they do have to play?"

Morrow rubbed his chin. "It'd be dangerous, but quick. No more than one hour, and there could be some, uh, you know, dying."

Nate stared across the table at his friend.

Morrow knew Nate was waiting for a number. "I was going to offer fifty, but I think seventy-five is probably appropriate."

"They might need a hundred," Nate said. "I think if you offer ten for being ready and a hundred if they're needed, they'll go for it."

"You got two guys with the smarts to pull it off?" Morrow asked, his tone sounding like the fate of mankind hung in the balance.

"I'll have an answer for you tomorrow. You want me to help? Anything *Nate* can do?" he asked, referring to himself in the third person.

"If you can come up with those two guys, that's a lot. I, um—Nate, I appreciate that I have somebody in this world I can talk to. Having somebody I can tell the truth to. You know?"

Nate nodded. "I know. You got this, I know you do." He flashed an easy smile in Morrow's direction, trying to buck his friend up. He knew Morrow well, and he'd never seen him this worried. The best thing he could do was just be there for him.

"I do," Morrow said, mostly talking to himself. "I've got this. I've made a few mistakes. Underestimating how difficult this might be was the first one. I'm kicking myself. That was Edwin's second rule, and I charged into this gig, forgetting it. But now I'm ready." He finished his beer, and his hand shook as he set the empty glass on the table. His lip twitched as he fiddled with his silver watchband. "I got this," he said, again mumbling to himself.

"You want one more beer?" Nate asked.

"If a shot of Jack goes with it, I do."

The two friends sat together for another twenty minutes. They didn't say anything more. They didn't have to.

31

6 days left.

Tara finished work at 5:40 and checked the time. Tonight, she was having dinner with her father at a pricey steak restaurant in Glendale at six thirty. She gathered her things, one of which was today's decoy painting. She placed it in her art portfolio carrier, a leather 37x28 Carry-All Portfolio case with a wired frame. Tara bought two of them in France months ago when she first came up with the idea to steal the Steed. With the painting measuring 24x36, it was the perfect size. She zipped it closed and went, once again, through the entire charade of taking paintings home to reframe them. None of the paintings Tara took were precious, just extras that LeBlanc had in storage. When she first suggested it to LeBlanc, he said he didn't want *any* paintings leaving the mansion, but Tara wore him down. She showed him how she could replace a poor painting's frame with a cheaper one and save the suitable frames for more valuable paintings. In that way, the poor paintings were still worth the same—next to nothing—while the more valuable ones could fetch a better price with a higher quality frame. Once he did the math, he was fine with it. Tara convinced him her love of art compelled her to do it as a hobby at no charge to him.

Truth was, she was so experienced at swapping out frames, it would only take her twenty minutes or so to finish the job. All, ostensibly, because she loved art. But, far more importantly, it created a consistent scene. One night soon, she would leave with her art carrier and *Gabriel's Steed* inside it. No one would pay any attention.

She grabbed her purse, coat, and decoy case and headed out the front door. Arriving at her car, she placed the carrier with the painting into the trunk and turned around. Two men approached her.

One flashed a badge and said, "Detective Fuller, PPD. This is Agent Sawyer." He nodded to the other man, having decided to take a little literary license and refer to Mr. Sawyer as Agent Sawyer. He reasoned that the man was an agent of the insurance company, and if anyone wanted to assume he was an FBI agent, that was fine with him.

"Police?" Tara said, instantly slipping into her dumb blond routine.

"Yes," Fuller said. "We'd like to ask you a few questions about your employer."

"Is he in trouble?" Tara asked, pretending to be in awe of the officer.

"No, of course not. We're working on a case, and one of the people we are following up on may have had some dealings with Mr. LeBlanc. That's all."

"Oh! My goodness," Tara said, laying it on thick. She was more than comfortable with adopting the chatty secretary defense. It had worked for her so well in the past. "Well, this is very exciting. I'd like to help with your investigation. What can I tell you?"

"You are Tara Violet, right?"

"I'm Tara, but my last name is Velloitte. You know, first, it's Vell, like rhymes with bell, then oitte, like the sound a pig makes, oink, except it's oitte." She spelled it out. "How did you know my name?"

"DMV records from your license plate. Ms. Velloitte, it might be best if you come down to the station with us so we can talk there. It's better than standing here in the open, you know."

"Oh my, yes, we can't just stand here," Tara said, thinking fast. "I'm supposed to pick up my elderly father in twenty minutes. Um, what about over there?" She pointed to a bus stop bench with a shelter. "That's in the shade."

Fuller scrunched up his face and then gave in. "Well, it's not normal, but I guess we could do that." The trio walked over to the bench, mostly shielded from the sun in the west, and sat down. Tara was at one end, with Fuller sitting next to her and Sawyer at the other end.

Fuller got right to it. "What can you tell us about Mr. LeBlanc and his business?"

In full effusive mode, Tara started in. "Oh, my gosh, there is so much to tell. Mr. LeBlanc is a wonderful boss. He lets me do all my work in any way I want. It's so fun to work there around all that art stuff. And he dresses impeccably. Today he had on this fantastic tan-colored suit with pleats perfectly ironed, and his shoes are always clean and shiny. My mother used to tell me you could judge a man by how he took care of his shoes. She said a man with clean and polished shoes always had the four best characteristics of a single man. Want to know what those four are? I'll tell you, first he—"

Fuller couldn't take much more of Sawyer's nudging in his ribs, so he cut her off. "Please, Ms. Velloitte, stop. All we want to know is about his business. What does he do?"

"Well, you said you wanted to know about *him* and his business. I was telling you about *him*. My mother used to always say that if a man can't make himself understood, it's his fault. Nobody else's."

Fuller dropped his head and stared at his shoes. They were scuffed and far from shiny. "I'm sorry. Let me be clearer. Does Mr. LeBlanc buy and sell paintings?"

"Yes, oh yes. All day long. He's a very busy man. But he's so nice about it. Do you know he took me out to lunch twice in my first week? He always wears such fine ties and his manners—"

Fuller cut her off again. "Are you familiar with all the paintings he has in the mansion?"

Tara shook her head. "Does a movie star know all the names of her fans? No, of course not. There's too many. He has rooms and rooms full of paintings."

"Like the one that's in your trunk?"

"That's one of the sad ones. Nobody wants them. Do you think a painting knows that? You know, that it's not wanted? I think it's so sad. My mother used to say—"

"No, Ms. Velloitte, no. Please stay on topic. The painting you walked out with—what is it?"

"I don't know the name. It's one of the sad ones nobody wants. I take one home every night and take the good frame off of it and replace it with a lower-cost one. It's not going to sell anyway, so we might as well get something out of it."

Sawyer was about ready to explode. "Perhaps you haven't seen all the paintings, but you have seen a lot, right?"

Proudly now, Tara said, "Oh, yes. I like to walk around at lunch and eat my sandwich and look at all the good ones. Have you ever eaten a tuna fish sandwich while you're walking? It's hard to do without spilling on the floor, so I—"

"Ms. Velloitte, please keep your answers short and to the point," Sawyer said, his voice straining to stay in control. "Just one more question. Have you ever seen a painting called *Gabriel's Steed*?"

"Gabriel's Sneeze? No, is it famous?"

Sawyer put his head in his hands and started to rock back and forth.

Fuller stepped back in. "No, Ms. Velloitte, you misheard him. The painting is called *Gabriel's Steed*. Steed, like a horse. It's a picture of the Archangel Gabriel holding the reins to a beautiful white horse."

Tara was having too much fun to stop now. Her eyes went wide, and she started to speak, but no words came out. She gulped, recovered, and said, "They have horses in heaven? I had no idea."

Fuller glanced at Sawyer and said, "Thank you, Ms. Velloitte. I think we've heard enough. You better go pick up your father."

"Did I help you with your case?"

"Immensely, thank you," Fuller said as graciously as he could.

Tara beamed. She gave a soft peck on the cheek to each of the men and walked back to her car.

As she walked away, Sawyer looked at Fuller and shook his head. "I have seen bags of rocks smarter than her. That was brutal."

Fuller nodded. "Welcome to my world."

Forty minutes later, Tara was seated with her father at the Rancher's Grill. She finished describing her reason for being late. Her father was in a good mood. He hadn't seen his only daughter in six months, and he enjoyed every minute of her story.

"Suze, the chatty witness gig works every time for you. I bet those two went straight to a bar and downed a few after that."

"I'm Tara here, Pops. Don't mess up and blow my cover."

"Simple Suze. They take one look at you and assume you're all looks and no brains. It's like the greatest built-in edge a player could ever have. And *you* know how to make it work for you."

"Tara, Pops. Tara, OK?"

Her father made eye contact with her and said, "OK, got it. So, tell me about your gig and why it's not working, Tara."

Tara told him her entire plan and how she felt she had reached the home stretch until Chuck Dawes showed up and ruined everything. She explained her tactics about getting into the safe and sidestepped her failed attempt at seducing LeBlanc. No father wants to hear that kind of thing.

They ate slowly. Tara realized how much she missed her father. Pops was the one constant in her life. They had pulled off more than a dozen cons working together, but she knew she had to set her own course.

Pops was Arthur Tanning, a fifty-eight-year-old man with distinguished looks. His hair was graying gracefully, as was his neatly trimmed beard. Tara thought he had put on a bit of weight since six months ago, but he was still very fit and energetic. She found she couldn't imagine him as an old man.

Arthur interrupted her reverie and said, "You want some dessert?"

Tara smiled and said, "You know I always do. Something wicked we can share?"

"There's a blackberry cobbler on—"

"Sold!" she said.

He ordered one as their entrée plates were cleared, and they sipped on the last of their red wine.

"Tell me about this Morrow fellow. What kind of man is he?"

"He's irritating. And he's obnoxiously optimistic. I mean, he's working on plan E now, and he still seems certain of success."

"A good leader needs to be an optimist. He carries the hopes and dreams of the whole team in his palms."

Tara nodded. "I know, but his confidence bugs me. I mean, he screwed up my whole play, and then he forced me to join them. Even if we pull this off, my cut will be peanuts."

"So he's sure of himself. Remember what your mother used to say..."

"I know. I hear her voice in my head every day. I can hear her now. Success is the ability to go from failure to failure with no loss of enthusiasm."

Both Tara's and Arthur's eyes glazed up a bit. Unnecessarily, Arthur added, "Winston Churchill said it first."

Tara nodded and dabbed her eyes.

The blackberry cobbler arrived. In what appeared to be some kind of secret ritual, the two of them smacked their spoons against each other's as though they were Sirs Galahad and Lancelot doing battle over the dessert. They both won and shared the treat.

As they were wrapping up their meal, Tara said, "Pops, I, uh, I sort of have a different plan in mind."

"Different than what?"

"Different than what Morrow is planning. I joined their team, but I did as you taught me: I never gave up on my plan. They think I did. It's almost too easy, but my plan calls for a, you know, a switcheroo. I have some muscle boys lined up to help me leave with the real Steed while Morrow and his team get stuck with a worthless painting. You, um, wouldn't want to participate, would you?"

Arthur flagged down the waiter and said, "Better bring us both one more glass of wine."

32

5 days left.

Morrow started his day on the phone. He called Walter again. There was no answer. He didn't leave a message this time. He'd already left three.

He rose from the couch in his dark living room and poured a shot of Jack for himself. After staring at it for ten seconds, he left it on the counter. Too early in the morning to start drinking.

Think, Morrow. If Walter won't play the role of Santangelo, who will? My other sources have nobody for me. I can't trust a complete stranger in this role. It's too key.

He called Tommy. There was no answer.

Lying flat on the couch, trying to relax, Morrow closed his eyes and forced himself to think of nothing. Old Edwin used to say, "Just give yourself over to the universe. Sometimes, a brilliant idea will be handed to you. You just have to be ready to receive it."

Nothing came to him, but he was patient. After a short time, Morrow thought he might have dozed off. He sat up, and his first thought was about his friend, Nate. He dialed his number. It was answered immediately.

"I was wondering when you were going to call, Morrow."

"Progress?" Morrow asked.

"I got two guys for you. The first, he's a dead ringer for what you want. Since he'll be doing the talking, he wants an extra twenty. I bet you can get by with seventy-five or eighty for the other, so same difference."

"That's great news, Nate. When can I meet them?"

"I'll bring them by the pub tonight, late. Say ten thirty?"

"Works for me. Thanks, Nate. Now I gotta ask you one more thing."

Morrow explained the problem he was having with Walter and asked if Nate knew anyone who could play the mob boss if Walter bailed.

"That's a tough one, Morrow," Nate said, then went quiet.

Morrow felt he could hear the wheels of Nate's mind turning, searching his memory. The twenty seconds of dead time dragged on so long it felt like a scoreless soccer game.

"Morrow, seriously, what you're asking for is next to impossible in our biz. I mean, conmen are generally younger, and they have a glorious heyday, and then they burn out like an old candle. There aren't very many guys in this business long enough to play a sixty-year-old power player. They've all retired or..." Nate let the thought drift off.

"Or they're dead," Morrow finished it for him. "Like I'm gonna be if I don't find a solution." Morrow paused and then quickly added, "Just kidding. I'll work this out. See you at the pub later tonight. Thanks."

Morrow hung up and set the phone down on the coffee table. He pressed his lips together. *I wasn't kidding, but I didn't need to share that thought with Nate.*

Leaning back into the sofa, he drummed his fingers on his knee and called Lou next. Lou answered on the first ring.

Trying hard not to sound desperate, he said, "Hey. What's up, Lou?"

"Nothing. *You* called *me*."

"Right. Look, I'm at that stage where the plan is done, and I'm just looking for hedges and building more backup plans that I'll probably never use. Just stuff to keep myself busy, you know."

"Always a good idea. That was Edwin's fourth law, wasn't it?"

"I think it was his fifth."

An awkward silence ensued. Morrow cleared his throat and said, "Yeah, well, I'm working on what to do if Walter changes his mind and doesn't want to do it."

"You heard from him? He's in?" Lou asked, sounding excited.

"Oh sure, he's in, but honestly, he seemed a little nervous about it," Morrow lied smoothly. *I can't have anyone on the team worrying about things they can't control. That's my job.*

"You think he might bail?"

"Nah, I'm just trying to plan for everything. You know how it is."

"Yeah, well, we need him," Lou said. "Not many guys could pull that role off and be convincing. Walter is one of the few."

Finally, a point he could segue from. "So, yeah, that's my point. Like, who else could do this, ya think? Maybe I should call around."

"What are we thinking he'd have to look like again?" Lou asked.

"Well, Santangelo is about six feet, a bit hefty, early sixties. You know, the kind of guy nobody wants to mess with. Who else do you think could do it?"

"What about Emerson? He could make himself look a little heftier."

"Emerson is on vacation in Europe. One of those river boat things. I think he blew most of the money from his last gig on the trip. Gonna have to be somebody else."

Another long silence. "I'm too short, Morrow, if that's what you're hinting at. And I don't know anybody else off the top of my head. Gotta be someone out there, I guess."

"Yeah, well, hey, good talking to you. Won't be long now till payday. I'll call you when there's some news," Morrow said, trying hard to sound chipper.

They hung up, and Morrow called Tommy again ten seconds later. No answer. He hung up.

He got up from the couch and retrieved his shot of Jack. He downed it in one gulp and poured another. Without Walter, the only alternative was to do a violent takeover inside the mansion. People could get hurt or killed. Again, Morrow wondered if he, himself, might be the mark. He felt manipulated with all the ups and downs. Edwin always said, "Give the mark a ride. Make him feel he's on a roller coaster. Up and down to make him want closure. Then close him." He poured another shot for himself and tried to reconsider his options. He knew they were slim and none. The whole con was falling apart. Again.

PART THREE

33

Morrow fixed a sandwich for himself, ate his lunch alone in the confines of his apartment, and decided on a course of action. He grabbed his keys and headed over to Tommy and Connie's house. His sixth sense was kicking in. Something was wrong.

Arriving thirty minutes later, he knocked on the door. Connie answered. She shuffled back a step or two and let an involuntary gasp escape her lips. Recovering quickly, she said, "Morrow, I was—I was expecting the neighbor."

"Oh, I thought maybe you were shocked to see my face without new bruises."

Taking a second too long to react to the joke, Connie opened the door and said, "Ha! Good one. Come on in. Is something wrong?"

"I've been calling you two all morning," Morrow said.

"Oh my! We must have left our phones off or muted. I'm very sorry. Is the whole team coming over?"

Morrow shook his head. "Just me. I wanted to pick your brains. Is Tommy in?"

"He's in the backyard, uh, trying to fix the barbecue. I'll get him."

A few moments later, they both returned. "Morrow, good to see ya. What's up?" Tommy said.

Connie handed Morrow a glass of lemonade and brought two for herself and Tommy.

"We've got a little challenge. I wanted to run it past you. Get some ideas."

"Sure, sure, you bet," Tommy said.

The three of them sat down, and Morrow explained how he'd been unable to reach Walter. He discussed the ramifications of

Walter bailing on the job and asked if they had any suggestions for an alternate actor.

Connie and Tommie exchanged glances, and both shook their heads at the same time. "Morrow, it's a tall order. I mean, an older dude who can play a mob boss? That person has to carry himself in that special way of authority. It takes a good actor to do that. Hell, just finding anyone who might look the part is tough in this business. I thought Walter was in."

"He made it sound like he was very interested," Morrow said. "He asked for a day to think it over. That was two days ago, and I've called him a dozen times without an answer. I think I have to assume he's not going to play."

Connie put her hand to her forehead and said, "Shit! Without him, we're a bit screwed, aren't we?"

"You got nobody you can recommend?" Morrow asked, knowing the answer already.

"No one. We'll need a new plan," Tommy said.

"I'm still looking," Morrow said. "I've got a friend in the theater business, and he may have a down-and-out actor who would fit the bill."

"A rookie? The pressure alone will break him the moment the mark senses something wrong," Tommy replied.

"Maybe," Morrow muttered. "Just in case, I think we may have to go in and brute-force it. Take down his guards and steal the damn thing. Not my first choice."

"Not mine, either," Tommy said. Connie nodded her agreement with her husband.

Morrow finished his lemonade and thanked both of them. Rising from his seat, he said, "Keep thinking. If you come up with any ideas at all, give me a call. And please, keep your phones on from now on. We'll be meeting soon with the team to go over the new plan."

With a half-hearted wave, Morrow left out the front door and headed to his car.

Tommy and Connie returned to their seats on the couch next to each other. "Damn it. This sucks. Maybe we should tell him."

"No," her husband said forcefully. "No way. We have to look out for ourselves. They know where we are, and, hell, they're probably watching. We're going to have to give them more info soon, or their next visit won't be so cordial."

"I know," Connie said. "It's just that Morrow seems like a good guy, and I feel crummy about us doing this to him. Barger's men will destroy any plan he comes up with. It's over."

Heading to Sadie's for a drink-and-think session, Morrow's phone rang. He reached for it and caught himself whispering a prayer that it was Walter. The screen displayed a number he wasn't familiar with, but he answered anyway.

"Morrow," he said.

"Morrow! It's Rafe. How are you doing?"

"Rafe, good to hear from you. Why the call?"

A short silence was followed by a more subdued version of his former coworker. "Well, I, uh, I still feel bad about getting you into this. I figured if you were going to pull it off, it'd be happening any day now, right?"

Morrow wasn't interested in committing to anything right now. "Rafe, get to the point."

"OK, well, I have some news for you that our um, mutual friend suggested I pass along to you."

Morrow hesitated, trying to read between Rafe's lines. "Go ahead."

"He says the fellow you are expecting to arrive on Saturday is scheduled to, um, show up at Goodyear Airport at 3:15. You know, touchdown time, and he planned to go straight to LeBlanc's. He thought that might help you plan your, um, your day."

Morrow breathed a sigh of relief. Only Westcott would know Santangelo's schedule. "Yes, Rafe, that helps a lot."

"Oh, good. Our mutual friend also said that, um, you know, Santa bragged to him that he was buying a painting for six point five mil. Does that help?"

"Help? Like an ace reliever helps a bullpen. You bet it helps. Thanks, Rafe."

Morrow could almost hear Rafe smiling through the phone. "Well, like I said, I, um, felt bad about—"

"Forget it, Rafe. Look, I could still use a driver if you change your mind. It's likely that anyone joining the team this late won't be on, uh, the chopping block if you're still interested. Won't be a ton of money, but probably five large in it for ya."

"That's something I'll think about. Thanks, Morrow," Rafe said and hung up.

Morrow knew that was a polite no. *Who can blame him? Half the town probably knows what deep shit I'm in by now. I wouldn't join me either.*

He parked on the street across from Sadie's pub and headed in.

After an hour and a half, utterly devoid of any new ideas emanating from his weary brain, Morrow's phone rang again. It was Tara.

Staying on the cautious side, he said, "Chuck Dawes."

"How are you doing, Chuck?"

"Swimmingly. Everything is coming up roses," Morrow said.

"My pops is in town, and we were wondering if you'd care to meet us for dinner."

Feeling a bit like Hannibal Lecter's next victim, Morrow tried to smile into the phone. "Sounds like fun. Where and when?"

"We'll get reservations somewhere and text you in a few minutes."

They wrapped up the conversation, and Morrow remained seated in his booth, wondering what else bad could happen to him today.

At six thirty, Morrow joined Tara and her father at a prominent Mexican restaurant in Scottsdale. Introductions were completed along with the usual small talk that occurs at a first-time meeting. Entrées were served, and the small talk continued for a few minutes more.

After a brief silence, Arthur broke the ice. "Morrow, I'm assuming you know what line of business I've been in all my life."

"I'm aware."

"Tara tells me you have a unique plan coming down this Saturday, and you were actively adding a few more players. I wanted to offer my services for any role. I wouldn't be insulted if it was a very minor one. I'd just like to see my daughter in action and, well, I'm going to be here anyway, so..." Arthur let the sentence complete itself.

Thinking fast and making sure to keep his options open, Morrow said, "Mr. Tanning, what would you think of being an understudy?"

"I'm not sure I understand your meaning."

"My man, Walter, is supposed to play the mob boss coming in to close the deal for the painting. I won't insult you by pretending that Tara hasn't told you everything. It's a very significant role requiring experience, calmness under fire, and an actor who could assume the role with understated strength. I'm sure you know what I mean by that."

Tara interrupted. "What's wrong with Walter?"

Thinking on the fly, Morrow quickly invented a cover story and filled in the blanks. "Nothing. However, his mother is old and sick, and he's waiting for the call that says 'come now or it'll be too late.' He told me upfront that if he gets the call before our play goes down, he's gotta go. It seems unlikely, but I'd like to be prepared. Your father, with his experience, could play this role—maybe even better than Walter."

Arthur smiled broadly. "The man's prepared. I like that. Backup plans are too often overlooked. I'd be happy to take that chore on."

Morrow fought the urge to look around at all the suddenly emerging lucky stars that had fallen on him. He extended his hand, and they shook on it. Wasting no time, Morrow launched into training mode, walking Arthur through the gig. His student was a fast study and understood completely how the role needed to be played.

As they wrapped up the evening, Morrow checked his watch. It showed 5:20. He shook his head, knowing he'd forgotten to reset the time early this morning. He pulled his phone out and glanced at the display. It was 8:35. He had plenty of time to get to Sadie's and meet Nate and his two players.

He wanted—no, he *needed* to talk to Arthur more. It was vitally important they be on the same page completely. "How about a little dessert? God knows I drank enough margaritas tonight. Let me pay for their famous Shortcut Tres Leches Cake. It's outstanding! And let me cover the tip too."

Graciously, Arthur agreed. He knew he could buy and sell Morrow ten times over and never miss a dime of it, but the young man had style, and he liked that.

The dessert came, and Morrow included another round of drinks for everyone. He had the time, even if he didn't have the money. He'd burned through most of Almeda's fifty grand advance already.

After peppering Arthur with many questions about his experiences and style, Morrow sat back, very pleased with himself. Providence had gifted him Arthur Tanning to take Walter's place, and he was enjoying every minute of it.

Arthur came back on him. "OK, turnabout is fair play. Tell me about Morrow. How did you get into this racket?"

Morrow warmed to the task. Blithely, he told them the same lies that he always told everyone. He never talked about his mother dying young and how he lived on the streets at twelve. He didn't mention his three-year stint in the pen and how he swore he'd never go back. He didn't mention his sister. It was none of anyone's business. Of course, he never talked about Katie or the promise he failed to keep to her. As usual, he mixed in enough that was true to keep the story straight. He talked about Edwin, the old man who took him in and taught him the trade. When he finished his story, he gave it a pleasant spin. Everyone loves a happy ending, he reasoned.

Arthur seemed to enjoy the story while Tara looked a bit skeptical. Morrow expected no less.

"So, Edwin taught you the ropes, and now you're on your own?"

Morrow nodded.

"And Edwin?"

Morrow bit his lip and looked away for a moment. Coming back from wherever his brain led him, he locked eyes with Arthur and said, "Edwin had one tough assignment. He...he ended up one backup plan short of enough."

Arthur knowingly nodded his head as if to say, "As so we all shall someday." He wasn't done yet, though. "Tara tells me you're not much of a fighter."

Morrow smiled unashamedly. "She's right. I guess I don't have enough anger in me. I don't get a kick out of hurting people, and so I go with my strengths. Brute force isn't one of them. I just, you know, try to outthink them."

They all finished their dessert, and Arthur announced that he had enjoyed the meal immensely and wanted to finish it in style. "I have one last question for you tonight, Morrow."

"Ask away."

"Everyone I know in this business says they run their cons like a game. Some see it as football, and they employ strategies to march down the field and score the touchdown. Others see it as poker, and they know every hand could win, so they bet and bluff it that way. There are dozens of other approaches as well. Tara says you're a baseball fan. Is that how you see this game?"

Morrow took the last swallow of his dessert drink and licked his lips in thought. "No, it isn't baseball. With me, it's all about chess. The goal is to place all the pieces on the board in the right position. If you do it right, you limit your opponent's options and you force him to do exactly what you wanted him to do all along. When it's their idea, their plan, they will stick to it, and when you already know what they're going to do, you're only a few moves away from checkmate."

34

4 days left.

Morrow rose at six in the morning and fixed a light breakfast. He'd had a tough time getting to sleep the night before. He knew he was far too late and deep into this con to have so many loose ends.

His meeting with Nate and his two men, Carter and Wilson, went well late last night. They were both sharp and quick studies. Morrow was thrilled that Nate had matched the new players with their parts so perfectly. It would be pricey but worth it, especially if they were needed to play the roles out. He fervently hoped they wouldn't have to.

But it wasn't that issue that kept him awake. It was the new, all-too-convenient addition of Arthur Tanning to the team. It was as if Tara and Arthur knew how desperate he was to find a replacement for Walter. Manna from heaven would have been less of a surprise than landing an experienced player like Arthur. And as Nate said, there weren't many conmen around in that age group.

While Arthur's addition meant the con could continue with a less violent approach, always preferable in Morrow's book, it also meant that Tara had an ally. That changed the group dynamics significantly. Edwin's rule number three: better to have most teammates who don't know each other than too many who do. If they know each other well and trust each other, the leader could find himself getting outmaneuvered. Never a good thing.

Is that what happened? Morrow wondered. *Did Tara call her father in so they can work together against me? Or was he here for the reasons he mentioned at dinner? I shouldn't have to spend time thinking about these kinds of questions.*

Morrow got up from the couch and started pacing the room, talking out loud to himself, which he preferred when it came to logically considering all his options. Something different happened in his mind when he talked aloud, and he needed all the edge he could get today.

"If they are planning against me, I need to be prepared. What would I do if I were them? How would I steal the Steed?" He paced back and forth while he pondered that. "It would have to happen right there at LeBlanc's mansion. We'd get the painting after convincing LeBlanc that he had no choice but to give it up or die. Something would happen, allowing Tara and her father to escape with it. They may have men outside to jump us, or somehow they'll escape and our vehicles will all have flat tires, and we won't be able to catch them. Think, Morrow, think. How do I stop that?"

Pacing more, Morrow focused on defense and started to relax. He gradually gained confidence he could avoid any surprise moves by the Tanning duo. "More men on my team outside than in. Ghost will have a rifle with a scope, so he can shoot out their tires if they try a fast escape. When the painting is handed over to Arthur, I'll have my guys take it immediately and place it in Tara's unique portfolio tote bag, and we'll carry it out. The trick is to keep them away from it and keep our eyes on it at all times. We can do this."

Tommy and Connie sat on the couch staring at Tommy's cell phone.

"We have to give them something," Tommy said. "I think we should tell them we now know *what* we're stealing and *when,* but we keep it a little vague. You know, hold back a few details, so we have something more to tell them later. Maybe we can buy enough time for Morrow to still pull it off."

Connie nodded her agreement, picked up the phone, and handed it to her husband.

Tommy dialed the number he was given and waited. It was answered on the fourth ring.

"Yeah?"

"This is Tommy. I, um, got some news for Wayne."

A moment later, Wayne came on the line. "I was just getting the team ready to come over to your house and firebomb it, you fuck! You were supposed to call me yesterday."

"I know. I know!" Tommy said, the urgency in his voice coming out clearly. "We didn't have anything yesterday, but Morrow called us this morning and set up a meeting. He told us what we're doing."

"I'm waiting."

"There's a valuable painting that the fence, Conrad LeBlanc, has. It's called Gabriel and the Steed or something like that. He was talkin' fast, and I didn't catch it all. Anyway, he says it's worth millions, and it's a big secret that LeBlanc has it. Someone is coming this weekend to buy it from LeBlanc, and we're going to take it from those guys."

"When?"

"We don't know yet. Could be late this week. Morrow said he'd be finding out the buyer's schedule within a day or so, and then it would happen. We're meeting again to discuss the step-by-step process."

There was a long silence on the line. Then Wayne said, "You call me again the moment you find out the exact time. Got it?"

"Yes. Yes, of course, but I have a question. Are you gonna try to take it from the buyer? And if so, I can help with that, you know, for a cut of some kind. Doesn't have to be a lot."

Again, another silence ensued. "I'll get back to you on that." The line went dead.

Connie looked at her husband and said, "I don't want to work with those assholes."

"I know, neither do I. They won't give us anything anyway. I wanted to sound dumber and more clueless. And I want them to believe we are totally on their side now."

"Preserve thy options," Connie mumbled under her breath.

"Yup," Tommy agreed.

Morrow was feeling more confident that he was back in control. He called Tara and invited her and her father to dinner. He told her that Walter had bailed, which meant her father was in the play. He insisted on another walk-through to be certain they both knew their parts.

Morrow scheduled the meeting at the Park Place Pub at seven o'clock. He was there by six thirty, going over his notes.

Sadie brought him his seltzer water and said, "Lots of meetings lately. Does that mean you're ready to make your move?"

Morrow eyed her. "There's no move, Sadie. We just like to talk. I'm lonely, so I try to invite as many friends to eat and drink with me as I can."

Sadie smiled and nodded. "Got it." She returned to the bar.

At 7:02, Tara walked in alone.

"Your father's coming too?" Morrow asked.

"He's going to be late. Had some things to do. He said to eat without him, and he'll join us for a drink or two."

"Something is more important than what we have cooking?"

Tara just shrugged.

Sadie arrived at the table and took their dinner orders.

Tara started off the conversation. "You're not going to be at the event, are you?"

"Obviously, he knows me, and Chuck Dawes has no reason to be there. If I tried to be there, like a coincidence or something, LeBlanc would ask me to leave, so I wouldn't be around to see the exchange. I have to stay out of view. I'll be a block away in my car listening to the bug that your father will have in his pocket."

Tara showed a brief smile. "That'll be like slow torture for you, won't it?"

"I imagine so. You like that idea?"

"Yeah, I do," she said. "Anything that gives me a little payback for you spoiling everything makes my smaller cut a little easier to take."

"Glad to be of service," Morrow said cheerfully. *Interesting comment,* he thought to himself. *Either she really is willing to take the smaller cut and I'm imagining the whole theft and escape with her father and the painting, or she's trying to lull me into a false sense of security. Back to where I started from. I still know nothing more than I did before.*

Picking up again, Tara said, "I want to be there."

"It's a Saturday afternoon. You don't work on Saturdays. That would be hard to explain," Morrow replied. "You could wait with me in the car."

"Too much torture for me. Look, I'll just drop by like I've made a habit of doing. I'll tell LeBlanc I had a few unfinished tasks, and I'll go to my office and work there out of view."

Morrow pursed his lips and thought about it. "There may be some advantage to that," he muttered. "If a call comes in from the real Santangelo or one of his men, you could intercept it. They might call and say they're running late. That would mess up our scene. The flight is scheduled to arrive at 3:15. With the usual pace, it's almost a twenty-five–minute drive from the airport, so LeBlanc might be expecting them around 3:45. I was planning on our team showing up at 3:40 as if they had made really good time."

"I could handle the calls if they try to reach LeBlanc while my father is there, pretending to be Santangelo. Getting a call from the real mob boss would be a bit awkward."

"To say the least. OK, you can be there," Morrow said agreeably. *She'll want to protect her father, and that's fine by me. With both of them in our sights, this could work well.*

The two of them enjoyed their meal while they finished walking through the plan together. Morrow pulled out some diagrams showing an X where he wanted everybody to stand. The bodyguards for Mr. Mob were spread out while Arthur was in the middle facing LeBlanc. He added another spot for Tara to stand in the event she was summoned to be there.

They discussed strategies and minutia about every move. Morrow felt more confident that she wouldn't go that deep into the process unless she was fully on board. Still, he knew he had to be wary of her.

By eight, they had finished their meals and ordered another glass of wine. Morrow was ready to find out a bit more about Tara. Just as her father had done with Morrow at the dinner, he wanted to know as much as possible about his ally and/or nemesis.

"So I met your father, and he's a very impressive man. I bet your mom is as well," he fished.

"My mom passed when I was sixteen."

"I'm sorry, Tara. That had to be rough."

"Yes and no. She had cancer and knew it was terminal three years before that. We spent a lot of time together near the end."

Morrow just nodded.

After an awkward silence, he said, "I think all of our lives are fashioned when we're young. You grow up with mom and dad and what you learn from them sticks with you all your life."

He waited to see if she would bite. She didn't, so he continued, "I think every kid learns life lessons that affect their entire lives going forward. From their fathers, they might learn business or functioning in the real world, as you did from your pops. What do you think you learned from your mother?"

Tara checked her phone for the time. Her father was due any minute now. She knew she had to fill the time, so she answered Morrow against her better judgment. "My mom was, oh my gosh, she was so smart. She could have had a career in almost any field and been successful. And she had a good heart. She taught me manners and how important they are. And she taught me to look for the good in people, even the ones you don't like."

"I'm probably a challenge for you," Morrow said, a glimmer in his eyes.

"That's true. I'll keep looking. I'm sure I'll come up with something. Maybe you like dogs or something."

Morrow was about to fire off a snappy retort when Tara's father walked in the door. He spotted Tara right away and joined them at the table.

"Quite the spot, Morrow. I like your booth. Very private."

Morrow rose from his seat and extended his hand. "Glad you made it. I have some news. My man, Walter, decided against the gig, so we could sure use you if you're up to it."

"You bet," Arthur said. "I'm ready."

Morrow fought off the grin he felt coming on. Not wasting any time, he moved on. "Tara and I walked through her role and decided she'd be there when it all comes down. So, now, I think we should walk through *your* play step-by-step."

Sadie brought another round of drinks, and by 8:45, they finished.

As they wrapped it up, Morrow said, "We'll have a meeting of the whole team late Friday night. I'll text you the location and time."

"Cutting this all pretty close, aren't we?" Arthur asked.

"Yup, scoring the painting on the 1st and delivering it to the client on the 2nd. That makes Tuesday, or probably Wednesday night payday. You'll both get a handsome cut."

"Music to my ears, Morrow. See ya then."

Morrow watched them leave and moved over to the bar. He ordered a Jack and a chaser as usual, then stared at the wall as he nursed his drink. He took on that faraway look Sadie had noticed so many times before.

"Whatchya thinking about, Morrow?" she asked.

"Oh, just thinking about a chess board. It's, well, it's all about getting the pieces in the right place at the right time."

Sadie nodded, not fully understanding but knowing that Morrow did.

Morrow relaxed at the bar for another fifteen minutes. His mind went to the bottom line and the true value he'd secured tonight.

I learned something new tonight. Tara, or whatever her name really is, values manners. And she said her mother had a good heart. That was a mistake. She shouldn't have said that. Now, I know something about her that I bet she doesn't even know herself.

35

3 days left.

Wednesday, May 29th. Tara worked her regular schedule, walked out with a painting in her case, and headed home. An hour later, she wiped her brow as she stood in the middle of her apartment. A furious clean-up process was taking its dying breath, and she put away her dust rags and cleaning spray. She hustled into her bathroom to freshen up.

Eight minutes later, the doorbell buzzer sounded off. She pressed 99 into her cell phone and went to the kitchen to pour two glasses of Pinot Grigio. Her dad entered through the partly open door as she put the bottle back in the refrigerator.

"Pops! You're right on time."

"I made it as quick as I could because I knew you were pouring," Arthur said as he strolled around the living room. "This is nice," he added.

"Have a seat. I'll be right with you."

She entered with her wine and a plate of cheese and crackers. "I know what you're thinking. You're wondering how long the lease is for."

"You know me too well. Six months, I hope."

"Yup. And it looks like I'll need every last day of it. Cutting things pretty close."

"We might be out of here with our prize in three days," Arthur said.

"That's what I'm planning on."

Arthur made a show of looking around the room and commenting on her artwork on the walls. When they both knew it was time to end the small talk, he said, "You asked me over here so you could show me something. What is it?"

Tara took another sip of wine and raised one finger. "Give me a minute." She rose from her seat and walked to her bedroom. She emerged with her portfolio case, unzipped it, and pulled a painting out, backside to her father.

"I wanted to show you this."

She turned the painting around and held it up. Arthur's eyes went wide, and his mouth fell open, competing with the Grand Canyon for the largest chasm.

"You got it! How—when did you—"

"Looks good, doesn't it? It's a fake, but a really damn good one."

"Are you sure? Maybe—"

"It's fake, Pops. I paid to have it made." Tara walked it nearer to her father so he could examine it more closely.

He let out a long, low whistle. "How much did it cost you?"

"Thirty grand. I tried to paint it myself, thinking, you know, that I had such intimate knowledge of the artist, Bandeaux, that I could surpass my normal talent level and create a great fake. It took me three failed efforts to realize my art skills are too minimal for a task like this."

"How were you going to use it?" her father asked.

"I was going to steal the Steed from LeBlanc's safe and leave it in its place. LeBlanc really knows very little about art, and I was betting the buyer was the same. I needed to stick around and work for him for a while longer to eliminate myself as a suspect in case the theft became news."

"Seems like that plot is toast. What are you going to do with it now?"

"I thought I might keep it for my own amusement, but now, I have a better idea. Now that Morrow has agreed that I should be there during the takedown, well, let me show you instead of telling you."

Again, she left for her bedroom. Returning a moment later with another portfolio, identical to the first, Tara added, "I bought two of these 37x28 cases. Identical in every way. I'm going to put my fake Steed in one and place it in the basement stairwell."

"Perfect! I get it already," Arthur interrupted, beaming with pride. "You'll give your empty one to Morrow to have the real Steed placed in after LeBlanc and his guards are taken down. Then we'll swap them, um, somehow. They'll be watching—they aren't fools."

"We'll need a diversion, and I have it all figured out. You're really gonna like the rest of this plan. More wine?"

Arthur laughed. "Yes, for both of us." He smiled broadly, knowing that the apple hadn't fallen far from the tree.

Morrow rented the private party room at Spaghetti Haven in Peoria. One by one, the entire team entered, including the three men Westcott had loaned him. Missing were the two men Nate recruited, Carter and Wilson. They were only going to be part of things if the whole con bombed. Morrow knew it was better if he didn't reveal that backup plan.

And two others were missing as well: Tara and her father.

Once everyone arrived, a grand Italian meal was served on multiple plates for everyone to share.

Morrow began his spiel. "Welcome, everyone. You all know each other, and I'm sure you remember Vic and Jayden. They're here on loan to us again along with their friend, Mel." He looked down the table to where the three of them were seated and gave them the signal to stand. Vic and Jayden, strong and muscular men, rose first, followed by the third man. Mel started to rise and just kept right on rising, standing a full six inches higher than the other two and nearly wide enough to fit two men into his body.

"As you can see, I'm counting on these fellas to be our bodyguards, or the fake mob boss's bodyguards, actually."

The team laughed and called out their welcomes. The men sat back down, and Morrow continued. "Tonight, we're going to hear from Lou, Brady, Tommy, and others about the delaying strategy we're going to employ to keep Santangelo from arriving at LeBlanc's on time. Instead, our fake Santangelo and his bodyguards will arrive at the mansion. For those of you who don't know yet, Walter is unable to play the mob boss for us, so I have replaced him with a very experienced player. That is Tara's father."

Morrow waited for the din to settle down and for the inevitable question.

Brady shouted it out. "How come they're not here? We should go over the plan inside the mansion. That's the key."

Morrow nodded. "You're very right, Brady, and all of us together will go over it on Friday night. But tonight, I want to focus on the airport only, and after we're done, I have something to discuss related to our two missing teammates. Lou, you have the floor."

Lou walked everyone through his plan to be recognized as a TSA officer with the right to close down the airport if necessary. He explained how he would confront the pilots and passengers on the Santangelo Lear jet upon arrival at the smaller local airport. He was confident he could stall them for ten to twelve minutes before they started throwing around their power and demanding to be let go. Then he had a few extra ideas on how to get another five to eight minutes before he pretended to be satisfied and would release everyone.

After explaining all of it, he turned to Tommy and said, "You're up."

Tommy told everyone how he and Shady would be doing a city work project that blocked the main exit out of the airport. Being a small airport that was already going through massive construction, it was hardly being used, so there would be very few customers inconvenienced and complaining. The Santangelo driver would be redirected to a detour road that, if used properly, eventually leads to the main highways into Phoenix.

Brady jumped in. "But they won't use it properly. They're gonna miss the first turn and take the second. It's a very long dead end. Somehow, the dead-end sign will be missing. Right, Shady?"

Shady nodded knowingly, and everyone knew he'd simply pull it out of the earth.

The three of them went on adding more details about uniforms and truck decals and all the tiny steps they'd taken to create the illusion of a legitimate detour. The net effect was to delay Santangelo by a minimum of twenty minutes and, hopefully, more. When they finished, the rest of the team gave them a round of applause and downed some more wine.

Everything Morrow did tonight was to fill them with confidence in the new plan and make it an enjoyable evening. He knew he might need these players again someday.

As the meeting came to a close, Morrow stood at the head of the table and asked for everyone's attention. "We have one other issue to discuss. Most of you know that Tara is not happy about joining us. She's in the game too, but mostly on her own side. Her father came to visit her, maybe at her request—I don't know. He's also a very sharp and experienced player. So, bottom line, I believe it is likely that they will try to steal *Gabriel's Steed* from us after we take it from LeBlanc."

The room was instantly filled with angry looks and unhappy chatter.

"What the hell, Morrow?" Brady yelled out. "If you think her father is in on this, why did you hire him to play a key role? That doesn't make any sense."

Morrow didn't answer. He looked around at the veteran players and waited.

Connie spoke up. "It's brilliant. First of all, we needed somebody older and sharp who could play the mob boss role. With Walter out, we needed somebody, and Morrow talked the dad into doing it."

Lou picked up where Connie left off. "Tara and her dad are probably underestimating Morrow and think he doesn't know about their plan. But he does, and I bet he can tell us better what, uh, precautions we'll take." He nodded in Morrow's direction.

Morrow gave a crooked smile to Lou and Connie and said, "Ghost will be in a building two blocks from the LeBlanc mansion with a high-powered rifle and a scope. He's a damn good shot, and his job is to blow the tires out of any getaway car that shows up to take Tara and her father away separately from us. If this happens, it'll be ten or more minutes after our play starts. The airport crew will be on their way to the mansion and should be in a position to assist if we need it. But there's another aspect that Ghost knows. I'll let him tell you."

Ghost looked around the room and said, "When you are expecting something like this to happen, you don't want surprises.

Having Tara and her dad *inside* the building puts them constantly in our line of sight. That's way better than letting them ambush us on the street or something. Now, we're controlling events more. We know right where they are, and they'll have to take down three large guards and all of us outside the building to get out. Morrow's seen the blueprints, and we'll be watching every exit. I don't see how they can do it."

Morrow stood back up again. "Here's the deal, guys. I could be wrong. I hope that I am. Maybe they'll be good team players. There's only one way to find out. I've got no proof one way or the other. This is me, just trying to be prepared."

"What can we do, Morrow?" Tommy asked.

"Two things. First, stay focused on your job and do it perfectly. Second, I want—no, correct that: I *need* every one of you to put your doubts about Tara and her father on hold and treat them nicely. I want everyone to be friendly and make them feel comfortable and also make them like us more."

"I don't get it, Morrow. Why do you need us to be nice to them?" Brady asked.

"It's a hedge. If I'm wrong and they don't try to steal it, then they damn well deserve to be treated nicely. If I'm right, being nice will give them a false sense of security. We want them to believe they've outsmarted us. That will make it easier for us to stop them. There is no downside to being nice." Morrow finished his pitch, thinking to himself. *No downside to being nice. Sounds like something Mom might've said.*

It took twenty minutes for everyone to say their goodbyes and file out. Ghost was in a position to observe and make sure no one was followed. Morrow asked Connie and Tommy to stay late.

When the last pair, Brady and Shady, left, Morrow seated himself across the table from the married couple and eyed them. "Tommy, you trying to copy me? You know, getting your face all smashed in, just like me?"

"Oh, no," Tommy replied. "I didn't choose this. It's nothing, Morrow. I had a little disagreement with a loan shark. My fault for misunderstanding his terms. It's all settled now."

"OK, you can always talk to me about stuff like that. I may be able to help. You need any cash? I mean, before next week's payday?"

Tommy shook his head. "I'm fine." They both rose from their seats.

Morrow waited until they were almost to the door before, speaking a bit louder, saying, "Connie? How about you? Everything cool?"

She glanced for just a second at her husband, then said, "Oh, yeah, we're good."

"It wasn't you that beat Tommy up, right?" Morrow asked, a glint in his eye and half a crooked smile on his face.

Once again, both of them took a half-second too long to laugh.

Morrow continued, "You know, I had a mentor once. His name was Edwin, and he taught me a lot of shit. He once told me how a team member was in trouble and didn't want to tell him about it. Edwin was fearful that the trouble would spill over and mess up the con. He got the player to admit what the problem was. I don't remember what he said, but the player thought it was a terrible problem, and he was so close to it, he assumed it was unfixable. But Edwin solved it in a few hours. He wrapped it right into the con and took advantage of the team member's predicament to create a happy ending for everybody. I remember being really impressed by that."

Tommy and Connie stared back at Morrow, saying nothing.

Morrow gave them a reassuring nod and said, "Thanks for being here. Almost to the finish line. Have a good night."

The pair smiled and hustled out the door. Morrow stayed in the room and finished his drink.

Twelve minutes later, Ghost called. "No tails. You want me to watch out for you?"

"No, go home. If they're gonna get me, I'm dead already. See you Friday."

36

2 days left.

Morrow woke up Thursday morning at seven and lounged in bed for another hour. He realized that he had nothing to do today. Every piece was on the board and in the right place. With a whole two days to spare, he had finally gotten the play to where he wanted it.

Late last night, after getting home from the meeting, he received one phone call and made two others to add some more muscle, solving a problem. He did both and now had everything covered. Nothing left to do for the rest of the day.

He got up at 8:15 and ate an English muffin with some coffee as he read the sports section. Packing up some hiking essentials and taking two cold water bottles out of the fridge, he left his apartment with the items in a knapsack. Morrow drove to the Echo Canyon Trailhead off of East McDonald Drive and started out on his hike. He'd done it before, but it was always invigorating.

When he reached the Echo Canyon trailhead, he moved quickly into a vacated parking space. It was the only spot available he could see. There were a lot of hikers out today on this well-used trail.

With plenty of water and energy bars, he walked the trail, moving high up Camelback Mountain. Phoenix isn't where you go if you want to spend time by a lake, but Camelback provided some exercise, a good way to lose a few pounds in water retention, and a fantastic view when you reached the end.

Morrow took his time, enjoying the outing. Reaching the summit, he collapsed on a nearby rock and downed the rest of his first bottle of water. He took a few deep breaths and caught a rare view of downtown, absent the normally ever-present industrial haze that usually clouds the vista. He broke open his second water bottle and took a short sip. He was dirty, sweating profusely, tired, and loving every minute of it. He felt like a new man, one with a bright future. Clouds had moved in, partially blotting out the sun making the day darker than usual, but cooler too. He didn't mind. For the first time in a month, he was at peace.

Returning to his apartment after enjoying a late lunch at an outdoor restaurant near the base of the mountain, Morrow pulled his Toyota into the garage. Parking in his space after doing one lap of reconnaissance, as usual, all looked normal, so he headed up the stairs. His fourth-floor apartment was only five flights up, and he tried to force himself to avoid the elevator and use the stairs for the exercise.

He arrived on the fourth floor and walked down the hall to 412. He entered, dropped his keys off on the counter and his knapsack on the floor. Already looking forward to a long cool shower to clean up, he walked into the dark living room. His blinds were eternally pulled shut to cool down the room, but even without the light, Morrow knew something was wrong. Moving quickly, he reentered the kitchen and grabbed a steak knife from the drawer.

Steeling himself, he called out, "Who's there? I'm armed."

Silence.

"I said who's there? I know you're there. Speak up. I'm in no mood for games," Morrow said as forcibly as he could.

Still no response.

He shut off the kitchen light and bent down, so his head was no more than eighteen inches off the ground. He peered out into the living room. It looked like two figures were standing against the wall on the south side of the living room.

Two. Probably armed with guns. Here I am with a dull steak knife. Might be smarter to exit. Of course, they could have somebody in the hall too. Fuck.

He rose to his full height. "Don't be shy. I know there are two of you. What do you want?"

Silence still.

Morrow waited another thirty seconds and decided to take his chances in the hallway. Stealthily, he picked up his keys and moved toward the apartment door. That's when he heard it.

"Payback's a bitch, isn't it, Morrow?"

"Tara!" Morrow cried out. He reversed himself and walked back into the living room. Flipping on the ceiling light, he could see Tara and her father standing against the wall.

"It's my fault, Morrow," Arthur said. "Tara told me about Ghost and you and Connie breaking into her apartment, and I thought you deserved a bit of your own medicine."

"Jeez! OK, OK, I get it. It's a terrible feeling. And if it makes you happier, Tara, I'll be thinking of it every time I enter this place now."

Tara smiled. "Actually, yes, that does make me feel better. Thanks."

She turned another light on and looked Morrow over again. "Gads! You're a mess. We got some things to talk about, but we'll help ourselves to a beer while you take a quick shower, OK?"

"Maybe I don't have any beer."

Tara laughed. "Nice try. You've got four Coronas and a six-pack of Heinekens on the second shelf. We got bored waiting for you, so we already downed a few and did inventory too."

Morrow rolled his eyes and headed to the shower. Fifteen minutes later, he joined them in the living room, looking, feeling, and smelling better.

"Well, what an unexpected visit this is. I won't insult you by asking how you slipped through the front door and got into my unit. Or how you even knew I was gone."

Arthur smiled. "I put a tracking device on the bottom of your car last night."

"Last night?" Morrow asked.

"Yeah, last night, while you were meeting with everybody except us."

"Oh, did I hurt your feelings?" Morrow asked, buying time while he dreamed up a story. "I was going over the roles with everyone. We already did yours the night before. No need to go over it again. Tomorrow, Friday, we'll have a full meeting with everyone."

Tara and her father exchanged glances.

Arthur turned to Morrow and said, "I have some concerns about the role you want me to play."

"Such as?"

"Such as I don't think it'll work," Arthur said.

Morrow stared back at him. "Because…?"

"I've done some research. Conrad LeBlanc is an experienced man. He's a scum bucket and a scoundrel, but he knows what's up. I don't think he's going to believe that we'd kill him for the painting. And if he doesn't produce it, and if we assume it's in the mansion, then aren't we right back where we are today?"

Morrow went on the offensive. "You don't think you're a good enough actor?"

"Don't play that game with me, Morrow. That might work with a rookie, but I know what I can do. The problem isn't my acting skill. The problem is that we need to demonstrate our willingness. Somebody has to die. Then he'll believe us."

Morrow dabbed his forehead. It was damp, and he was uncomfortable with the sudden turn in the conversation. "I, um, I try not to, uh, you know, kill anyone in my cons."

"First time for everything," Arthur said.

"If you're talking about shooting one of LeBlanc's guards, I'm against it. And this is my con, so we'll do it my way. Period."

"I wasn't talking about killing a guard."

"Who then?"

"Look, Morrow, now that you agreed to let Tara be in the building at the takedown, she still has to be in character. I can kill her. She's an innocent bystander. I'll threaten to shoot her if LeBlanc doesn't produce the painting. When he says he won't give it up, we kill her right in front him."

"You mean fake her death, right?" Morrow said, thinking out loud.

"Of course, genius!" Tara said, rolling her eyes. "Excuse me, I'm right here. Would Pops be talking about killing me for real right in front of me?"

Morrow nodded and appeared to be deep in thought. "Have you got siblings?"

"What does that have—? No, no siblings. Why?"

"OK, forget that," Morrow said. "I was thinking maybe, you know, you weren't his favorite." A half-smile flashed briefly on Morrow's face.

Tara looked at her father and said, "See! This is why I hate him."

"OK, good," Morrow said. "I just want to make sure I know what the plan is. So, killing Tara is off the table. I'll make a note to myself."

"I shouldn't have to put up with this," Tara said. Her pops chuckled.

"So, what do you say?" Arthur asked. "I've killed her before. She dies great. And let me tell you, when Suze plays the scared employee and starts begging for her life, no one's better."

Tara glared at her father.

Morrow let loose a crooked smile. "Suze? Her real name is Suze?"

Arthur pressed his eyes closed for a moment and cringed a bit. Turning toward his daughter, he said, "Sorry, honey."

"You know what you two guys are? You're screw-ups! Both of you. Pops, you can't keep my name straight, and Morrow, you're working on what, plan F now?"

Being chided by a twenty-one-year-old didn't sit well with either of them, but they had to admit her point.

The three of them spent the next thirty minutes walking through Tara's murder and how they would deal with the aftermath. When they were satisfied, it was decided that Tara would explain it at Friday night's meeting.

37

1 day left.

Friday, May 31st, was another hot, sunny day in Phoenix. At eight in the morning, Morrow turned the air conditioning on again and tried to make himself comfortable.

Everything was in place with the exception of a few loose ends. Detective Red Fuller was one of them. He called Fuller's cell number.

"Detective Fuller."

"Detective, this is Chuck Dawes. Remember me?"

"What if I do?"

"Then it's your lucky day. I have a gift for you."

Fuller shifted in his seat. Grabbing a notepad and pen, he replied, "It ain't my fuckin' birthday yet."

Undeterred, Morrow continued. "That painting, the one with the angel and the horse—"

"Yeah?"

"I know where it is. Are you still working with Sawyer, the insurance guy?"

"I never said he was—"

Morrow interrupted. "Of course he's with the insurance company. You know, oh, forget it. If you're just going to give me a bad time, I'll keep the news to myself. Thanks for nothing." He hung up.

He waited. He knew his burner number showed up on Fuller's phone. Now he just needed to be patient. Patience wasn't a problem for Morrow. He had a cornucopia of things to think about. Today, he was playing with numbers, trying to figure out faster ways to compute cube roots. He loved math and found the language of numbers something far more trustworthy than people. *And more consistent too. Four plus seven is eleven. What was it in 1865? Eleven. How about 1492? Eleven. 600 BC? Eleven. Find something in another field that hasn't changed.* He was close to being amused by his reverie when his phone rang again.

It was Fuller.

Morrow let it ring eight times.

"This is Chuck," he said when he finally picked it up.

In his droll voice, Fuller said, "You sure are sensitive, Chuck. OK, no more games. Where is it?"

"What's in it for me?" Chuck asked.

"I, um, I don't know yet. I'll have to ask Sawyer. You looking for a finder's fee?"

"I'm thinking like maybe 3 percent. That's about the usual, isn't it? The painting's valued at six mil. If I find it, I should get rewarded, right?"

"A hundred eighty grand is a chunk of change for doing nothin', Chuck. I'll see what Sawyer can do. Meanwhile, where is it?"

"Hang on a minute, Fuller. I'm lookin' for that pumpkin truck I must've just fallen off of. Tell you what, I'll give you that info when I see a contract, signed for 3 percent. You can email it to me. Keep it short. And one other thing, Fuller."

"Yeah?"

"I just want to be clear. When I say 3 percent, that's not to be confused with 2 or 2.5 or even 2.99 percent. Let Sawyer know if he wants to negotiate the price, he should find someone who likes to dicker. Is that a ten-four?"

Fuller sighed. "Ten-four."

"Thanks. I should have all the info ready for you by Sunday. Keep your afternoon open. I can tell you this now: the painting is not in Phoenix, but it's nearby. I'll be waiting for that contract."

Morrow hung up and crossed that off his to-do list.

The next meeting was, once again, at Spaghetti Haven. It was easy to tell when Morrow was working with his last dollars. Meetings were always held at the Spaghetti Havens of the world.

Everyone showed up. They were all good sports about the venue. Would they have rather gone to an expensive steak house? Of course. This site was within the budget, though, and the food was still diverse and delicious.

One by one, every player walked through his or her role. Word for word, sometimes giving the dramatic version, striving for an Oscar if necessary, until every player knew their part. There were mistakes, and the error-maker had to do it all over again. There was no "start at where you messed up" allowed. They had to get it all completely correct in one try. Lives depended on it. When Morrow ordered everyone to do it one more time perfectly, the groans could be heard throughout the restaurant.

The last walk-through was virtually error-free and moved along much faster than the first one. Morrow employed Edwin's fourth rule: imagine all the things that could go wrong. He asked more questions to test everyone. When Tommy finished his spiel about the construction at the main gate, Morrow asked, "What will you say if someone asks why you don't have a company van?"

Tommy laughed and said, "We've got that planned out, don't we, Shady?"

Shady grabbed his head in his hands and moaned. Tommy laughed with Shady and then explained what they were going to do. When they were finished, Morrow made them play-act it again. Everyone laughed, and Morrow stood up and gave them a one-man standing ovation.

"Now that is preparation," Morrow announced to everyone. "Always ask yourself what could go wrong and then make your response appear natural. Damn fine work, Tommy, Shady," he added with a genuine smile.

There was always a method to Morrow's madness. During the longer meetings, everyone grew more comfortable with each other. Tara and Arthur seemed to be enjoying themselves, and the rest of the team was being friendly to them, as advised. He knew that all his players were tired of meetings and practice. They wanted to do the real thing. They were looking forward to it. That was key. Morrow wanted them to look forward like a man looks forward to seeing a beautiful woman. He didn't want them looking away, fearful of death, like a D-Day soldier.

Near the end, Morrow made everyone stand up and tell a short joke. Their favorite joke, no matter what it was, no matter how many times they'd already told it. Morrow wanted more bonding, more trust, and less nervousness. Laughing was a good release. What they were all going to do tomorrow could end badly. The last thing needed in a gig like this was fearful and edgy players. He wanted them confident and sure of themselves.

Some of the jokes were raunchy, some corny, some hard to understand. When they had to be explained, the ambiguous humor clarification was always funnier than the joke. At one point, as if he could read Morrow's mind, Arthur made eye contact with Morrow and gave him a knowing nod, as if to say "nice meeting."

For a moment, Morrow thought he'd get off the hook. He began talking about payday and when they could expect it. He didn't finish his first sentence when Brady said, "Wait, Morrow. Everybody told a joke except you."

"You weren't supposed to notice that, Brady. I should make you tell another one for that."

The boos rang out, and everyone was calling for a joke from Morrow.

Morrow was the last person who should tell a joke. He rarely laughed and seldom smiled. Telling a joke in public wasn't in his wheelhouse. It didn't matter. He knew that running a con required him to play a role. He was the leader, and the leader had to be able to make people laugh.

He paced the open floor at the head of the table, pretending to be deep in thought, as though he had a million jokes to pick from. He only had one. A joke Edwin had told him years ago.

"Jeb and Ted visit their sick uncle in the hospital. Tubes running into his nose and throat. They take up spots on each side of the bed. They get up tight and close and speak softly to him. He looks distressed. He tries to say something. He grasps his throat. Jeb moves over closer to him, trying to hear what he's saying, but no words come out. Jeb looks at Ted and says, 'I can't hear him.' Quick thinking Ted gets a notepad and pen and hands them to his uncle. His uncle, fading fast, finishes writing something, then his eyes glaze over, and he dies. Jeb and Ted are inconsolable. 'He's gone,' says Jeb. Ted says, 'Well, at least we were here. He wasn't alone in his final moments.' Jeb looks at the notepad. 'What did he write?' Ted asks. Jeb reads it out loud: 'You're standing on my air hose.'"

Morrow was the leader, and he got some good laughs, mostly because of who he was. He didn't care. He was uncomfortable being in the spotlight, and he was relieved that it was over. He reminded everyone that payday would probably be Wednesday night and announced the payday event and celebration of a successful con would be held at Quincy's Steakhouse. That, alone, got a rousing ovation.

As the meeting started to break up, Morrow let Ghost go first so he could get into position. Then everyone drifted out, one car group at a time. Again, Connie and Tommy left last. While they were waiting, Morrow asked, "Everything all set up?"

Tommy gulped hard and replied. "It's set. See you just after four."

They left without looking back.

38

June 1st, Gig Day.

Lou walked into what passed for the main terminal at GYR, Phoenix Goodyear Airport. New construction had been going on for years, and everyone simply worked around it. The airport served mostly as a parking lot for unused jets when the airlines had a surplus. The amount of daily traffic was limited to an occasional commuter plane and many private aircrafts.

He strolled up to the front desk as though he'd done it a thousand times and said, "I'd like to see Richard Gelling, please."

Gelling was the airport manager who Lou knew was in DC today for a mandatory FAA meeting. Fate played into their hands that day, but if it hadn't been Gelling, he would have asked for someone else who was on vacation or inexplicably unavailable. It took a skilled player very few phone calls to figure out who to ask for.

The young lady at the front desk had no idea what Gelling's schedule was, so after calling his office and hearing he was out of town, she said, "I'm sorry, sir. Mr. Gelling is out of town. Perhaps someone else can help you?"

"Matters not. I'm William Trent from the TSA." Lou flashed a badge he had forged for the occasion and added, "If you'd be so kind as to give me a pass for field access, I will complete my spot inspection."

"Oh, oh, my gosh. I don't know. I—"

"Miss, you actually don't have a choice on this. This is a surprise spot inspection. I see you have passes right there." He pointed to a stack of them on her desk. "Just give me one, so I can get started. I have two other airports to hit today, and I need to stay on schedule."

"I don't know if I have the authority to—"

"You do. Section 18, Paragraph B, of the Domestic Airport Procedure Manual gives you the authority because it grants it to the TSA. I'm the TSA."

Clearly flustered, the young lady said, "I'd feel better if—"

Once again, Lou cut her off. Sighing, he said, "I'll need your name for the records and the citation on your status."

"I'm in trouble? Look, I just started last week. I don't know—"

Smiling now, Lou said, "I understand. I'll try to put in a good word in for you, but Section 31 of the code addresses errors during probationary periods, and it isn't—"

Thankfully, she cut off Lou this time. "I get it. I really need this job. Here you are. I'm sorry for the delay." She handed him the pass. He thanked her and left the terminal. He passed through the first employee barrier and onto the tarmac. Now, doubling his efforts to walk as if he owned the place, Lou made a beeline for Hangar 3, where Santangelo's plane would park within the next fifteen minutes.

Standing in the shade, his pass and his TSA badge prominently displayed, he gave several knowing nods to repair workers and other airport personnel working in the area. Most of them gave him a very wide berth. In general, there were so many TSA rules and regulations that no employee at the airport could ever be 100 percent in compliance at all times. Everyone cut corners, so no one wanted anything to do with him. In many ways, that made playing a TSA inspector the easiest con you could imagine.

Santangelo's jet touched down at 3:12 Saturday afternoon. Lou texted Morrow that it had landed and he was in position. Morrow, in turn, texted everyone else. The plan was simple. Delay them. Santangelo expected to walk off the plane and get into a waiting limo. That would be a thirty-second exercise. Lou's job was to turn those thirty seconds into fifteen minutes or more.

Hanger 3 was usually reserved for dignitaries, celebrities, or other noted personalities who requested a low-key arrival. To a large degree, it was to treat those people more appropriately as their rank required. Passengers of routine Lear jets and commuter flights had to disembark on the red hot tarmac and walk to the terminal or a shuttle bus. It wasn't the glamorous way to enter Phoenix.

The private jet carrying mob boss Ian Santangelo rolled into Hanger 3 six minutes after touchdown. Immediately, Lou began walking around the jet, looking at everything and anything. When the stairs were moved into position at the jet's door, Lou stood at the bottom of them. A man who, by his build, appeared to be a bodyguard walked down first. Hardly looking up from his clipboard, Lou asked, "Number of passengers?"

The guard looked at Lou. "Who are you?"

Lou acted perturbed and pointed to his TSA badge. "TSA spot inspection. How many passengers?"

The man thought for a moment and said, "One, no, uh, four."

Lou gave him a look that made the big man feel small. Lou, himself, was five-foot-nine and overweight. Not someone considered a threat, yet the guard felt inadequate in his presence. It was a technique Lou developed over years of practice.

Another guard came down, and Lou directed him toward the other, saying, "Stand over there unless otherwise instructed."

Santangelo walked down next, followed by one more bodyguard.

"Is there a problem?" he asked.

Lou shook his head. "Not so far. TSA spot inspection. I just need a few answers, and you can be on your way." Looking directly at Santangelo, he said, "I'm assuming this flight is something you ordered? I'll need your name." He poised his pen over his notepad as casually as if he were taking his order for lunch.

Morrow checked his watch. He shook it and double-checked the time with his phone. 3:20. Speaking into his com device, he said, "OK, the plane's on the ground in the hangar, and we have to assume that Lou is going through the whole TSA gig by now. Connie, if they were on the road now, how long before they'd get here?"

Connie said, "Traffic is light. He'd sail right on through. I'd say fifteen minutes tops. Less if he goes a little over the limit."

"Alright, everybody in position. Vic, Jayden, Mel, Art, it's 3:21 now. I want you to pull up in front of LeBlanc's in fifteen minutes. Sit there for two. A man like Santangelo would have specific directions he'd want to give to his bodyguards. It would be normal for him to stall two minutes before getting out. Bodyguards out first to recon the area, and then you surround Art as he's walking up to the building. Everybody good to go?"

Vic answered yes for them all.

"Art, any last questions?" Morrow asked.

"I'm good. I know my routine. It'll be fine, Morrow," Arthur replied.

"Ghost, got your viewpoint?" Morrow asked, already knowing the answer.

In his usual uber-succinct style, Ghost said, "Yup." Morrow would have liked to hear more detail, like how his angle was or if he had any blind spots. He resigned himself to live without it. If there were any issues, Ghost would have told him.

It was beginning again—Edwin's calm before the storm.

"I told you already, the trip is for both business and pleasure," Santangelo said, exasperated at the length of time the TSA man had cost him.

"Gonna do a little golfing?" Lou asked, offering a fake smile as if he really cared.

"Is that for the TSA records too?" Santangelo barked. "Did you want to know which restaurants I'm going to and what I'm going to order?"

"No, I think I've got enough. I just need a few minutes with the pilot and the attendant next," Lou said.

"We'll be on our way then," Santangelo said as he started to get into the limo.

"Oh, sorry," Lou said. "No one is allowed to leave the premises until the full inspection is completed. I'm sure you understand." Without waiting for an answer, he turned to the pilots and said, "I'll need your names and home addresses."

210

As the pilots gave their information, one of them had an address with an unusual street name. Lou pounced on the opportunity to stretch out more time. He made the pilot repeat it twice and then spell it. Purposely, he read it back to the pilot, inserting an extra letter. The correction took another forty seconds.

Santangelo got into the back seat and slammed the door.

Inside the mansion, Tara was already in place. Morrow called the main line at LeBlanc's business, getting Tara on the first ring.

"LeBlanc Enterprises," she said.

"Tara, time to tell him that the customer is only ten minutes away."

"Why, thank you for calling, sir. That is so considerate. We'll see you soon," she said, staying in character.

Using the intercom, she buzzed Mr. LeBlanc in his den and said, "Cust is ten minutes out, sir."

He said, "I want you to greet them at the door and escort them into the den."

"Yes, sir."

Tara tried to calm herself. Her hands dripped sweat. Her heart was beating at a steady extra-fast pace. Breaths came with difficulty. She was so close now. So close.

"I think that's all I need for now. You've both been very helpful. Of course, I'm sure you've been through many other TSA spot inspections before," Lou said as pleasantly as he could.

The pilot shook his head. "Never one like this."

"Oh, well, it's a new procedure. Came out of the FAA meeting in Atlanta two years ago and is just now being implemented." Lou had a hard time keeping a straight face. This was almost too easy. "Oh, I'm sorry. One other thing. I'll need to take a look at your flight plan."

Santangelo had his window rolled down in an effort to torture himself, listening to one TSA request after another.

"That's it! That's it! Enough," he screamed out. Leaving the back seat of the car, he walked over to where the pilots and Lou were standing and said, "Look, I have an appointment I am going to be late for if this keeps going on. I insist we be allowed to leave. Now!"

Lou stared back at the taller and larger man and gave a cursory customer-service-like smile. "I appreciate that, and I'm sorry, but national defense takes precedent over your tee time. After I look at the flight plans, I'm sure you'll be cleared to go."

Santangelo stared down at the little man. "I have connections. If we're not out of here in the next three minutes, I'm going to make sure that my government friends hear about what I think of"—he paused to peer down at Lou's ID badge—"William Trent."

Lou just turned back to the pilots. "Flight plan?"

The pilot handed it to him as Santangelo walked back to his limo.

Lou knew he'd pushed it as far as he could. More delays would be up to the rest of the team. Still, he was pretty sure he could push the envelope and hold them for an additional two minutes or so.

He knew he needed to get back on the offensive. Holding the flight plan, he pointed to an unreadable note and looked up into the pilot's eyes. "Could you tell me what this is supposed to say? And is it written in English, or is this some kind of obnoxious flight acronym?"

The limo with mob boss Arthur pulled up in front of the LeBlanc mansion. Once there, a second car with four more men pulled up behind them. Vic and the bodyguards all tensed up. The com device sounded off.

"Vic, the car behind you is some extra folks also on loan from our, um, mutual friend. One will go in with you, and the other three are backups. I decided late last night we needed more muscle."

Vic let loose a long breath. "Thanks, Morrow. Had me worried there for a minute. We like the idea of more backup."

Arthur, unsure what to think about this late change in plans, checked his watch and waited the required two minutes before the guards got out and eyeballed the area to make sure it felt safe. Mel opened the door for his boss and took the position behind him, carrying the empty portfolio case, as they walked up to the front door. One guard from the other car joined him and whispered, "I'm Decker," as they headed to the mansion. Mel whispered back, "Mel." There wasn't time for anything else.

Seconds after they rang the doorbell, Tara opened the door and welcomed the gentlemen in. She guided them down the long hall and into the den where LeBlanc was watching a Yankees–Red Sox game on his giant white screen at the far end of the room. LeBlanc's lair was larger than the floorplan of some one-bedroom homes, so he enjoyed the look of awe as most men recognized the room for what it was—a giant man cave.

"Welcome, Mr. Santangelo!" LeBlanc said. The two men shook hands as Arthur's bodyguards spread out in the room and positioned themselves in a semicircle.

Two of LeBlanc's bodyguards suddenly stepped into the picture from out of the darkness of two different corners. Vic's immediate thought was to wonder how many more there might be.

Lou pushed his luck as long as he could, but when he saw Santangelo put a cell phone to his ear, he announced that he had finished and they could leave. The limo pulled out immediately. The driver returned to the main entrance, the one he'd used twenty minutes ago when they entered the airport, but it was closed off. A van with a magnetic Phoenix City Electric sign on the door blocked half the road while two workers were chalking up the street for some emergency repairs, effectively obstructing both lanes.

The limo came to a stop. The guard in the passenger seat got out and stood by his door. "We need to get through," he called out to the two workers.

"We won't be long," Tommy said. "Should be done in twenty minutes or so. Just gotta break the surface and check a relay connection."

"We have to go now," the guard said.

"Well, sorry. You can go out the south entrance. That'd be faster."

"Where is that?"

"Just turn around. The only road is Perimeter Road, running alongside the airport. Keep going, uh, to the south to the end of the runway, and there's a gate there and a guard. He'll let you out."

"Son of a—" Santangelo mumbled out loud, letting the end of the exclamation die off. "Is there any other delay we could run into today?"

The guard got back into the car, and the driver started to turn it around. As he did, Santangelo's side got a closer look at the van. It was a rental. The mob boss ordered the driver to stop. Santangelo, his suspicions rising, rolled his window down and called out to the worker closest to him. "You work for the City of Phoenix?"

Tommy stepped up to cover for Shady. "No. We work for Phoenix City Electric. We're a vendor for the city."

"Big company?" Santangelo asked.

"Huge fuckin' company. Why? You lookin' for work?"

"You got a nice contract with the city, but you can't even afford your own vans?"

Shady grabbed his head with both hands and groaned.

Tommy, almost giddy about his advance preparation, cried out, "Ha!" He turned toward Shady and pointed at him as he did a little dance. "Pony up! You owe me ten bucks, Sam! I told ya. Didn't I call it? I said somebody would make some snarky comment about the van. You didn't think so. Ha! Pony up!" Looking back at the man in the car, Tommy said, "Sorry. Yeah, it's a big company and an inefficient one. I go to the motor pool today, and they got no truck for us. Nobody plans ahead in that biz. It's all fucked up. Dooley, that's the motor pool manager, he hands this fuckin' magnetic sign to me and tells me to go rent a fuckin' van, charge it to my card, and submit a reimbursement request. Meanwhile, we lose ninety minutes, and do you think they take any workload off of us? No. Same amount of work."

Tommy stopped and looked at the ground. "I should quit this fuckin' job."

Santangelo, his suspicions quelled, rolled his window up and said, "Head to the south gate."

"I'd like to see the painting, Mr. LeBlanc," Arthur said, getting right to business.

"I'd like to see the money, Mr. Santangelo."

"It's here on my computer. I'll send it to your account when you give me the number."

LeBlanc walked over to his desk in the den. Tara stood next to it. He looked at her and said, "You can go back to your office now, Tara."

"No," Arthur said forcefully. "I'd prefer nobody leaves the room until this transaction is complete."

LeBlanc rolled his eyes. "OK, stay right there, Tara."

He picked up a notecard on his desk and handed it to Mr. Santangelo.

Arthur accepted it and set his laptop down on a counter. He turned it on and looked at the card. The bank routing and account numbers were neatly typed on the card. "OK, I have your number. After I see the painting and verify it's what we agreed on, I'll order the money sent to your account."

"Yeah, about that," LeBlanc said, walking back to his original position. "I'm afraid the price has gone up. I have another buyer who offered me seven mil for it."

Arthur stared at him. He tried to summon up the anger that the real Santangelo would feel at this cheap attempt to get more cash in the transaction. He flashed an angry look at him and said, "We had a deal."

"No, not really. We agreed that six point five mil was the highest offer I had, and if you could come and pay that, I would sell it to you," LeBlanc said. "Now, I appreciate you coming all this way, but I have another offer on the table. I could sell it for seven million tonight. That is unless you agree to pay something more than seven."

"How about this," Arthur said. "I pay you seven million exactly, and I won't kill you afterward. Sort of like a bonus."

LeBlanc tried to laugh, but it came out as more of a cough. "OK, I don't particularly like the way it was put to me, but OK. I'll take that. Transfer the money."

"I need to see the painting first."

"I'll give it to you after the money is in my account. If I show it to you now, you've already threatened me with death. What's to stop you from shooting me and just taking it?"

Arthur shook his head. "I don't do business that way. It's not unrealistic to see the painting. Hell, based on what you said, I could kill you and tear this place apart until I found it. And then I'd have the painting *and* the money. But I won't because that would be bad business. How would I ever buy another painting from anyone?"

"You'll never find the painting," LeBlanc said, smiling like a Cheshire cat. "This is the most talked about and, currently, the most fascinating painting in the world. I'm making you a hell of a deal. Just transfer the money, and it's yours."

"Maybe the painting is all wrong. Maybe Gabriel is standing with a zebra."

Instantly, hearing the code word they'd agreed on, Vic and Jayden pulled their guns and pointed them at LeBlanc's guards. Arthur pulled his gun, too, and leveled it at LeBlanc. Mel walked over to each of LeBlanc's guards and liberated their weapons from them. He pushed them down to their knees, which allowed Vic and Jayden to easily hold their guns at the back of the guards' heads.

"So, here's the deal, LeBlanc," Arthur said calmly. "I don't like renegers. We had a deal at six point five. I'll pay you that amount and not a penny more, and you will thank me for it."

The limo approached the south gate. It was now 3:48, and Santangelo was steaming. A guard, Brady, manned the gate and opened it as the car approached. Staring through the front windshield, Brady could see the driver turn back toward a passenger and nod. Brady walked around to the driver's side as the driver rolled the window down.

"Do you need some directions?" Brady asked.

"Yeah, how do we get to I-10 from here?"

Playing the helpful guard, Brady said, "Well, first of all, turn left and head north. The first right, that's Sarival Avenue; it's what most folks take to get to I-10, but don't do it. It's rush hour, and as soon as you get within a half-mile of I-10, it's a parking lot. What most folks don't know is all you have to do is go about four blocks farther south, to South Lambard Street. I think there's a sign there for I-10. Just turn right, and although it's all residential, you just keep going, and boom, all of a sudden you're right at the entrance to I-10. You can get anywhere from there fast."

The guard nodded and said, "Thanks. So no turn at Sarival and keep going to Lombard and turn right?"

"Yeah, except its *Lam*bard. Lam, not Lom."

"Got it."

The guard rolled his window back up, and Santangelo mumbled, "Now, we're getting somewhere."

Brady waited until the car was out of sight before he replaced the chain and lock on the fence and called Tommy. "He's off doing just what we want. Open up the main gate and get out of there."

"80 percent done already. Nice work, Brady."

Morrow was listening in on the play that Arthur was making. It was all on schedule so far. He called Connie. "Con, what's up? Where is he now?"

"Morrow, I just watched them drive out the south gate. Hopefully, he doesn't turn on Sarival. Hang on, he's coming up to the intersection now."

Morrow waited while Connie reported events. This was a big one. In practice drives, it had taken four minutes to reach the dead end of Lambard Street. That meant at least an eight-minute round trip, and then he'd have to get back to Sarival. Morrow was worried that Arthur's play was taking too long. They needed every minute of delay they could get.

"You transfer the money. The painting is here. And it can be yours upon payment. You'll be happy you did." LeBlanc was back in sales mode, doing what he did best, close big deals. *Make them want it*, he thought to himself. *Make them want it so bad, they'll do anything.*

"I'm not going to ask again, LeBlanc. I don't buy anything sight unseen. Show it to me," Arthur barked.

"Or what?"

"I'll end this with a bullet in your head," Arthur tried.

"No, you won't. Kill me, and you'll never get the painting." LeBlanc said, smiling back at him. "Besides, you don't do business that way. You said it yourself."

"You're right. OK, how about this. If you don't show me the painting now, I'll kill your pretty little assistant."

Tara's eyes went wide, and she mumbled, "Mr. LeBlanc—"

"Now, wait a minute. She's got nothing to do with this. Leave her out of it."

"LeBlanc, I'm sick of this. Show me the painting now, or I'll do it myself."

"Conrad! Oh, God!" Tara took a step back and started crying.

Arthur yelled at him, "LeBlanc, last chance, on the count of three."

"Conrad!" Tara screamed.

"One, two…" Arthur didn't wait until three. He fired his blanks twice. Tara twisted around, propelling herself off her feet and back, so it looked as if the force of the bullets had caused her to fly backward. When she hit the floor, a blood sack taped to her chest exploded. She lay face down in an instant pool of blood.

"Oh, God," LeBlanc said. "Fuck you, Santangelo. You didn't need to do that!"

"Show me the painting," Arthur said.

218

"They bought it, Morrow. They passed Sarival and are heading to Lambard. You've got yourself an extra eight or more minutes before they even get onto I-10."

"That's great, Connie," Morrow said. "Let me know when they get back to Sarival. How long did you say we'd have until—wait a minute—"

He pushed his earbud in farther and leaned his head unnecessarily to hear better. He listened for forty seconds and then got back on the phone. "Tara just got killed. We should be getting the painting any minute now. Keep me up to date."

"Will do, boss," Connie said. She started to hang up but suddenly stopped. "Wait! Morrow? Are you still there?"

"I'm here. What's wrong?"

"Shit, Morrow! They turned around. Now they're turning on to Sarival. He's fifteen minutes away!"

LeBlanc stared at Arthur and said, "I can't believe you did that. She had her whole life ahead of her."

"Shut up. Show me the painting."

"Or what? Gonna start killing my guards now?"

Arthur locked eyes with LeBlanc's. "No. The next bullet's for you. I don't care anymore about the painting. If I don't get it, nobody else will either. You show me that painting now, or I'll have Mel here practice his aim on your forehead. And then I'll burn the whole place down."

"You can't be serious. I—I'm just trying to get a good de—"

Arthur turned to Mel. "If he doesn't show me the painting by the time I count to three, pump two rounds in his forehead."

Mel, remembering Connie's suggestion for how he should react to the kill order, smiled like a maniac would and said, "My pleasure."

Not waiting at all, Arthur said, "One, t—"

Recalling how brief Tara's countdown had been, LeBlanc screamed out, "OK, OK, look over there!" He pointed to the giant white screen covering most of the north wall. He pressed a remote in his pocket, and the screen slowly disappeared into the ceiling. Lights came on instantly—all focused on a 2x3 piece of art: *Gabriel's Steed*. The display made it all the more impressive. The room was silent as everyone gazed at it.

Several of the guards fought the urge to say, "Wow!"

Gabriel appeared to be looking directly at everyone in the room. Not collectively, but individually. The steed, replete with folded wings on its torso, was magnificent. The horse's long face was reflected eerily in the Archangel's shield. It appeared that the right eye of the horse was also looking at everyone individually. Anyone who saw it would swear the horse knew some dark secret about them, as though he could read their minds.

Arthur looked at Mel, the tallest of the guards, and judged he'd have the best chance of reaching the high-hanging painting. "Mel, see if you can remove it from the wall."

Mel did as told and, very cautiously, took the painting down and carried it back to Arthur, who placed it in the portfolio case and zipped it closed.

LeBlanc said, "And the money?"

Arthur looked at him and said, "We really don't have that much money, so we're just going to take it. Vance, James," he called out, using fake names for Vic and Jayden, "all of you, tie up LeBlanc and the guards and put them in a different room, one with a door you can close. Leave them in there. Don't worry, LeBlanc; we won't burn the place down."

The guards got busy with their assignments.

"Tara, you can get up now. Don't worry about cleaning up. You feeling OK?"

LeBlanc took on a wide-eyed look as he realized he had just been conned. "Tara, you bitch, you damn—" He continued on, but it was all muted as Vic stuffed a gag in his mouth. Tara paid him no attention. Holding her chest, covered in blood and looking like she was in great pain, she exited the mansion out the front door and headed for her car.

Morrow had listened to it all play out and was clapping by himself in his car. *Arthur was right. It did take faking death to scare LeBlanc into displaying the Steed. And they played it so well.*

He got on the com device and blared out. "The Steed is ours. Everybody get out of there. Now. Santangelo is fifteen minutes away. Maybe less."

Back to the phone again, he called Connie. "Where are you?" he asked.

"Following them down Sarival. He's already on the entrance ramp for I-10."

"Shit! OK, keep following him. We'll have to escalate the Liberation Two timeline. Connie, make the second call to the Barger goons and tell them where to go."

"I'm on it."

Arthur watched as Vic, Jayden, and Mel moved LeBlanc and his guards to another room. He picked up the portfolio case and told the new guard to get out the door. He told him to run, and Arthur followed, hot on his heels. They both ran down the long hall, but as Decker practically flew out the main entrance, Arthur pulled a sharp left into another room. The door to the basement was right where Suze had told him it was. He opened it and headed down the stairs as quickly as he could. Twenty seconds later, he left the house via the basement back door, carrying his treasure. He reached ten feet out before a six-foot-four, two-hundred-fifty-pound ex-linebacker wrapped his arms around him and held him tight and nearly motionless. Arthur was in good shape but no match for a former Pro Bowler.

Morrow showed up fifteen seconds later. "You disappoint me, Arthur. I was starting to think I was wrong about you two. Jenkins, take him back to the other car. I'll take the painting."

"Nothing personal, Morrow. Just business, you know." Arthur said, a hint of remorse in his eyes.

Morrow said nothing. He nodded to Jenkins to head out front, and he followed him. His phone rang. It was Connie.

"Morrow, they are flying on the freeway. He must be doing ninety. You better get out of there quick."

"OK, on our way. We have the Steed. See you back here at the designated spot in ten minutes."

Lou was now standing out front. "Congrats, Morrow. We got it, right?"

"We got it, Lou. Well, wait a minute." Morrow set the portfolio down on the grass and unzipped it. He pulled out the painting just far enough to confirm it was the Steed.

Vic was yelling at him. "We gotta go, Morrow!"

He zipped the portfolio case back up and smiled to himself, knowing that they caught Arthur in time.

Back on the com, he said, "Ghost, where is Tara?"

"She went back to her car. She didn't look well, and she sat in it for a few moments. Hell, the next time I looked, the car was gone. What happened, Morrow?"

"Oh, hell. I'm not sure. But we've got the painting *and* Arthur. All we're missing is Tara." Still talking so Ghost could hear him, he said, "Lou, put the painting in the trunk and secure it so it can't bounce around. Tell Vic to drive carefully and get out of here. I have to stay. Got a little housekeeping to do. Go! Now!"

Lou took the painting and secured it in the trunk as Morrow watched every moment of it. As instructed, the car pulled away from the curb at normal speed. Turning at the first corner, it was out of sight in no time. Morrow hurried around the corner a mere thirty seconds before Santangelo's limo showed up in front of the LeBlanc mansion.

"Morrow, what's going on? Why are you sticking around for this?" Ghost called out, still on the open line.

"Later, Ghost. Stay low."

The line went dead.

39

Morrow slipped into the copse of trees to the south of the LeBlanc mansion. He worked his way through the woods for twenty yards and came out on the cross street, 18th. Tommy was already there waiting for him.

"Glad to see you made it. I hear virtually everything went well at the airport," Morrow said.

"It did, with the exception of they must have smelled a trick. They didn't fall for the Lambard Street ruse. Connie said they sniffed it out somehow and shot back to Sarival."

Morrow coughed. "Must be pollen. I'm struggling this spring. Yeah, Santangelo and his team just arrived. Connie should be here any minute now."

"Morrow, I hate to be dense, but I'm not following how this setup solves our problem. When Connie called you the other night and told you what was going on, I was mad at first. Then you called back and said you had a plan, and you laid this out, so I felt better. But now we've got Barger's thugs showing up here any minute, and Santangelo will be inside. How does that help us?"

"You told him that I was going in disguised as an older bearded man, right?" Morrow asked.

"Yeah, so?"

"So, that's what Santangelo looks like. They're going through you to get to me. They don't like me. I made them look bad when they failed to blow up Westcott's car a month ago. Everything I heard tells me they don't even work for Barger anymore, so they're operating independently. I just had you give them what they wanted and—"

"There they are," Tommy said as the white Cadillac sped past and pulled in just behind Santangelo's car.

Connie approached Morrow and Tommy from behind. "Was that them?" she asked, causing both of them to jump like scared children.

"Jeez, Con! I hate it when you do that," Tommy said.

"You're the one who taught me how to be sneaky like that, honey," Connie said, smirking at both of them.

"Yeah, that was the ole Barger boys, all right," Morrow said. "Let's go back into the trees here and find a good vantage point. I gotta call Ghost, too."

"We really got the painting, right?" Connie asked, her face trying to mask her fears.

"Yeah, we got it," Morrow said, then turned his attention to his phone.

"Morrow, what is this all about?" Ghost asked, wasting no time with a hello.

"Just watch, Ghost. Don't do anything. We're pitting two rivals against each other to solve a little problem, uh, some of your teammates had. Kind of a two-fer."

"Tommy and Connie, right? I figured something was up when I saw the creative alterations to Tommy's facial features."

Morrow gave the "shh" signal to Tommy and Connie and whispered to Ghost, "Gotta go now. See you at my place within the hour." He hung up and motioned the pair closer to where he was. They had an unobstructed view of the yard in front of the mansion.

Quietly, Tommy leaned over and said, "Barger's guys are getting out of the car. You didn't tell me what this accomplishes, Morrow."

"They think they're taking me down. They're going to rush Santangelo instead in hopes they'll secure the painting as their reward. Sadly, they won't."

"'Cuz we already got the painting, right?"

"No, not because of that," Morrow whispered. "See, what we have here is a classic mismatch, and a tragic one. Sending Barger rejects up against Santangelo's trained staff is like pitting Mother Teresa's School for Girls against the Green Bay Packers."

"Oh! Oh, shit!" Tommy said under his breath.

"Santangelo's coming back out," Connie said, just a little too loudly. One of the Barger thugs glanced back at the woods at the same time the mobsters exited the mansion, empty-handed.

What happened next took the blink of an eye. The four Barger boys pulled their guns out, and the three Santangelo bodyguards went down to one knee, brought their pistols up, and fired rapidly at the attackers. All four went down almost instantly. The one who had glanced back at the woods didn't even have time to turn around fully. He took two rounds in the head and was dead before hitting the ground. Two of the others got off a few shots, missing their targets. They both got hit in the chest and went down.

Morrow guessed they might survive, but their interest in following up with him would be dead. The other shooter wasn't smart enough to stay down. He bounced back up and was hit by no fewer than six shots. He fell to his knees and then to the ground. Santangelo's men piled into the limo and shot out of the area like a rocket.

"Oh, jeez, that was brutal, Morrow," Connie said, shaking. "We gotta get out of here."

Morrow agreed. He led the way back through the trees and hitched a ride with Tommy. Before they left, he reminded both of them that they should drive away slowly. Cops would be descending on the mansion grounds in droves in minutes, and cars speeding away from the scene were what they'd be looking for.

They drove toward Morrow's apartment, where they were all told to meet after the heist. About ten minutes into the ride, Tommy glanced over at Morrow and said, "I, um, I didn't think, you know, it was going to be such a permanent solution."

"I know," Morrow said evenly. "But think about it. You live here. Lots of folks know you. You either had to give me up completely to them, or your ass was grass. Nothing would have stopped them from going after you and me. This was dog eat dog. Those boys picked the wrong side, and they got what poor decisions always reap. We just helped it along a little bit."

Tommy nodded and swallowed hard. "Still, it was brutal. I suppose that what goes around comes around. Maybe next time it'll be us."

"I don't believe that," Morrow replied. "They chose a dark path. They chose anger and fear, and they innately enjoy violence. That's what you get. We aren't saints, but that's not who we are."

Tommy nodded again and continued on to Morrow's home.

40

When the three of them arrived, the party was already in full swing. Lou had the extra key to let everyone in, and champagne had already been spilled everywhere.

Morrow entered amid cheers and multiple slaps on the back. A bottle of beer was handed to him as another was poured on his head as though it were Gatorade and he were the winning coach.

"OK, OK, enough of that. We may have scored a victory today, but there are still a few things to do to reach payday. Where's the painting, Lou?"

"It's on your bed. I thought it might be bad form if we had it displayed and sprayed it with champagne and stuff."

"Good idea," Morrow said, pointing a finger at him and winking as he walked to his bedroom. He carried it out into the living room and gently set the portfolio case on the floor. Everybody gathered around.

"I tell ya, that's some painting," Mel said. "When LeBlanc unveiled it, everyone had to catch their breath. The way that angel and the horse looked back at us was, I don't know, eerie or something. You'll understand what I mean when you see it."

Morrow asked everyone to turn on all the lights and open the drapes so they could view it better. He noticed Arthur was sitting on the couch next to Lou, his hands tied in front of him and his ankles bound. He was the only one in the room that wasn't smiling.

"Who's got flashlight apps on their phone?" Morrow asked. Nearly everyone raised their hands.

"OK, turn them on and gather around me. I need as much light as I can get so I can find the one thing that proves this is the original."

Everyone turned the lights on and held them over the painting as Morrow pulled it out of the ornate case. Quiet reigned as they all held their breaths for a moment. He laid it down flat and stared at it. "My gosh, that is something, isn't it." Struggling for the right words, Morrow continued, "I mean, I don't know much about art, but this is—this is—"

"A fake," Arthur said, breaking the silence and the mood.

"What?" Morrow asked, his jaw dropping.

"If you're going to look for the artist's tell under his signature, you'll find nothing. It's a fake. A really good one, but as phony as a three-dollar bill."

Morrow's wheels were spinning. The party atmosphere frosted over, and everyone looked to Morrow.

"How? And how'd you know?" Morrow asked, looking directly at Arthur. "Did LeBlanc not know it was phony? Maybe he did and he was trying to pawn it off as the real thing."

"Mel's right," Arthur said. "Leblanc's painting was the real thing. It's a remarkable, some say heavenly inspired, piece of art, and you don't have that one."

Mel interrupted him. "Morrow, when you unveiled this painting, I didn't get the same feeling from it. It didn't grab me like the one I saw at LeBlanc's. I tell ya, I was kinda mesmerized by it. Art's not telling lies. It's in the eyes. Hey, I made a rhyme. The eyes of both the angel *and* the horse. This one here, it's—it's missing something."

"I've read the same thing from people who have seen the original," Arthur confirmed.

"Arthur, finish your story. What happened to the real one?" Morrow asked.

"I put the painting in the portfolio case and ran with the new guy toward the main entrance. While he kept going, I took a sharp left and then hustled down the stairs. I stopped at the bottom and left the real Steed there in plain sight in the stairwell. I picked up this one in a duplicate case. You caught me with the one that Tara had paid thirty grand to have made. As we expected, after I was caught out back, you took the painting I had and marched me out front. Tara waited till we were gone and came in the back way, got the real painting, and left with it."

Brady and Shady sat down against the wall in defeat. Tommy and Connie looked at each other and shook their heads. Ghost said, "Oh, fuck! Morrow, I'm sorry. I switched my gaze to the front yard and the activity there. Last I saw of Tara, she was lookin' shook up, sitting in her car. She must have been waiting for her dad to get caught. She just slipped in there, picked it up, and put it in her car. Nobody was looking at her."

"Not your fault, Ghost," Morrow said. "It's Arthur's fault and mine for believing he...for believing he—oh, shit," He looked to the ceiling, then back to Arthur. "Oh, good grief. It was never you, was it, Arthur?"

He slapped his forehead and shook his head as if to clear the cobwebs of his brain. "She played me." He started to laugh.

Everyone in the room watched as the man they knew who rarely smiled was sitting on the floor laughing to himself.

"Morrow, what happened?" Connie asked.

Again looking at Arthur, he said, "It was *her* idea all along, wasn't it? She suggested that you kill her. That would give her an excuse to leave early. I know. Even when it's staged, getting two bullets or blanks to the chest is a scary ordeal. It made sense to me that she was upset. But she wasn't. She planned the whole thing. And, oh, of course, you never *expected* to get away. She sacrificed you to us so we'd believe the painting you left the house with was the same one LeBlanc had. You switched it on the way out. Probably only took three seconds. And we fell for it."

Arthur said nothing.

Morrow stood up and kicked Arthur's feet. "Where is she?"

"Probably halfway to Vegas by now."

"Morrow, we know what her car looks like," Tommy said. "Who do we know in Vegas who can—"

"Forget it. If she's smart enough to outwit us, she's smart enough to switch cars. She probably had a backup car staged in Wickenburg or Kingman on Highway 93 long ago. Or hell, maybe she went to Albuquerque. Back roads, whatever. Either way, she's gone."

"We got her father!" Vic said. "We can threaten her with killing him if she doesn't bring it back."

Morrow shook his head. "Never work. She knows me. She knows we don't do the whole violence thing. That's why she left Arthur with us. She knows we wouldn't hurt him. Empty threats don't work."

He leaned over and cut the ties binding Arthur's feet and hands. "Connie, get Arthur a beer. At least one of us ought to be celebrating tonight."

Vic and Jayden got up and said, "It was a good try, Morrow. It was fun, too. We'll work with you anytime, but we're gonna head out now." They waved to everyone and left.

Mel followed them, shaking Morrow's hand and saying, "Sorry. We, uh, we still gonna get something?"

"We're still on. I still plan to pay everyone. I just have to switch to plan F now. And no, in case you're wondering, I don't have a plan G. It'll have to be plan F or nothing."

Arthur accepted his beer from Connie and watched with interest as Morrow was literally forming a new plan in front of everyone.

Tommy raised his hand like a schoolboy, fearful of asking a question but more afraid of not asking. "Morrow, can you tell us what plan F is?"

Morrow held up one finger as if buying another minute from this cruel universe that thwarted his every try. He nodded to himself, seeming to be brokering some kind of agreement between his emotional lobe and his logical lobe.

Lowering his finger, he allowed himself a comforting smile, mostly designed for everyone else's benefit. "Yes, in plan F, we will show up at three o'clock tomorrow, at Doctor Almeda's home, and deliver the actual painting to him. He will hand me the remaining five hundred fifty grand that he owes, and we'll be done with it."

Arthur smiled. Everyone else exchanged glances and wondered if Morrow had lost his mind.

Tommy spoke up. "Morrow, um, it's been a long day. You know, the real painting is with Tara, and she's a hundred fifty miles away from here by now."

"Not quite. More like a hundred twenty or so. Minor detail." Morrow spoke quietly as if he were talking to himself.

"Morrow, we don't have the painting," Brady said. "Did you mean we'll take this fake and try to convince him it's real?"

"No. I meant what I said. We'll deliver the real painting tomorrow afternoon."

Tommy exploded. "Oh, for crying out loud. Morrow, you're living in a fantasy world. You've lost it. We don't have the painting. It's gone. Maybe you better go lay down for a bit."

Morrow calmly shook his head. "No, I understand this now. I didn't before. We'll deliver the real one and get paid for it."

Everyone in the room exchanged glances. Arthur continued to have an odd smile on his face.

Lou broke the silence. "Morrow, would you share with us how we are going to get the painting in time to give it to Almeda?"

Morrow nodded. "Tara. Tara will bring it back to us."

"What?" The word came out of at least three mouths simultaneously.

"Are you nuts?" Brady asked. "Morrow, she stole it from us. She isn't going to bring it back."

"She will."

Lou had seen Morrow's mind work under pressure a few times before. He decided to coax more information out of him. "It seems a bit counterintuitive. How do you know she'll bring it back?"

"Connie," Morrow called out. "You're a fast study. I have a few faults. Can you name them?"

Connie shook her head. "How much time we got? You didn't do your research before you started this con. You're always too confident each step will work. You micromanage our plays. You took too long to size up the marks. You're apparently a terrible fighter and can't even protect your own face. You—"

"OK, that's enough. I think we all get the idea," Morrow said, glancing at Arthur. "When you want the truth, just ask a woman."

Arthur chuckled and nodded his agreement.

"Connie, you did so well on that. Can you tell me, do I have any strong points?"

Every eye in the room turned to Connie as she contemplated that question. She sat on a counter stool silently, thinking. Ten seconds turned into twenty. Lou moved forward in his seat. Tommy started to open his mouth to answer, but Connie raised her hand to his mouth to stop him.

"I guess you do have one strength, Morrow. You're a student of human nature. You seem to know what people are thinking and what they'll do."

Morrow said, "Thanks, Con. I better use that skill now." He looked at Arthur. "Tara's mother. She had a good heart. Am I correct?"

"You are correct," he answered simply.

Connie glanced at Lou and started to smile. "He knows something we don't. Morrow, why is it important that her mother had a good heart?"

Ignoring her question, Morrow started talking more to himself again. "She'd be about thirty, maybe forty miles outside of Kingman by now. That's where it would start."

Looking at Arthur again, he continued, "She had to prove to you she could do it. That was her win. This is about the time that she'd start realizing it and worrying just a bit about her pops."

He shifted his gaze back to his team. "She'll realize it wasn't the money after all. It never was. It was her quixotic quest to do the impossible. That was all that mattered. She never wanted us, specifically, to lose. She knows Almeda doesn't forgive. She'll be looking now for a place to pull over and think. She'll do that and then turn around."

Nodding to himself, he asked, "What time is it?"

"Seven thirty," Ghost said.

Again Morrow nodded to himself. "Two and a half hours. Three tops. She should be arriving around ten. We should all have another drink or two and relax."

No one spoke for three long minutes. Connie broke the silence, going back to the question that was ignored. "Morrow, why is it important that her mother had a good heart?"

Looking more alert now, as though he had just awakened from a dream, Morrow said, "She told me about her. How she learned from her. How her mother still talks to her in her mind. She knew."

Fighting the urge to scream at Morrow to be more specific, Connie said, "So, she knew. Knew what? And why is that important?"

Morrow looked at Arthur and said, "Feel free to correct me if I say something that's not true."

"Everything you've said so far is true," Arthur said.

"Connie, her real name is actually Suze. And it's important that Suze knew her mother had a good heart. She recognized it; that was key."

Feeling she was finally close to the answer, Connie pushed one more time. "Why is it key, Morrow?"

"Because Suze recognized it for what it was and honored her mother for it. And the thing about a good heart is this: it takes one to know one."

41

Ten o'clock came and went.

Ten fifteen passed with some questioning looks.

Ten thirty was just another stop for the minute hand on the clock.

"Morrow, I think we have to face facts. Shady and I are going home."

"She'll be here any minute," Morrow said.

"Look, Morrow, nothing personal," Brady said. "But we can't sit here all night. We'll get some sleep and if you have any news for us, give me a call."

The brothers both got up, Brady said their goodbyes to the team, and they looked at Morrow with long faces. "Let us know if we should get out of town for a while."

There was a triple knock on the door. Everyone tensed.

Morrow got up from the floor and said, "I got this." In case it was an enemy bent on violence, he motioned everyone to get out of the line of fire. He didn't have to suggest it twice. Those who were armed pulled out their weapons.

Morrow walked to the door, stepped to the side, and called out, "Who is it?"

There was no answer.

As Morrow considered his options, a voice finally answered back, "You know who it is, Morrow. Open up."

The rest of the team could hear it, and smiles abounded.

Morrow opened the door and said, "Tara, what a surprise."

"Stuff it, Morrow. You telling me you didn't know I was just messing with ya?"

"We were kinda fifty-fifty on that."

"Which side were you on?" she asked as she entered and passed him by. "I come bearing gifts. Well, not plural, just the one gift. Hi, Pops."

"Suze, you're late. We expected you a little earlier."

"You're damn lucky I'm here at all. I only came back because I was afraid Murderous Morrow would hurt you. Did they torture you at all?"

"Made me drink this cheap beer. How was Kingman?"

"How would I know? I turned around about forty miles shy of it. It's a boring drive at night."

Morrow closed and locked the apartment door and joined everyone in the living room. Pointing to her portfolio case, he said, "I remember some woman telling me how that case was one of a kind. Unique. Unmatched. Never duplicated."

"I lied," Suze said. "It was almost too easy. You're kinda gullible sometimes."

Morrow glanced at Connie and said, "There's another weakness you can add to my list."

Connie chuckled and nodded.

"We got any beer left for the guest of honor?"

Connie left her stool and went straight to the fridge. "We got a few."

"Bring me one too," Morrow said.

Suze took the opened bottle of Corona and raised it to Morrow.

He raised his in return and said, "Time for a toast. To our team—efficient, brave, and staring victory in the face! Drink 'em if you got 'em!"

Everyone downed a swallow.

Morrow quickly added, "And to the woman of the hour who has a damn good heart."

A chorus of "hear, hear!" rose from the ranks.

Suze took another swig, losing some of it down her chin. When she wiped it with her sleeve, she turned away and dabbed her eyes at the same time. Then, looking at the team, she said, "What are we all standing around for? Doesn't anybody want to see this painting up close?"

42

The team left Morrow's apartment at twenty minutes past one in the morning. Although they briefly discussed the handoff to Almeda and the process of dispensing the cash, most of the time was spent admiring the painting.

Mel was right. The eyes were captivating. Everyone stared at *Gabriel's Steed* up close and then moved farther away and off to the side, continuing to claim that the eyes followed them wherever they went. Brady went out to buy some more champagne and wine to extend the celebration. No one wanted to leave. It was one of those nights they were sure they'd remember for the rest of their days.

The highlight of the evening, however, was watching Suze study the painting with a magnifying glass, looking for the artist's tell. Suze had some members of the team use their phone flashlights to enhance the wee bit of light she had to work with in Morrow's gloomy apartment. After a tense twelve minutes, Suze got excited and said, "Oh, hey. What's this? Here it is. I found it!"

Everyone closed in to try to see, but it required a magnifying glass. She showed everyone one by one. "See, the wind is clearly blowing from left to right. The horse's mane and Gabriel's golden hair are blowing to the right. Down here, on the ground, the blades of grass are all bent to the right. Except for here, under his signature, five blades are leaning to the left. That's not possible. It's Bandeaux's tell. This is very definitely the original *Gabriel's Steed!*"

Whoops and hollers followed, and everyone poured some more champagne. Suze told everyone about the other paintings and gave them a rundown on all the different ways that the artist left his telltale mark. Her story mesmerized them. Morrow watched the event unfold and marveled at her tenacity and focus. With the alcohol consumed and their energy sapping, the night ended.

The next morning, Suze and Morrow met for breakfast at a café a few miles away from her apartment. Morrow had his favorite: scrambled eggs, bacon, and a mountain of hash browns. Suze had a fruit plate.

"How's your Cholesterol Special?" Suze asked.

"It's perfect. I think I may make this a permanent ritual on the morning that a con ends."

"You're quite the optimist. You think you'll live long enough to run another con?"

"Eat your pineapple, or I will," Morrow replied, dodging the question.

The waitress refilled their coffee cups, and as she walked away, Suze asked, "Why'd you invite me to breakfast? Aren't you a little pissed at me?"

"I'm pissed at myself. You're what, ten years younger than me, and you still ran circles around me. This gig wasn't exactly a confidence-builder."

"I'm not ten years younger. Lou said you're twenty-nine. That's only about six or seven years older."

"Lou's wrong. I'm thirty-one. Only poor math gets you that close. Fact is, that was one fine move. You made me focus on your dad because I thought it was his idea to steal the painting. I figured you were just along for the ride, but it was *your* plan all along."

Suze smiled. "It was really fun. I had the Steed! I was on the road, outta here, but, I don't know, the escape kinda lost its appeal. I thought about Connie and Lou and Tommy, Ghost, the brothers, and all maybe getting killed by our client, and I kinda like them. So I came back."

"Doesn't sound like you cared too much if Almeda killed *me*."

Suze eyed him. "Morrow, you're a mystery to me. You don't seem to think like I expect. You don't enjoy this work much. You look miserable most of the time. Part of me thinks, you know, maybe you wouldn't mind it that much if you were put out of your misery."

Morrow forked another mouthful of hash browns up and in. He didn't answer.

Suze let it be and returned to her previous thought. "Besides, I figured you can take care of yourself. You didn't screw *everything* up. You suspected us and hired more guys to cover the exits. Of course, Pops and I were sure you would. I was counting on you catching my dad as he exited the basement, and you didn't let me down."

"You mean I fell right into your trap," Morrow said, grimacing a bit for her benefit.

Suze laughed softly. "OK, we'll go with your version if you insist."

They ate in silence for a short time. As they were getting ready to leave, she asked, "Are you going to have enough money to pay everyone what they expect?"

"It may be a bit tight, but I think we'll be OK. Long as I make a dollar, I'll be happy. Part of me doesn't really want the money."

Suze's posture stiffened, and her eyebrows rose. "What? Why wouldn't you want the money? I mean, isn't that what you did this for?"

"Not exactly," Morrow mumbled.

"Why did you do it, then?"

"I thought I was helping. Rafe, a guy I worked with who put me on this trail, he needed the money and wanted to help. And Almeda, I misjudged him. I saw him as a wronged victim who had a fabulous painting stolen from him. I thought, you know, how cool it would be to use the skills I have to solve both problems. It'd be kinda fun, and I'd make some cash too."

Suze just stared at him. "Fun? You got beat up twice and lost your whole first team because it became a life-and-death thing. How is that fun?"

"It all turned out OK. So there were a few unfun parts. Such is life. We got through it. I made new friends and met you and your pops. Wasn't so bad."

Suze shook her head. "And now you don't want his money?"

Morrow finished his coffee and started to get up from the table. Suze reached over and forcibly placed her hand over his. "You're not leaving yet. Answer me. You don't want the money?"

"I *do*, but it's not about the money. Almeda lied to me. He's not even close to who I thought he was. If I take his money, that means this painting, this incredible piece of art, will be sold to the highest bidder, or Almeda will keep it for himself. Either way, its beauty will be lost to everyone else. It belongs in a museum so people can experience it on their own. All I'm doing is helping some warped old man enjoy it all by himself."

"Morrow, that old man is your *client*. You got the painting; now get the payday. Forget the rest. Your feelings about it shouldn't be part of the equation."

Morrow patted her hand. "You're right. We'll just do it and get it over with. I called Almeda and moved the meeting up to one o'clock. I'll bring the painting and pick you up at your place at twelve thirty. Brady and Shady are providing the security in case we need any help. It should go pretty smooth."

Morrow left a fifty on the table to cover the bill and the waitress's tip. That was nearly all that was left of Almeda's advance.

Suze decided to walk home. Morrow had just a few last housekeeping chores to do. And a phone call to make, too.

43

Morrow picked up Suze at twelve thirty in front of her apartment and headed to the Almeda mansion. They traveled the first few miles in silence.

Suze broke it. "I'm trying to figure out why I'm here. And, excuse me for being nosy, but are you packing?"

"That obvious?" Morrow asked.

"To the trained eye. I can see the bulge under your jacket."

Disappointed, Morrow replied, "I have my Glock. This could be a bit dicey, and I felt I needed a little firepower, just in case."

"Loaded? I mean, with real bullets?"

"Yes, hollow point. If this gets bad, I have to damage what I hit."'

"Jeez, doesn't sound like you, Morrow."

"I'm adaptable. It depends on the circumstances."

Suze mulled over that thought for a moment and returned to her original question. "I still don't understand why I'm the one you want to accompany you to this event."

"I want you to watch him when he looks at the painting. You know exactly where the wrong-leaning grass blades are, and I want you to tell me if you think he knows about the tell too."

Suze angled her head to the right. "I don't get it. Why would that make any difference?"

"If he knows, then others do too," Morrow explained. "That erodes my confidence that what we have is the real thing."

"Morrow, stop the car! I want to look at it one more time. I should double-check. After all this work, the thought that I'll never see it again is really troubling. I'd like to take a picture of it too."

"Nope. We'll be late if I stop now. Shoulda thought of that before."

"So we'll be late. We can be fashionably late," Suze said.

"I don't do late. It's bad manners. Just hang on to your hat. You're along for the ride."

"You are such a bastard, Morrow. I was just starting to think you might be OK after all, and instead, now I'm sure I was right the first time."

"Just do your job, and you'll get paid a reasonable amount," Morrow said, his voice betraying no emotion.

Eight minutes later, Morrow pulled the car to the curb in front of Almeda's place. It was 12:58.

Led inside by the same butler he met four weeks ago, they were escorted into the grand library to await Almeda. Morrow counted the number of steps.

Doctor Almeda, dressed in a fine suit, his snowy beard perfectly coifed, appeared at the entrance to the room. He smiled broadly. "You didn't disappoint me, Mr. Thompkins. Cut it a bit close, but today is my deadline, and here you are."

"I try to be punctual," Morrow said.

Suze rolled her eyes.

Pointing to the portfolio case, Almeda said, "I assume that is my prize."

"It is," Morrow said stoically.

"Well, may I see it?"

Morrow looked at him and said, "Well, may I see the money?"

"Oh, my, are we having a little bit of a stand-off here?" Almeda asked. "I always pay. You can trust me. But I need to see my painting first. How about a sneak preview?"

Morrow unzipped the portfolio case and started to raise the painting out of the case. He pulled it up about four inches and got an expectant smile out of Almeda. Then there was a loud knock on the front door.

Morrow froze as Almeda called out to his butler, "Jon, see who it is and tell them I'm busy."

Jon's steps across the hardwood floor could be heard as he approached the front door. He opened it, fully prepared to shoo away whatever type of pest this was.

"Detective Red Fuller and Agent Sawyer," the man said, holding his badge up high.

They didn't wait for permission to enter. They started walking into the foyer, and the detective's loud voice could be heard down the hall. "Where is Almeda? Take me to him and then scram."

Morrow listened as their footsteps echoed more loudly. One second per step. He continued pulling the Steed higher up so Almeda could see the top of the horse's head. The moment the eyes showed, a somewhat disheveled man with a mop of red hair walked in along with a shorter, well-dressed man in a suit and tie. Still holding his badge out, Fuller said, "Well, well, what do we have here?" He glanced at the painting. "Looks like an illegal transaction is in play."

Morrow immediately placed the painting back in the portfolio case.

"You can't—you can't just come in here," Almeda yelled out.

"We can, and we did. We know this man and woman have ill-gotten goods, and we were tailing them. Lo and behold, they led us right here. I assume that you, sir," Fuller said, pointing to Morrow, "are in possession of stolen goods in the form of *Gabriel's Steed.*"

Morrow seemed stunned. He didn't move or speak.

Fuller looked at Sawyer and smiled. "It's the jackpot! The painting, the thieves, and the illicit buyer all in one."

Almeda quickly disagreed, "Uh, you have this all wrong. I was returning it to—"

Fuller pulled out his .45 and said, "Save it for the trial. Hands up, everyone. Hope you like the prison you'll be going to."

"This is an illegal search!" Almeda screamed out, drawing Fuller's attention.

At that moment, Morrow reached into his jacket and withdrew his weapon. "I'm not going back to prison! I'm not!"

Before the last syllable left his mouth, Morrow fired wildly, hitting a vase nearby, shattering it. Then he adjusted and fired two shots into Fuller's torso and another into Sawyer's chest. They both flew backward and to the left, blood spraying everywhere. Crumbling to the floor, Fuller looked dead before he hit it. Sawyer lay stunned, gasping for one last breath that never came. Then his head fell to the side into a pool of blood.

Suze screamed and backed away.

Almeda went wide-eyed and stood like a statue in the middle of the room, his mouth gaping. "What have you done? My God, I have lawyers! You didn't have to do that."

Morrow stared at his handiwork, and his gun hand shook.

"Morrow! What did you do? You can't shoot a cop!" Suze screamed at him.

Brady and Shady arrived at the library door seconds later. They'd entered through the front door, left open by the butler on his frenzied way out.

"What happened, Morrow? What'd you do?"

Morrow walked over to a chair and slumped down into it. He let his Glock fall to the floor. "Oh, God, what have I done?"

Brady looked to Suze for guidance.

"Oh, jeez, we have to get out of here," Suze said.

Almeda looked at all of them and said, "No! You can't just leave. You have to fix this. I'm—I'm ruined! I'm the one who has to get out of here."

Morrow stood back up and shook his head. "OK, listen up. I'm sorry. This is terribly unfortunate. We need to clean this up. And we have to get all traces of this mess out of here."

"What about me? I have to get out of the country," Almeda said, still sounding stunned. "I can't be associated with this. You have to help me get out of here."

Morrow stood up and took charge again. "Brady, call Tommy. He's nearby. Get him here to take Almeda to the airport." He walked over to the doctor and handed him the painting. "Here. Take it. Get out of here. My man will take you—um, he'll, um—I know this guy. He can make a new passport for you. A new name. He can get you to Brazil, and you can go where you want from there."

"Tommy'll be here in two minutes, Morrow," Brady called out.

Morrow looked at Almeda. "I, uh, I did get you the painting. You need to pay."

"Fucking hell! You've ruined me. I'm not paying a dime. You get me and my painting on that plane and out of here. Do what you want with the rest of it. I wash my hands of this mess. You, Thompkins, or Morneau, or whatever your name is, you're a fucking disaster!"

Tommy showed up at the library door. Seeing the two bodies on the floor, he said, "My God, what happened here? Morrow, what—"

"No time, Tommy," Morrow said, interrupting. "I fucked up. I need you to take our client to Loki's, you know, the forger. Almeda needs a passport and a new name. Then get him on the next flight to Rio. Now!"

"OK, Morrow, OK." Looking at Almeda, he said, "Come on. Let's get you outta here."

Tommy led the way, and Almeda followed, carrying the only thing in this world he cared about—the Steed.

"Oh, God, Morrow," Suze said, tears flowing down her face. "He's right. You are a fucking disaster. You killed a cop and an FBI agent. I was *part* of it. You've doomed me. Two men dead, the painting gone forever, no money for anyone. You idiot!" She screamed it at the top of her lungs as she headed for the door.

"You can't leave now," Morrow called out to her. "Don't you want to stay and help me clean up?"

"I can't—I can't believe you said that. This is the worst day—"

Cutting her off, Morrow said, "Guys, looks like we'll have to clean ourselves up."

At that moment, Carter and Wilson, Nate's secret recruits, both sat up in their pools of blood. "That's OK. I hate lying around in blood all day. Happy to help clean up," Carter said.

Suze stopped in her tracks. Brady and Shady smiled broadly. "Worked pretty good, boss," Brady said.

"Suze, you sold it! Just like I hoped you would," Morrow said, flashing a short victory smile. He didn't feel bad about smiling this time. Every successful con deserves at least one fine smile when it's over.

Suze looked at Brady and Shady and instantly knew that they were in on it and she wasn't. Then, turning back to Morrow, she said, "But the painting? He took it with him."

"He did. A small sacrifice," Morrow mumbled.

"Not small. Why'd you do that? Almeda's gone, but so is the painting, and we got no money from him."

Morrow turned to his men. "Guys, find a mop and clean up. I need to take Suze for a little walk."

The men all nodded and began their duties. Morrow put his hand under Suze's elbow and walked her into the great ballroom. "Take a look around. See all the paintings on the walls?"

"Morrow, why are we—"

"Humor me. Look at this painting. Nice, huh?"

She looked at a painting of Dante's Inferno. Flames, despairing souls, devils everywhere in chaos. "Yeah, it's nice. Actually, it's very good, but it's also a fake." She walked five feet over to peer at another. Saint Teresa in her moment of ecstasy. "This is well done, but a fake too. They're all probably fakes. What's your point?"

Morrow waved his hand around the room. "The room is filled with fakes. Every other room is too. There's well over ninety of them."

"So?"

"So, Almeda won't be able to show his face in the U.S. again. The only passport he'll own is Brazilian, and if he even gets that far, he doesn't want to come back to murder charges. He can't hurt any of us now. And I have a buyer lined up. He's already agreed to take all these fakes off my hands for nine thousand apiece and resell them for twice that amount. With just our share, I'll have more than enough money to pay everyone well and still have some left over."

"Why didn't you tell me about all this?"

Making eye contact with her, he said, "You have a good heart. Murdering those men was unforgivable. I didn't bring you along to see if Almeda knew the tell. I brought you along so someone would be abhorred by my actions. I needed someone who would cry for the dead, decry the atrocity, and make Almeda believe it was all real. I didn't want an actor; I needed the real thing."

"You conned me."

"It was for a good cause."

They walked out of the library as Rafe and three men walked down the hall.

"Hey, Morrow. I got all the gear you asked for out there in my truck. And I got the extra guys here to help me move everything."

"Good timing, Rafe. Mr. Almeda has bequeathed me all the paintings on the walls. Go through the entire house and place each one in the leather cases I bought. Then deliver them to the art dealer and bring me the check. I'll be at the Park Place Pub at six. You know where it is?"

"I know where every bar in town is. We'll see you there."

"Good! Bring your friends. There'll be a cold one waiting for you."

Rafe, all smiles, nodded and started directing the crew.

Suze chuckled a bit. "From horse's ass to man of the hour in five minutes. Pretty good, Morrow. Still, I would have liked to see the painting one more time."

"It'd be nice if everyone could, but life is full of tradeoffs."

Morrow stopped and looked at Suze Tanning. "You were magnificent. Even when you were conning me, you were amazing. See you at the pub tonight. I gotta go. One more thing to do." He leaned down and gently kissed her forehead. Then he was out the door.

44

The scenery on I-17 northbound from Phoenix was nothing to write home about. The highway cut through nothing but flat prairies, cacti, and a few brief moments passing through small towns. All very forgettable. As they continued north, the mountains made it more interesting, but overall, it was a drab trip unless you had someone to converse with. Morrow did.

"Look, Chuck, I'm really losing patience here. You said you were going to show me where *Gabriel's Steed* was, but you haven't told me nothing yet," Red Fuller said.

"You have to be patient. I handed you Almeda, didn't I?"

"Well, the Phoenix PD nailed him at the airport. I only get partial credit."

"They caught him because you provided them with his new name on his passport. Now you got him, so sweat him, and he'll tell you how he staged the original Steed's robbery and sold the painting that the insurance company paid him for."

"Got no proof of that," Fuller said under his breath.

"He doesn't know that. He knows what I am now, and you can tell him that I figured it all out and will testify against him. He'll crack."

Fuller shook his head. "I guess I still don't follow. If he stole his own painting and then sold it, why did he want it back?"

"He had to get it back. My guess is that he sold it to a collector under the proviso that it not be resold. He collected the cash on that sale plus the two million the insurance company paid him. But when the painting resurfaced, he knew that it could be traced back to him, so he hired me to steal it back. He'd gotten plenty of money out of it, so he probably just wanted to hold on to it."

Fuller rubbed his chin. "So the two drivers of the armored car service, they helped Almeda steal it for cash or something, and then they, um, met a—a—"

"An untimely demise," Morrow said, finishing the sentence for him.

"Yeah, and you think Almeda had them killed to shut them up?"

"Why else? He had to. So tell him that you know, and he'll crack."

They rode in silence for another ten miles, then Fuller suddenly broke the silence. "You know, it doesn't seem right, you getting nearly two hundred thousand from the insurance company just for telling them where it is. You should just admit where it is as a public service."

"You work for free, Fuller?"

"Well, no. But I'm out there putting my life on the line every day."

Morrow just looked at him and said, "I don't work for free either. Almeda had a pair of cement overshoes with my name on them if I didn't give him the painting. I think I earned it."

Fuller scratched his head, messing his hair up more than it already was. It didn't seem to matter. "You had a team too, right? How you gonna pay them?"

"That's what the two hundred K is for," Morrow lied. "I won't make hardly nothing out of this."

Fuller mulled that over, then blurted out, "When we gonna get there?"

"Patience, Fuller, patience."

"Fuck that. I got things to do. You haven't even told me where we're going yet. It better not be fucking Utah."

"We're almost there. It's in Sedona."

"Oh, excellent," Fuller said. "We're less than ten minutes out. Some collector has it there or something?"

"Nope."

"It's in a gallery?"

"Nope."

"Oh, stop it," Fuller said. "You're overwhelming me with all the detail. Can't you give me something?"

Ignoring the question, Morrow fired off one of his own. "Have you ever seen the painting in person, Fuller?"

"You know I haven't. Neither has like 99.9 percent of the world."

"Well," Morrow said, "today's your lucky day. You'll like it. After you see it, you'll understand why it's so special."

"Yeah, well, I'm not much of an art fan. You shoulda asked Sawyer to come along with us. He'd be salivating to see it."

Morrow turned off the highway and made his way into downtown Sedona, a picturesque resort city that had multiple art galleries and the prime showcase, the Sedona-Hamilton Art Museum. He pulled into the museum parking lot, into a space near the front entrance, and turned off the engine.

"Did Sawyer ever talk to you about this place?"

"Well, not by name. He said the painting was in Sedona at a museum. I assume it was this one, right?"

"It was. Almeda sent it here to be viewed. He loaned it to the museum for three months but pulled it out, as his contract allowed, after six weeks. Allowed or not, it was very unexpected. The museum had to refund over ten thousand passes sold in advance for the viewing. Then they had to hire an attorney and defend themselves against Almeda's lawsuit against them. Reportedly, the museum settled out of court, paying a hundred thousand or more. Almeda claimed they picked an unworthy security team to move the painting back to Phoenix."

Fuller eyed Dawes and asked, "You're telling me this because?"

"Because as badly as Sawyer's insurance company got screwed, this little museum was damaged ten times more. Nobody cared. They were on the edge of bankruptcy, and my guess is they still are."

Fuller scratched his head. "Why do *you* care, Chuck? Don't you have enough problems of your own?"

"I like underdogs. And I don't like it when bullies kick them around. So today, you're along with me to be a witness. Now, come on. We have a four thirty appointment."

"To do what?"

"We're going to make a donation."

Morrow got out of the car, retrieved a handsome custom-made leather portfolio case, and carried it with him into the museum. Five minutes later, they were seated in the curator's office. Introductions were made.

"So, Mr. Dawes," Norman Hamilton said, speaking to Morrow, "you reportedly have a donation to make to us. You understand while we appreciate all gifts, we cannot guarantee the item will be displayed."

"I understand. Let me ask you, have you been with the museum for long?"

"As you may have guessed from my name, this is a family-run business. I've been here for over thirty years."

"That's good," Morrow said. "I think you'll appreciate this more then."

He unzipped the case and withdrew the painting with the backside facing the curator and the front exposed to both Fuller and himself. Fuller's eyes almost fell out of his head.

Morrow peaked out from around the side of the painting. Looking at Norman, he said, "Sir, I lied. This isn't a gift. I want to sell it to you for one dollar. I have a contract here."

Then he turned the painting around.

Hamilton nearly shot out of his seat. "Oh, my great gracious God! The Steed! I can't believe it. Is this real?"

"Guaranteed original. You know by looking at those eyes," Morrow said.

"Sir, I have to ask you, how did you come in possession of this piece of art?"

"Does it matter? I misplaced the bill of sale. There are only two conditions. I ask that you allow people to see it for free one day per month. And the other is that if a woman named Suze Tanning ever comes here, you give her free entrance, a grand tour, and you listen to her as she explains her remarkable method of proving that this painting is, indeed, the original *Gabriel's Steed*. I, uh, I think she'd enjoy telling the story."

Hamilton put his hand to his head and paced the room. "This is—this is very irregular. Not the way we normally do business. And you've got no bill of sale from the entity you bought it from?"

"Nope. And it doesn't matter that I don't," Morrow replied.

"Of course it does. This could be stolen."

"So, it doesn't matter. Possession is nine-tenths of the law. Correct, Detective Fuller?"

"Well, that's just a saying, but in essence, well, yeah, it sort of is."

Morrow rose from his chair and said, "Mr. Hamilton, when I sign that bill of sale, your museum will own the most talked-about painting in the world—for as long as you and your attorneys can keep it here. The insurance company will make a claim of ownership, and perhaps you can settle that with them, out of court, six or eight months from now. It would be, um, quite an interesting run, don't you think? Probably even a very profitable run."

Hamilton considered that for a moment, hesitated, and then signed the agreement.

Morrow immediately leaned over and added his signature. Looking directly at Hamilton, he said, "My one buck, please."

EPILOGUE

A good con always ends with a well-planned cool out. The goal of the cool out is to cover everyone's tracks and ensure that the mark won't seek revenge upon them. With Barger's old crew obliterated, Almeda headed to prison, the painting displayed publicly for now, and headed back to the insurance company eventually, Morrow felt all his people were in the clear. That included himself.

The con scored almost nine hundred thousand dollars from the resale of the quality copied paintings left at Almeda's mansion. The hundred and eighty thousand in reward money from the insurance company all went to Morrow as taxable earnings. After laundering the other cash, the con netted a fraction over three-quarters of a million dollars, and that was what he was distributing today. As Morrow pulled into the parking lot at Mickey's Mash House, he found himself dreading the meeting. He didn't enjoy being the center of attention, and since he was the one with the cash, there was no doubt he would be welcomed as such.

He'd rented the private room and had the entire team assembled. Told to be there at seven, the con participants all started rolling in by six p.m., wide grins of victory pasted on their faces. Subtlety was in short supply.

As he approached the front entrance, Morrow took a deep breath and talked to himself. *Just do your job. You're the leader, so act like one. Tell them all how wonderful they are and make them want to work with you again. Yes, Edwin, I can hear you. I won't ruin it for them just because I can see all the flaws and my own failures. They earned this. It's time to celebrate. I'll let them.*

Upon entering the private room, all hell broke loose. They were all equipped with colorful party-favor inflating blowouts and noise-makers. Pointing them at Morrow as he entered, the props all unfurled as a cowbell rang out, and a horn blew while everyone acted like youngsters at their first party.

Morrow looked around the room. Even Arthur and Suze had party hats on. Suze was laughing. The imp in Morrow couldn't resist.

He took on a very serious face and raised his hands in the air, lowering them slowly in a plea for quiet.

As the room grew still, Morrow said, "Bad news, everyone. The cash was stolen from me last night. I'm sorry."

Dead silence. Then Morrow displayed his own victory smile. "Wow, you're so gullible. I have all your payments here," he said, holding up his overstuffed briefcase. The celebrating started up again.

Morrow placed his briefcase on a table, opened it, and began removing envelopes of various sizes and calling out people's names. He started with the muscle men who, while important to the cause, were not the highest paid of the bunch. That was reserved for the key roles with a lot of verbal interaction or intense danger. As he passed them out, he shook their hands and thanked them personally for their efforts. Some conversations lasted longer than others.

Every envelope was filled with bands of one-hundred-dollar bills—all untraceable, tax-free earnings. The muscle men typically earned some multiple of ten thousand, depending on the degree of danger they experienced. Help like Rafe and his crew got five to ten thousand each. Nate got fifteen. His two recruits, the ones playing Detective Fuller and Agent Sawyer, were paid handsomely prior to this meeting. Morrow and Nate wanted to keep them out of contact with the others for security reasons. Brady, Shady, Mel, and Vic got thirty K each. Players like Tommy, Connie, Lou, and Ghost, each landed fifty to sixty thousand apiece.

Brady brought Morrow a beer and stood nearby, observing him closely. Quickly, he emptied his briefcase with the exception of a few remaining envelopes.

Looking out at the crowd, Morrow said, "I have two more. Arthur, you saved the day. Without you, we could never have pulled this off. I want to thank you for all you did."

Morrow held out the envelope. It was stuffed, holding a hundred K. Everyone applauded, and a smiling Arthur stepped forward to accept the payment.

"That wraps it up. The last envelope is for me for my brilliant planning and smooth execution. Did I miss anybody?" Morrow asked.

Hands on her hips, pouting in the corner, Suze tilted her head and looked at Morrow. "I think I missed all your flawless planning and that smooth execution you mentioned. Maybe you're thinking of a different con. And, yes, you did miss someone."

There was a spattering of nervous laughter going through the room. No one was too sure if Suze would get paid or not.

Morrow's face broke out into a hint of a second smile, and he nodded vigorously. "She's right. Sure, she stole it from us, but she did bring it back. What do you guys say? Should I give her five hundred bucks or something?"

Suze's face began to grow red.

Morrow opened up his briefcase and made a big show of looking into it. One overstuffed manila envelope was all that was left.

"OK, I think I have something here. Yup, I do. I almost forgot. This is the largest payout of all." Morrow paused and stared back at Suze. "This one goes to the lynchpin. The young lady whose long con we interrupted. The woman with the good heart."

The crowd erupted into hearty applause.

Trying hard to suppress her smile, Suze stepped forward and accepted her payout. She raised it over her head and waved it around. Everyone cheered. Enjoying her moment in the spotlight, Suze held the envelope close to her chest as her eyes glistened.

Leaning over toward Morrow, she whispered in his ear, "Just for the record, I still hate you."

Morrow nodded, mumbling back, "I know."

ABOUT THE AUTHOR

I'm Earl James. I live in Seattle with my wife, Kat, and our cat, who still doesn't have a name. I didn't start writing until my sixties and I experimented writing various genres under different pen names for the better part of a decade.

It wasn't until 2020, that I began to write the one series I had the most hope in – the Morrow's Con series. Morrow is a character I've had in the back of my mind for years, but I lacked the confidence to actually write about him. When I realized I'd better hurry up and write it before the grim reaper arrived, I buckled down and produced Morrow's Last Con. It was a long book intended to be a one-off. Fate intervened and Morrow's Last Con was never published. But I found I liked the character so much that I wanted to write more. So, the so-called final book of the series was set aside, and I began writing the prequels. Morrow's Con – Opening Gambit became the first story.

Before I began my writing career I filled all my time as a small business owner. I had a bevy of wonderful people working for me and with me and I experimented with different techniques to try to create a more motivated, happy, and engaged workforce. I studied people and learned what made them who they were. In other words, I educated myself about human nature. I developed a better understanding of people and what makes them tick—what motivates them to do what they do. I learned not only how to predict how the employees would react to changes, but also how to create an environment where they enjoyed working and performed productively. It was those insights that helped me to understand human nature—very much like the character, Morrow, does.

Now I'm having fun too. Writing more and working less. And by the way, as an unknown author, an honest review of any kind would help me immensely. I would appreciate it so much, maybe I'd even let you name my cat for me.

The 2nd book in the Morrow's Con story is ***KNIGHT'S TOUR***

Coming out soon!

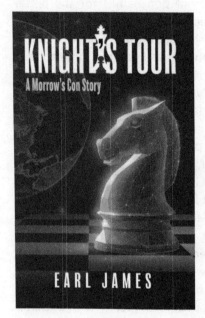

MORROW IS BACK

Usually, Morrow picks the con he wants to run. This time, it picked him.

His latest client is a public company in the oil industry that hires him for a very sensitive job. There are two parties involved, and it doesn't take Morrow long to realize he's found himself in a quandary. One party wants to avoid him, and the other wants to kill him.

Using all of his skills, Morrow builds his team of players and sets up a con that will solve both problems.

In the midst of the ruse, Morrow fights off distraction. He meets an intriguing young woman who becomes the key to unlocking this puzzle. But nothing is ever what it seems, and opening the wrong door may net the worst-case scenario.

Running a successful con can be very rewarding. But it's the funny thing about a con: the first time you fail is also the last.